Firestorm

Shadowed Embers Book One

Kayla Robinson

Paperback ISBN: 9798992918205
Hardcover ISBN: 9798992918212
Library of Congress Control Number: 2025926983

Cover design by: Magdalena Pietrzak (barn-swallow.carrd.co)
Published in Crab Orchard, Kentucky
Printed in the United States of America

For anyone who listened to *imgonnagetyouback* and thought that it would make the best soundtrack for enemies who turned into lovers that were still drowning in tension….

Swifties, this one is for you.

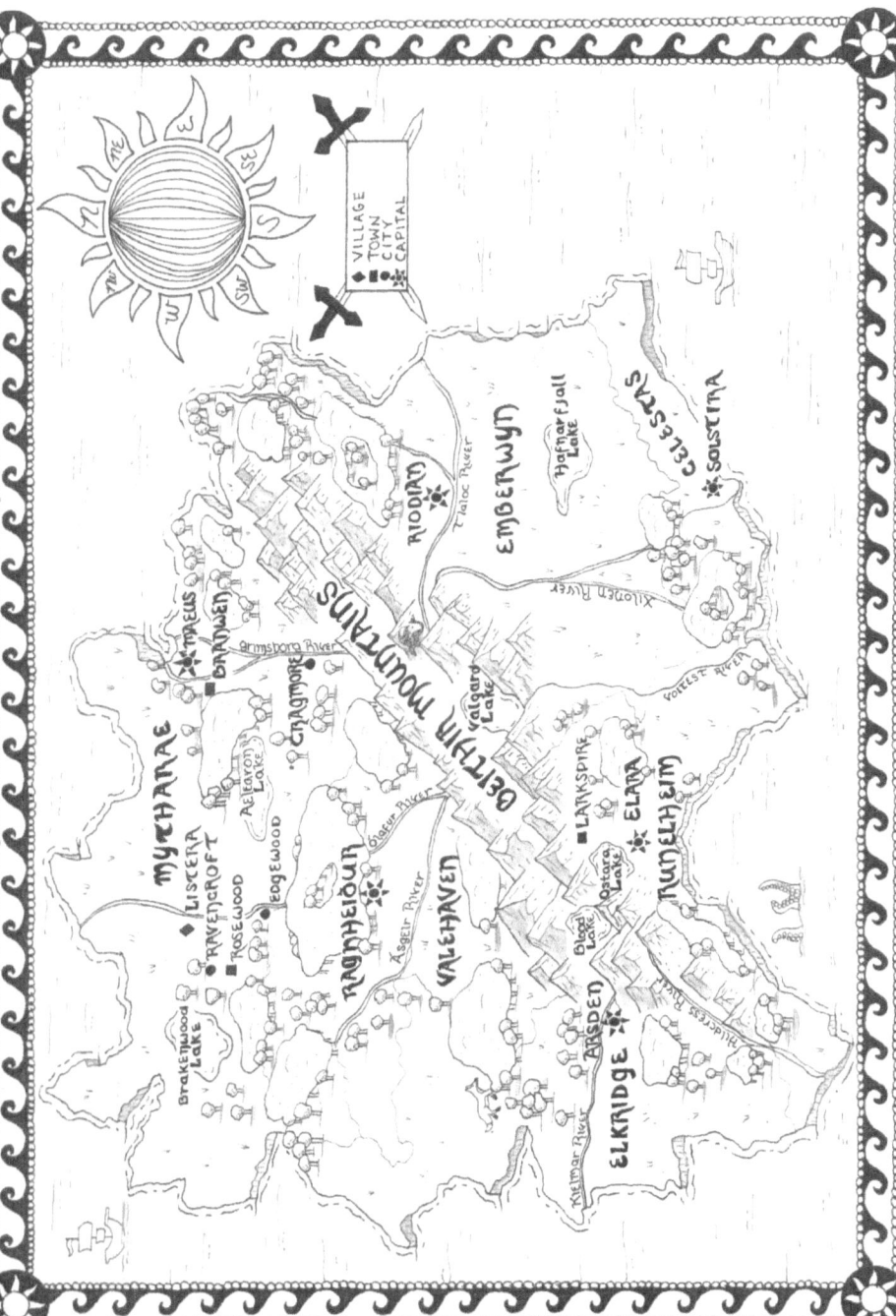

Glossary & Pronunciation Guide

Pronunciation:
Emberwyn - ember-win
Mytharae - myth-ah-ray
Runelheim - rune-el-hime
Azazel - uh-zay-zul
Maeus - may-us
Riodian - ry-oh-dee-an
Beithir - bay-her
Moira - moy-ruh
Leodric - leo-drick
Zephyr - zeh-fear
Nyvara - nih-var-ah
Aelearon - ah-lay-ron

Glossary:

Emberwyn
- Court Details
  - Queen Moira Cutwater - water mage
  - Princess Amelia Cutwater - water mage
  - Spymasters - Desmond, Azazel, Ezra
  - Elizabeth Cutwater/Liza Winters - fire mage - eldest daughter of Queen Moira
- Creatures/species
  - Mages
  - Halfbloods
  - Humans - slaves or lower class

Mytharae
- Court Details

- - - King Phillip DuMont - human
    - Prince Andras DuMont - human
    - Prince Edward DuMont - human
    - Captain of the Guard - Jesse Mercer - human
  - Creatures/species
    - Humans
    - Mages - slaves or lower class
    - Halfbloods - slaves or lower class

Valehaven
- Court Details
  - Not referenced
- Creatures/species
  - Elves

Elkridge
- Court Details
  - Not referenced
- Creatures/species
  - Werewolves
  - Humans
  - Halfbloods

Runelheim
- Court Details
  - Queen Nyvara - vampire
- Creatures/species
  - Vampires
  - Humans
  - Mages

Celestas
- Court Details
  - Not referenced
- Creatures/species
  - Fae
  - Halfbloods
  - Humans

Spotify Playlist:

Prologue

Fifty Eight Years Ago

I ran down the palace hall, throwing myself around a corner to gain some ground on Ezra, who was closing in on me with each step. It was midday, which meant that the queen would be in meetings and we would have the run of the place without worrying about getting in trouble.

I rounded another corner and slammed into Azazel, Ezra's older brother. He didn't budge an inch. He glared down at me. His bright golden eyes contained nothing but judgment and condescension. He was only three years older, but he liked to believe he was an adult already. He and Ezra were both in training to be spymasters for the queen, but he took the duty far more seriously than Ezra ever seemed to.

"You know better than to parade around the halls like that." He frowned at Ezra behind me. "They're in the middle

1

of a *very* important meeting that you would've interrupted with all your noise and chaos."

"Spare me the lecture Azzy. We weren't going to go running into the throne room." Ezra chided, earning herself an even harsher glare than the one he had settled on me.

A loud crash pulled all of our attention to the meeting happening beyond the large doors just a few paces away from us. The door was left slightly ajar, which explained Azazel's insistence that we would've been disruptive. They never forgot to close it.

"They've revolted and rather than handle it you've come here to *inform* me about it?" The queen's shriek could've probably been overheard all the way into the palace gardens.

The three of us hurried closer to the door, but kept out of sight so we could hear the discussion better. I was never very well informed, but a revolt was something that I *needed* to know more about. It was a thing I only ever read about in books.

"Apologies, your majesty. They took the city by force and declared their liberation from your rule before we could gather enough troops to suppress them." Desmond, Ezra and Azazel's father explained. "I shadow walked to inform you as soon as I was able, while the remainder of our forces fled the city in whatever ship they could find."

"I will *not* stand for this. How could you let this happen?" Her voice was laced with venom. I pitied their father.

"Your majesty, I–"

Someone cleared their throat and cut him off. "If I may, your majesty. It has become a hassle to govern that part of the country since the dragons effectively cut off our roads that pass through the mountains. It would take far more time and resources to fight back than we can realistically expend."

"I will not lose half of my land to *humans*." She spit out the last word like it was poisonous. I had never heard her speak of them in such a way.

"He's right, my queen." Her advisor cut in. "We will get it back, but we need to carefully determine *how* before we go barging in and begin a war over it. Let's think on this–"

"And what of my people who will undoubtedly be slaughtered or thrown from their homes?" The queen interrupted.

"We cannot help them now, but we *can* help them in the future if we play our cards right." The advisor explained.

The rest of his explanation and attempts to talk the queen down from her ranting faded as my own mind spiraled. I didn't understand. A revolt? Dragons? I couldn't have missed *that* much. Ezra usually told me some of the issues she overheard while attending meetings with her father as part of her training. Dragons and uprisings weren't among them.

A heavy shove from Azazel, followed by a stern but quiet, "move!" brought me out of my thoughts and back to the present. We were being shoved down the hall so that they wouldn't be aware we were listening.

When we were far enough away that I was certain they wouldn't hear me, I turned to Ezra and Azazel. "Dragons? Neither of you mentioned that."

Azazel gave me a condescending look. Ezra just shrugged.

"You mean you haven't noticed them flying over the mountains sometimes?"

I looked at Ezra incredulously. "No. I don't often stare out at the mountains."

3

She snorted. "Sorry, forgot you prefer to spend all day in the gardens with your nose buried in a book." She laughed at my expense.

"I'm not permitted beyond the palace walls. You know that." I snapped back. "It is useless to stare out at land I'll never get to see up close."

"Better to dream of a fantasy world you *also* will never see?" She teased.

I smacked her, but cracked a smile. "At least in a fantasy book I can ignore my *real* problems."

"Whatever you say." She rolled her eyes and turned to walk around the corner into the hall that led to her rooms. I let her walk away without me and turned to Azazel.

"There's something you're not telling me." I demanded.

"There's nothing else *you* need to know."

"I–" I started to insist, but a band of shadow wrapped around my mouth and silenced the rest of my protest. Azazel gave me a wicked smirk.

"Remember your place, *Liza*. You have no right to know anything Ezra tells you. I, unlike her, have no attachments to you and will not risk my future title to aid in spreading gossip." He turned on his heel and walked in the same direction as Ezra. The shadows disappeared when he was far enough away that I was sure he wouldn't hear me even if I shouted after him.

I hated the bastard. No wonder the queen seemed to like him and his father so much. They were cruel enough to fit right in.

Chapter 1

Liza

I followed Ezra to the throne room. Her long brown hair was tied up into a handful of intricate braids that wove together around the back of her head. I couldn't see how that was practical for someone in her position, but it wasn't my place to question it. I wondered sometimes if she kept her hair in such artful displays to keep people guessing about her *real* intentions, but I didn't dare to ask that either.

It was early. The sun had only just crested the horizon and it cast the soft cream stone of the castle walls in a beautiful pink color as we walked down the window lined hall. It was unusual to be summoned by Queen Moira this early, even for me. She rarely called upon me anymore. It was almost a relief, but that made each time she *did* summon me all the more nerve wracking.

The halls were quiet too, like no one but the guards had risen yet. It made my already uneasy stomach clench with a little more dread. She didn't want *anyone* to overhear our discussion this time.

The guards at the door nodded at Ezra when we approached, then stood aside to push open the large arched wooden doors that lead to the extravagant hall that Moira spent most of her days in. I followed Ezra through in silence to find Moira alone except for the two guards who always stood behind her throne.

Her blonde hair was done up into a simple bun atop her head, which would be mostly hidden by her gaudy crown once she put it on. It sat on the arm of her throne while she leaned back casually into the seat. I never understood how she could sit in such a solid and uncomfortable looking chair for so many hours. It wasn't ice, of course, it was just carved to *look* like it was ice, but there was no cushion to it. I imagined that most people would find it acutely uncomfortable.

Her pale blue eyes fell to me before we reached the dais and the displeasure was unmistakable. It took all of the self control I had to keep my own features neutral. A glare or even hint of irritation directed at her never ended well for me. Still, if she had an issue with my lack of formal dress, she had only herself to blame for summoning me so early. I had only just donned my chemise when Ezra came barging in.

Unlike me, the queen was in full royal dress already. She wore a sky blue gown that had a square neckline dropping to just above her breasts with long plain sleeves. The silver embroidery around the neckline was simple, but on her it always looked like so much more. The gown cinched in her waist and hung loosely from her hips, with the same embroidery design around the hem at the bottom of her skirts.

6

Ezra came to a stop at the dais and I stepped up next to her. Ezra bowed, while I tilted my head and curtsied.

"Rise." Moira's voice exuded boredom, which contradicted the disdain I still saw in her eyes. "Leave us." She gestured toward Ezra as well as the guards.

"Your majesty?" Ezra seemed hesitant, like she hadn't heard her correctly.

"I will not ask politely again." As though her first statement had been anything other than a demand.

Ezra bowed her head, shot me a sympathetic look, and quickly left the room. The queen's guards followed closely behind her. The throne room doors were pulled shut again, leaving me entirely at Moira's mercy.

I stared at her expectantly and raised a brow.

"I have need of you for a mission."

I sighed and crossed my arms over my chest. "A mission of what sort, exactly?"

"Do not give me an attitude, Elizabeth. It is about time you earned your keep."

"I didn't *ask* to be–

"Silence." She seethed.

I knew I was pushing my limits. Our complicated relationship gave me a little more wiggle room than most, but her eyes seemed to glow with rage. I knew it was only a matter of time before she lashed out with her magic. For once, given the murder in her gaze, I listened.

"The king of Mytharae has sent a messenger here to negotiate the terms of a trade agreement. I'm inclined to accept this agreement, with a few conditions of my own."

I reined in the desire to roll my eyes, instead opting for a look that told her to go on. She'd never given me a way to prove to her I wasn't a disappointment, like she so often pointed out to me. I doubted this would give me the chance to do that, but I was intrigued enough to find out more.

"We've been trying for years to get someone on the inside of that kingdom," she continued. "You will return with King DuMont's messenger and act as my emissary. You will attend to all decisions regarding our trade agreement and be sure to act in favor of *us*. But that is not all."

I raised a brow. She ignored it.

"I'm told that Prince Andras is…" She trailed off, seeming to try to find the right word. "…*Intrigued* by mages. He talks of equality among all their people and permitting other species to cross into their territory again. While I am sending you there as our emissary, I am also sending you there to woo the prince. If we can secure him in marriage, we can take back our lands more peacefully."

I laughed out loud at her, unable to quell the outburst as the shock and absolute absurdity of the demand she was making of me became apparent. Woo the prince? Was she out of her gods damned mind? Shipping me off like some prized cattle to a kingdom that barely tolerated our kind?

"You want *me* to seduce a prince. You're sending me off to be a broodmare? How ridiculous–"

My response was cut short as a cylinder of water shot up around me. I wasn't unfamiliar with this reaction, though I still didn't understand why I bothered to speak out at all. It never changed her mind and always resulted in my own discomfort.

That was the definition of insanity I supposed. Doing the same thing repeatedly and expecting a different result. Because this time, *this time,* I might get through to her. Not insanity, I realized. It was the definition of stupidity instead.

The water moved with me, no matter what I tried. Without oxygen, I couldn't do anything to save myself. I fell to my knees as I struggled to keep myself from attempting to draw breath and consequently drowning.

My vision started to blacken at the edges before she finally decided she was satisfied and withdrew the water. I choked and gasped, desperate to replenish the oxygen I'd been deprived of.

"Now, where were we?" She paused as though she had to think, for dramatic effect. "Ah yes, I was explaining your mission. Are you ready to listen now?"

I managed a nod, but did not rise from my knees and did not look up at her while I continued to try to calm my racing heart.

"Good. As I was saying, you will attempt to steal the prince's affections, and if we're lucky, accept his hand in marriage. When the king falls, he will ascend the throne, which you will promptly give over to *me*."

"What makes you think he'll even be interested in someone without a real royal title?" I kept all of the anger from my voice when I asked. I knew better than to provoke her again, and a small part of me thought this might actually prove to her I was worth being reinstated as *her* heir.

"I don't." I looked up at her to catch the end of a shrug. "You're either going to accomplish this mission, or you will end up dead. If you fail, don't bother coming back."

My mouth gaped which only resulted in a sick and twisted smile from her.

"You shouldn't look so surprised. I don't know which of the gods decided to curse you with fire rather than water, but you serve no purpose to me unless you succeed with this. Perhaps, if you're successful, I'll consider reinstating you as my heir.

"Of course, knowing the former king's distaste for magic and mages alike, if you fail, I imagine they'll send your head back to me as a reminder of why they split off from us in the first place." She raised her shoulders in another careless shrug. "They'll save me the trouble."

I had no words, no retort at all. For once in my life, she'd rendered me entirely speechless. She let me sit there like that, mouth gaping, basking in her own victory for several minutes before I managed to compose myself and rise to my feet.

"May I ask one question, before you send me on this suicide mission?"

She rolled her eyes, but waved her hand at me to proceed.

"Why didn't you just cull me when you discovered that I didn't have water magic?"

She allowed me to see a blink of surprise before she schooled her face back into neutrality. "Because I didn't go through the pain of *birthing* you to not get anything in return. I knew I could use you for something even if I didn't know what yet."

I was yet again stunned into silence. I wasn't sure that I had even wanted to know the answer, and now that I did I only hated her more. I was nothing more than a pawn in her games.

"Pack your bags, Elizabeth. You leave at noon."

Chapter 2

Liza

Nearly two weeks later, I was immensely thankful to finally be stepping off of the ship onto dry land. Eric, the emissary that King DuMont sent, descended the gangway ahead of me. It took more self control than I was willing to acknowledge to not push the man down the damned ramp and run past him.

His lack of haste gave me plenty of time to gauge my surroundings though, which changed drastically since the last time I had come here with Moira. These docks used to be rather beautiful, but they looked filthy now. The smell of fish was so strong that I nearly gagged. I was never fond of seafood, but I fear even if I had been, the overwhelming smell I faced here might change that about me. They clearly had a rather extensive fish market and fishing operation.

While I didn't hold the same distaste for the species as my mother, humans *were* quite gluttonous when it came to… well, everything. Their population grew with a fervor that I didn't see in any other species on the entirety of our continent and they ate through resources like they never feared they might run out. Gods, even the vampires had more self restraint than this.

This overpopulation turned what was once a beautiful and prosperous port into an overcrowded disaster of poverty that made me sick to look at, all smells aside. I was terrified to see what had become of our summer palace, certain they had destroyed that in a similar manner.

I shifted my focus back to the man descending the gangway ahead of me. He reached the dock below us and was greeted by a handful of guards. Most of them were rather plainly dressed, meant to blend in more with their surroundings with dull and inconspicuous armor.

One of them seemed even more regal than the rest. He was very out of place among the other impoverished and dirty looking dockworkers. His armor glimmered in the midday sun and he had a red cape strung over his shoulders with a large pin displaying what I presumed to be their royal crest holding it in place.

He glanced from Eric up to me and the two of them exchanged words quickly when his gaze returned to the emissary. They seemed to be quietly arguing, but I didn't catch a single word over the din of the other chatter and noise around us. By the time I reached the bottom of the ramp, they had silenced. I could have sworn that Eric's dark brown hair had a bit more gray than it did when we left, but I couldn't for the life of me understand what had him so stressed.

"Lady Winters." Eric gave me an amused smile. "This is Captain Mercer of the royal guard. He will be escorting you to the palace. I have unfinished business to attend to with the captain of our transport as well as a few of the merchants here at the docks, but will catch up with you eventually."

I shifted my gaze from Eric's tired hazel eyes to meet the captain's gaze instead. Up close I could make out his features far better, and he was younger than I expected. I would estimate him to be in his mid twenties, which was young, in my mind, for someone to hold such a title.

His eyes reminded me of aventurine and his pale brown hair, while quite short on the sides, blew in the breeze on the top of his head and hung low enough to nearly brush his eyebrows. He cracked a slight smile and dipped his head when introduced. He was surprisingly lean for a guard as well, but I imagined that if he earned his position that his looks were probably deceiving.

"Pleasure to meet you, Lady Winters." He stepped to the side and gestured for us to walk forward. "Allow me to escort you to the carriage we had waiting to transport the two of you back to the palace. The longshoreman will load up your belongings and then we'll be on our way."

"The pleasure is mine, Captain." I said with a smile that I realized was likely far too friendly for the situation, judging by the slight flush that rose to his cheeks as I moved to walk with him toward the awaiting coach. The four guards who previously flanked him now took places around us and escorted us through the crowd.

I got a few sideways glances from workers and what I assumed to be civilians walking around us. I was vastly overdressed for this area. Had I known what I was walking into, I may have opted for a more simple gown, but I wasn't sure who I might meet upon arrival, so I chose one of my best dresses. It was an emerald green velvet material with short sleeves and a dangerously low neckline that I hoped might catch Prince Andras' attention if I happened to run into him today.

I had even done up my hair to the best of my ability, despite the rocking of the ship as we floated into port. It was a bit disheveled, but up and away from my neck, which was a godsend in this heat.

Captain Mercer stepped up and opened the carriage door, then stood to the side to allow me to enter first. I assumed I would be travelling alone and he might join the driver, but to my surprise he climbed in with me after giving the guards a few hushed orders. He took a seat on the bench across from me and pulled the door shut behind him.

The silence stretched between us until the carriage began to move several minutes later. I gazed idly out the window and watched the city pass by. Even the homes and buildings we passed on the way to the palace seemed in more disrepair than I recalled them. It had been nearly sixty years though, I reasoned, and I was young the last time I set foot here. It was possible I wasn't remembering correctly. Surely.

"So you're a mage then?" The captain's question brought my mind back to the present, and to the situation at hand. I drug my eyes from the window and met his curious gaze. I gave him a brief nod.

"What sort of magic?"

I gave him a quick once over. "Are you asking because you can't quell your own curiosity or are you asking because you need to report it to the king?"

His brows lifted, but he quickly schooled his expression back to something more neutral. "A bit of both, I suppose." He gave me a second look now, like he hadn't expected me to know or care about the different motives behind the question.

I sighed, maintaining an air of boredom as I shifted to look out the window again. Moira hadn't specified that I couldn't tell anyone what type of magic I possessed. Surely if she was sending me as a mage, I could share it. "A fire mage, if you must know."

"Interesting." He muttered, mostly to himself it seemed, because the conversation ended just as abruptly as it began. When the carriage finally slowed to a halt he stood and reached for the door.

"I will show you to your quarters. I don't believe the king was expecting a woman, but I would venture he should have suspected as much from a country that seems to be mostly run *by* a woman. Should you find that you need anything beyond the accommodations provided in your suite, please let the guards know."

He pushed the door open and stepped out. I was surprised to find him waiting and offering me his hand to aid me in descending the steps to the cobblestone road beneath. Part of me wanted to be spiteful and ignore the gesture, but I had appearances to uphold, so I took his offered hand and carefully descended.

When I dropped his hand and turned to take in the palace in front of me I stopped dead, as did he, at the sight of the man descending the steps. He strode down the stone stairs like he owned the place, and given how expensive his outfit likely was I presumed that he *did*. He wore a white tunic with a brilliantly embroidered crimson vest. He traded style for practicality and finished out the ensemble with a black pair of riding pants and tall boots.

His auburn hair was windblown and falling to just above his eyebrows, like he'd just returned from a ride through the countryside. A soft smile rose to his lips as he looked me over the same way that I did to him and a glint of amusement rose to his deep brown eyes. I smiled and curtsied, just before Captain Mercer lowered into a bow.

"Forgive me, your highness, I was not expecting to run into you before seeing Lady Winters off to her quarters. Is everything alright?"

"Everything is fine, captain."

I saw him rise out of the corner of my eye, so I followed suit and smiled up at the prince. Which one he was, I wasn't sure, but at that moment it didn't matter all that much to me.

"I came to catch up with Eric and see if I could meet the emissary that Queen Moira sent back with him." He glanced between the two of us. "I assume Eric is still at the docks?" His attention settled on me and he continued before the captain could reply. "Lady Winters, was it?" He descended the last two steps and offered me his hand.

I took it and gave him a nod and smile. "Yes, your highness."

He kissed the back of my hand and flashed me a mischievous grin. "It's a pleasure to meet you. I'd be happy to show you to your quarters. I am certain the captain has other matters to attend to."

"I–" He started, but was silenced when the prince raised a hand.

"My father will want to speak with you. I can absolutely handle showing her to her room."

"She's a fire mage, sir." He pushed, a hint of warning in his voice, though I anticipated that the prince before me would ignore him.

As expected, the cautionary words seemed to only intrigue the prince and he tsked at the captain for his insistence. "Honestly, Jesse. If she intended to harm me, I'm sure she would've done so already. The mage queen would

16

not risk our tentative peace and trade agreement by sending someone to kill me." He didn't wait for the captain to protest again before he turned toward the palace and offered me his arm. "Shall we?"

I rested my hand on his forearm and found an amused grin rising to my lips as I mumbled, "of course."

We were quickly trailed by two guards, I assumed per Jesse's request. Though it was also possible they would've trailed the prince regardless. I didn't know how strictly they guarded the royalty here.

In Emberwyn the queen always had two guards with her even though I doubted their presence was actually necessary. She was the most deadly person in the room, perhaps aside from Desmond, but he rarely followed her around. He appeared when she requested him and when she didn't need him I never knew where he ran off to.

"My name is Andras, by the way." The prince said softly as we headed down a hall off of the large foyer.

I'd been so distracted I hardly noticed we'd even made it inside. To my surprise, the inside of the palace was not all that different from when I'd been here as a child. It was still just as extravagantly decorated, although the colors had been changed to reds and golds rather than the white and blue that would have been here for Emberwyn.

The portraits we passed were all new, which wasn't surprising either. I imagine they burned any reference to magic or the Cutwater royal family. We were heading toward the east wing, which I very rarely explored. The layout however seemed to be exactly the same as the palace I'd come from. This would at least make navigating this maze on my own a bit less confusing.

"You can call me Liza." I said in response. "Lady Winters is…" I trailed off as I gazed out the large windows that overlooked the city. "Far too formal." I gave him a half smile and then looked ahead of us again.

"Liza," He tested out my name and I could see the corner of his mouth lift. "I hope you'll come to like it here. I am not sure my father will know what to do with you though." He let out a low chuckle. "I don't believe he expected a woman."

I huffed a laugh myself. "That isn't the first time I've heard that today."

"I imagine not." He stopped before a door on our left. "Here we are."

The guards that had been trailing behind stepped around us now to push open the door. It opened into a small but beautiful sitting room, with two other closed doors which I assumed led to a bedroom and bathing room.

"Forgive me, but I do need to find Eric, so I will have to take my leave. Your meals will be delivered to you here. Should you need anything else, please request it from the maids when they make their rounds."

He didn't wait for my reply before walking off the way we had come from. The guards stood on either side of the door like statues, but their focus stayed entirely on me. I gave them a strained smile and stepped through the doorway. One of them very quickly closed it behind me.

My shoulders drooped and I exhaled. At least I didn't have to *start* more lies yet. The relief of that was short lived as I looked around the rather sparsely decorated room and realized that I'd just traded one prison for another. At least in Queen Moira's castle, I was permitted to roam. It seemed that here I would be restricted to my quarters.

The difference though, was now I had hope. She said all she'd give me was freedom if I succeeded, but perhaps I could prove I was worth more to her and regain my crown too.

18

Chapter 3

Slade

I leaned against the bookshelves of Leodric's study trying to hide the annoyance from my face while I waited for him. The bastard had the gall to call me here with no explanation of why, but then couldn't show up on time to his own fucking meeting. It was something I'd grown accustomed to by now, but I still expected that he'd give this up once I'd more than earned my keep.

The door swung open violently and he strode in with Naomi on his heels apologizing for whatever it was she'd done to piss him off now. I still didn't understand how she'd ended up as his *assistant*. She always got on his nerves. He barely spared me a glance as he walked between the large leather armchairs that sat in front of his desk and around to the mahogany chair behind it. The seat vaguely reminded me of a throne.

Papers littered his desk, along with a handful of daggers that were seemingly used as paperweights. Naomi halted in front of his desk, set down a folder with a few more papers inside it, then turned on her heel and left without another word.

Leodric's age was showing. It was obvious in the dim light from the chandelier. The gray strands peppering his otherwise midnight black hair glimmered like the stars visible in the sky beyond the large windows that lined the wall. He heaved a heavy sigh and ran his hand down his face as he leaned back and rested an elbow on the arm of his chair.

He gestured for me to have a seat as he reached forward and flipped open the folder. I didn't move. I just sheathed the dagger I had been cleaning and pocketed the rag before crossing my arms over my chest and raising a brow at him.

"Straight to business then." He murmured, without looking up from his paperwork.

"That would be nice."

He shot me a brief glare, but closed the folder and steepled his hands in front of his face. With either elbow rested on the armrests beside him, he slouched back in his chair as he examined me.

"Xavier broke the code."

Both of my brows shot up my forehead. We *all* knew the consequences. In all my time here I hadn't ever heard of someone doing it.

"You want me to kill him." It wasn't really a question. I already knew the answer, but I needed him to say it anyway.

He nodded. "And his target."

"Who was his target?" Xavier wasn't the type to accept a hit and not finish the job. There had to be a reason, and I wasn't about to accept this without knowing why.

"Valencia Altura. The daughter of the lord that presides over Listera."

I glanced away from him while I thought through the reasons he likely wouldn't have been able to follow through with it, but came up empty. None of us had many hard drawn lines in the sand as far as who we *wouldn't* kill. We could refuse the job, but once we accepted it was kill or *be* killed. There was no going back on it.

"What was his reasoning?" I asked when I couldn't come up with an answer on my own.

I glanced up at him again when I saw him move out of the corner of my eye. He reached into the inside pocket of his vest and pulled out a piece of parchment. He offered it to me. I pushed off of the bookshelves and stalked over to his desk. I snatched the paper from his fingers and opened it. It was Xavier's messy script, without a doubt. It simply read, 'You bastard. It'll be your head on a pike.'

"This tells me nothing." I dropped the paper on his desk. "Is there something I should know before I accept this?"

"I wasn't giving you an option." He shrugged a shoulder, reached out, took the note, and tucked it back into his vest. "You either kill him and complete the contract he refused, or I kill you and call in the next person on my list."

"That's not how this works."

"It is now." He picked up the dagger closest to him.

I could just kill him. The thought crossed my mind far more quickly than it should have, but less than a second later the realization that I had no desire to take his place at the head of the guild quelled the rage that rose up with his threat. I couldn't imagine handing it over to one of the others either.

"Fine." I snarled through gritted teeth. "Where was he last seen?"

"I assume that the messenger hawk came from Listera, but I couldn't tell you." He gave me another shrug. "Find him and bring me his head."

"Just his?" I mused, turning to leave his study.

"I won't need her head to know that the job is done."

I yanked the door open, shot Naomi a glare, and headed toward the front door. For the first time since I arrived at Leodric's mansion as a child, I found myself questioning my mentor's loyalties.

Chapter 4

Liza

It was the following afternoon before anyone came to call on me. I hadn't tried to leave my room, but was certain that I would not have been permitted to even if I had requested it. I spent my evening and most of the morning unpacking. If they hadn't sent me back yet, I didn't imagine they would.

There was a light knock on the door and I opened it to find Captain Mercer standing between the two guards on either side of the doorway.

"You'll be needed in the King's study in thirty minutes." He gave me a once over before he met my gaze. "However, if you're ready now, I can escort you."

I looked down at myself, then back up at him. I had put on another emerald gown this morning, similar to the one I had worn yesterday but a bit more modest. My hair hung loosely down my back, and the waves were more unruly than usual thanks to the humidity here. It seemed suitable enough for meeting the king.

"I suppose I am ready now."

The captain nodded and stepped to the side, motioning for me to walk around him into the hall. I stepped out, pulled the door closed behind me, and started off to the right without waiting for him to guide me. It occurred to me far too late that I probably shouldn't show how much I know about the structure of the castle.

He caught up with me before I made it five steps. "You seem oddly confident that you're headed the right direction."

I slowed my steps so I was moving at a more casual pace and shot him a sidelong glance. "Well, I imagine that the king's study is not in the same wing that I'm staying in, which means it must be back the way we came when I was brought down here yesterday."

He raised a brow and shook his head. "Right. Of course." He fixed his gaze ahead of us, but slowed to match my walking speed.

We walked for several minutes in silence and I took the chance once again to look around at the walls. The paintings and tapestries that covered them were lavish, but still nothing compared to what had been in the palace in Emberwyn.

"You certainly know your way around pretty well on your own." Captain Mercer observed.

I struggled to bite back a smile before I could rein myself in and realized I was giving far too much away. "This is nearly identical to the palace in Emberwyn. The only difference is the artwork and color scheme, really." I gestured to the walls around us. "I assume that he uses the same room that Queen Moira uses as her study."

I finally met his gaze and nearly stumbled at the amusement I saw there. I would have assumed his reaction to be something more like suspicion or concern, but his sly grin said otherwise.

"I assume that means you know all of the palace's secrets then."

Fine. If he was going to play into the game then so was I. "I'm sure there are differences where secret passages are concerned" I waggled my eyebrows at him. "I hardly have any interest in wandering through cobwebs though. I'll stick to the main halls."

He chuckled as we rounded the corner into the hall that would hold the king's chambers, and also held his study. I stopped at the doorway allowing him to open it and walk in first.

The room was more plain than I expected. A large round table sat in the middle of it. Book shelves lined either side all the way to the back of the room and they were packed full of books. I didn't bother to take the time to study them to see if I recognized any. Either they kept the books we had to learn more about how we worked, or they destroyed them in an attempt to erase the history.

Their lives were so fleeting it was easy to wipe out books and documents from a prior monarch and pretend it never happened, not even two generations later. My people lived so long that most of us were *alive* for the history that would've been in those books.

The vampires, they *never* changed. Gods, Queen Nyvara was nearly four thousand years old by now if I recalled correctly. The idea of living that long was horrifying, though I don't know that I would consider it *more* scary than dying itself. Surely at some point she grew bored.

The captain introducing me brought my thoughts back to the present as my gaze fell upon the king and I dipped into a curtsy.

"Rise." His voice boomed through the room, far more powerful than I expected. I did as he asked, but did not approach the table. A handful of men sat around it. Prince Andras was seated directly to the king's right. On the king's left sat a young man who bore a striking resemblance to Andras and to the King himself. I assumed he must be the other prince, Edward, per Desmond's notes.

He had hair that was darker than Andras'. It was more brown with very little red in it. His facial structure was nearly identical, but he seemed to have a permanent scowl on his features, which only deepened as he took me in. His eyes were hazel in color and held nothing but malice.

Andras rose from his seat and pulled out the chair to his right. "Please, have a seat, Lady Winters. We were just about to get started and were merely waiting on you."

The blush that rose to my cheeks was genuine. The captain had said we had thirty minutes. Surely we had not walked so slow that it had taken that long to get from one side of the palace to the other. Despite knowing that, I was horrified to have been late to my first meeting with the king.

I quickly took my seat, which he pushed in behind me, and he returned to his seat. The king's gaze never left me. I could feel the weight of it like a boulder sitting on my chest. It was almost hard to breathe. Gods. He had the same effect on me as Moira. I disliked him already.

"Yes," King DuMont mused. "It seems the moment that I informed my court that the emissary was a woman they were far more punctual than they normally are." He glanced around at each of them. "Quite early, in fact." His dark brow raised.

Much like his sons, the man was broad and well built. I was certain he could take down anyone in a fight if he chose to, except a fae or vampire of course. His hair was dark brown. I assumed the reddish hue of his sons' must have come from the queen. His eyes were a brilliant emerald, though right now they held a bit of annoyance which made their green color even more striking.

No one spoke. He let out a heavy sigh. "Let's get on with it then, shall we." He leaned forward and rested his elbows on the table, gesturing to me with one hand. "Lady Winters is the emissary that Queen Moira has assigned to stay here and monitor our trade agreements. She will make decisions on the Queen's behalf and aid Andras in managing trade in the ports. Any import and export related business should be routed through the two of them."

He looked at me now. "I will allow each of the members of my court to introduce themselves to you after this meeting has concluded. We have no trade matters to discuss at the moment, but anything that you hear in this room *stays* within this room or we will send your head back to Queen Moira regardless of the detriment it would cause our people from the loss of our agreement with her. Do I make myself clear?"

I blinked, the only part of the ice cold fear and shock that drenched me I was unable to stifle. I cleared my throat. "Crystal, your majesty."

He stared at me for a moment longer than felt necessary before his attention shifted to a blonde man across the table from me. The moment the weight of his gaze shifted from me to that man, my shoulders drooped in relief. I don't know what I had been expecting, meeting King DuMont for the first time, but an outright threat to my life was not what I thought I'd get.

A hand rested on my knee and I nearly jumped out of my skin. I quickly stifled the motion and Andras squeezed my knee. I glanced over at him and the question in his eyes was quite clear. I was most certainly *not* okay, but I nodded my head subtly anyway and he returned his hand to his lap.

Why the prince felt like he needed to check on me, I wasn't sure, but it solidified my hope that it might actually be possible to survive here after all.

*

By the time the meeting ended, I was starving and could not have escaped that room fast enough. Everyone was dismissed at once, myself included, and I quickly rose to my feet. I wasn't sure how I would stand another moment with all of them, let alone how I would remember their names. They were curious about me, sure, but once we got into the nitty gritty of the discussions among the court, which consisted of dukes from all over Mytharae, all I could take away from it was their hatred of mages and magic as a whole.

This trade agreement was a requirement for their survival and nothing more. Their land was so wooded still that they could not possibly produce enough crops to last through the winter for their entire population and that shortage had only gotten worse the longer the DuMont's had been in power here.

I was here because they had no choice but to agree to her terms. What I gathered in the hour long meeting was that Valehaven, as expected, told them to go fuck themselves, Elkridge was out of the question based on logistics alone, and Runelheim demanded humans be handed over in trade. The thought made me shudder. Becoming a living bloodbag was unimaginable. Celestas, well, that wasn't even on the table.

No one wanted to mess with a deal with the fae. My mother was the only one who seemed inclined to trust them.

Andras caught me by the elbow the moment I escaped the room. "Surely you must be hungry." He said with a warm smile. "Allow me to show you to the dining hall?"

I could feel Captain Mercer's presence behind me. I could have sworn the man had specifically chosen himself to be my personal escort. It seemed like an overreach of power to me, but I was not well informed when it came to the captain of a royal guard's duties, given that Desmond seemed far more important to Moira than anyone else.

I desperately tried to rein in my disgust and anxiety by plastering a smile on my face. "I'm famished." I breathed, which was not a lie, but it was the best excuse I could give to get me far, *far,* away from that room and those men.

The captain was not subtle with his scoff, but Andras paid him no mind. He led me down the halls with his arm looped through mine as if I had no idea where the dining hall was. But he wouldn't have known I could have found it myself. He had not had the chance to be informed by the guard nipping at our heels as we traversed the hallways.

When we finally reached the dining hall I stopped in my tracks and stared in disbelief. Despite the extravagant nature of the room, with the same red and gold colors as the halls in various decorations and curtains around the room, the food was almost *scarce* and rather insignificant. There was a considerable amount of fish and various seafood, but it was entirely lacking of much else. Servants stood at either end of the table of food and, noting our arrival, quickly began to prepare plates for us.

"Not what you expected?" Andras asked casually after stopping and turning to look back at me. He didn't give me the chance to respond before he continued. "As I'm sure you gathered from the meeting, we almost never have enough grains and other crops growing to support our population. Without any form of trade until now we've been forced to ration out most everything we can't get from the sea. We do what we can to make sure our people are fed."

I desperately rushed to regain my composure. "I'm sorry, I don't know what I was expecting, but it most certainly wasn't that you cared enough to limit your own meals as well."

He raised a brow. "They don't do that sort of thing in Emberwyn?"

"I'm not sure there's ever been a need for it, if I'm honest with you, but knowing Moira she absolutely would not limit herself for her people."

He raised a single brow and judging by the tick in his jaw, he didn't appreciate that. "Interesting."

I walked around him and took a seat at one of the tables that sat the farthest from the other court members and guards who were already eating and chatting around the large room. Andras followed me and took a seat across from me. The captain lingered behind him.

"You're dismissed, Captain. Please feel free to have a seat elsewhere and have dinner yourself if you don't have other obligations." Andras glanced over his shoulder at him for only a moment, before his attention returned to me. "I'm sure you have questions for me?"

Plates full of salmon and another type of fish I wasn't sure I had ever eaten were placed on the table in front of us. I picked up the fork they sat with it and pulled off a small piece of the salmon. It smelled delicious, but I couldn't put a name on the spices used.

"Several actually, but I doubt they'll be the questions you're expecting me to ask."

He stabbed a fork into his own salmon and ripped off a far larger chunk. He held the fork up and hesitated before bringing it to his mouth. "I have come to expect the unexpected where anything with Emberwyn and mages are concerned, but I'll answer whatever you'd like me to if it's within my knowledge and power to do so."

The corner of my mouth quirked up in a slight smile. "I've not heard much since Mytharae was... uhm, liberated?" I wasn't sure the word to use for it exactly, but tried to say something that he hopefully would not be offended by. His answering snort of a humorless laugh at least told me that he wasn't irritated by it.

He began to eat as I spoke. "What happened to the mages that lived here or held positions of power?"

"Most of them were stripped of their titles and wealth and tossed out of their homes. I don't believe that anyone has paid them much mind since. Some of them may have left. In fact I assume most would have." He looked down and pushed the food around on his plate while I slowly picked at mine.

"Truthfully, there were several who still fought back. They were either subdued and imprisoned or killed."

Suddenly, I'd lost my appetite, but it would be incredibly rude not to finish the small amount of food that had been given to me. I forced myself to pick up the final piece of salmon.

"I don't imagine that leaving would be possible if they were stripped of their money and homes." I mumbled, unable to stop myself.

He looked up and met my gaze again. "I never said I agreed with the treatment of them. The stories I've heard made mages out to be awful tyrants who enslaved humans or paid them barely livable wages. I imagine that anyone alive at that time was simply tired of the oppression they experienced under Queen Moira's rule."

My eyebrows nearly rose to my hairline.

"What?" His brows scrunched together. "Is that not the case in Emberwyn?"

"I–" I stopped myself and looked away, trying to think back to my time spent in either castle. I hadn't really recalled whether or not the few humans I did interact with were paid, nor had I ever inquired about their wellbeing. Suddenly, I felt far more out of touch than I'd been in my whole life.

I sighed. "Honestly I'm not sure. I haven't ever left the palace except to come here." I didn't go on to tell him that meant I had also been here before he was even a thought in his father's head, but that was a story for another time – if I ever felt that he deserved the full truth.

"You've never left the palace, at all?"

Was it concern I saw in his eyes? I couldn't be sure. Confusion perhaps? Regardless, I shrugged my shoulders and took a few moments to eat before replying. I had to concoct a lie. The first of many. What "lady" spends her entire life in the royal palace? Most of the other officials among my mother's court were permitted to come and go as they wished and often went on trips to other places in Emberwyn and in the world if they saw fit.

"My parents died when I was very young. I was raised by Queen Moira and her court. I haven't ever had the need to travel. Everything I needed was provided to me and I did not feel comfortable testing my luck and asking to travel too."

It was definitely confusion I saw in his face now as he tilted his head to look at me like I was some foreign being he hadn't known existed until now. "Simply leaving the palace to explore the capital city is hardly *travel*."

My cheeks flushed. *Shit*. Of course I hadn't considered just leaving the palace to explore the city. I nearly shook my head at myself for how stupid that story likely sounded.

"How about this?" He leaned forward and I looked up at him. "I'll take you on a tour of Maeus tomorrow. I know you saw some of it on the carriage ride from the docks to the palace, but there is *far* more to our beautiful city than the dreary roads you took to get here."

I smiled, my embarrassment falling away when it was clear he seemed to drop the subject and accepted my carefully woven lie. "I would be honored to have you show me the city."

Chapter 5

Slade

I left my horse at the stable on the outskirts of the village. Listera was small with buildings clustered close together which made surveying *anyone* a bit of a challenge. There were fewer places to hide when every home was practically on top of the next.

My first order of business was determining if Xavier was even still here. If he was smart, he wouldn't be. Shit, if I'd threatened Leodric I would've left the country as quickly as I could. He had to know that one of us would be sent to end him.

I strode down the dirt road farther into the village. The houses became more well constructed the further I went. It transitioned from small one or two room huts with thatch roofs to larger wooden homes with actual windows. The only sign of anyone with some kind of wealth living here.

I was a few buildings from the tavern when I was yanked by the shoulder into a tiny alley between two homes. I glared at Xavier. He pressed a knife to my throat.

"Tell me what the fuck you're doing here, Slade, or I swear to the gods I'll kill you where you stand."

"Good to see you too, Xavier."

He pressed the knife harder against my neck, but angled it so that it wouldn't draw blood. "I mean it, *Marbhadh*. Speak or die."

I sighed and rolled my eyes at him. Before he could make good on his promise, I grabbed his wrist, hit a pressure point that I knew would disable his whole gods damned arm and flipped us around so his face and chest were pressed to the wall instead.

"You know better than to threaten me Xavier. You also know better than to threaten Leodric and refuse to kill your mark after you've accepted it."

"He didn't give me a fucking name. He told me it was the lord's daughter. He knew damn well if he'd have given me her name I would've refused it."

"And why, exactly, is that? You see, I asked, but he didn't give me anything other than the note you sent him." I pressed him harder into the wall. "It would have been far smarter to simply *disappear* instead of threatening him and telling him you hadn't completed the assignment."

"He would have figured it out on his own eventually."

"Yes, and by then, you moron, you could've been on the other side of the fucking world."

"And let someone else kill her? Absolutely not."

"Which brings me back to *why*." I leaned in closer to him. "You're testing my patience now. Give me *one* reason I shouldn't follow through with his order to kill you in the next thirty seconds or I'll do what I was sent here to do without a second thought."

"She's my oldest friend. I haven't seen her in *years*. I don't know when or how her father became the lord over Listera but somehow Leodric found out I still had ties outside of the guild and sent me up here to kill her to test my fucking loyalty."

Against my better judgement I released him. "Several others have people outside of the guild. You'd have to have done something else to make him question you for him to pull something like this."

He grumbled something under his breath and turned to face me. "After my last assignment I told him I wanted out. I still owed him a *little* bit of money and told him my next assignment would be my last and I'd pay him off."

I shook my head. *No one* gets out of this life once they're in it. Xavier wasn't the brightest of the bunch but he had to know better than that. I didn't even bother asking why. It wouldn't matter either way.

"I have to kill you. He wants your head."

"You don't have to do anything." He rubbed his neck and leaned back against the wall. "You can tell him I'm dead and he'll believe you. You've been around for your whole gods damned life. He'd never question you."

"I have never completed an assignment without returning with the requested proof." I narrowed my eyes. "I am sure as shit not risking my reputation *and* being in his good graces over someone stupid enough to think they can just get *out* of the guild."

He snorted. "Right, because no one is ever allowed to leave. If they want to, they *mysteriously* end up dead on their next assignment. You've never noticed that?"

"I've never cared to pay attention to anyone but myself."

"Right, because the infamous Sàmhach Marbhadh is just as much of a ghost in his personal life as he is when out on an assignment for the fucking guild."

"What I do when I'm not working for Leodric is none of your business and bringing that up is not convincing me that I shouldn't just cleave your head from your shoulders in this disgusting alley."

He drew his sword now. "You aren't going to take me down that easily, and you're not getting to her without going through me first."

"All this for a childhood friend?" I tsked at him as I drew my own blade from the sheath between my shoulder blades. "Really Xavier, you should get your priorities straight."

"You mean to tell me there isn't a single person that you would protect with your life?" He was reaching now, trying to find something, anything to get me to change my mind. I admit, it was a little irritating that we couldn't leave. After all, at some point someone would notice I'd stopped aging and get suspicious. I would have to find an out myself, and faking your death was not as easy as it seemed.

"Not a single fucking one."

"No one is that alone." He lowered his sword half an inch. "You're lying."

"And you're going to force me to make a scene in a downtown alley, which will be terribly inconvenient when I have to find a way to drag your body off and dispose of it somewhere."

Something I couldn't place crossed over his features for a moment, but afterward I could see the desperation.

"What if I offer you a life debt? A blood oath if you let me live?"

"I have no use for whatever you could offer me in exchange."

"Even if I can help you get out one day too?"

"What would make you think that I'd want out?"

"I saw you shadow walk. I *know* what you are. It's a secret we unfortunately share, but for some irritating reason, being a water mage doesn't give me the ability to just walk to another location whenever I want."

I lunged for him and swung. If he knew that, he was going to die regardless of whether I'd been ordered to kill him or not. He only succeeded in dodging me because he froze my feet to the ground long enough for me to stumble and wind up on my back before I could recover my balance.

He was on top of me the next moment, his sword pointed directly at my throat. I was frozen to the ground in the next breath. A solid sheet of ice encasing my body beneath him. The bastard should count himself lucky that the move took me by surprise or he'd never have gained the upper hand. I hadn't ever fought a mage.

"Fine." I snarled. "And what, pray tell, is your fucking idea for how to give him your *head*."

"Looks like you'll have to come up with something."

"And her?"

"Leave that to me." He sheathed his sword and knelt next to where I still lay frozen to the ground. He slid his knife along the palm of my right hand, then his own. "I agree to creatively make sure she's perceived to be dead, then disappear with her. I will owe you a life debt, to be paid at your choosing. You will figure out how to lie to Leodric about killing me *and* her. Do you agree?"

"Yes." I snarled.

He clasped his hand in mine and the ice melted at the same moment. The insidious blood magic encased both of our arms. I couldn't see what form it took on either of us. He pulled me back up to my feet.

"So, what's your plan?" He asked.

"Where are you running off to?"

"Elkridge."

I considered that. "I think I've got an idea."

Chapter 6

Liza

I should have known when Andras offered to show me around the city that we'd have to ride horses to do it. Why I thought this would be a quiet and romantic carriage ride I wasn't sure. I, unfortunately, had absolutely no sensible clothing to ride in, which likely meant that I would have to ride sidesaddle.

Even worse was the fact that I'd never even sat on a horse in my life. I stood next to the massive chestnut gelding and stared at him as if he were literally going to be the death of me. I was convinced that he would.

Andras chuckled when he walked over to check on me. "Come on then, I'll give you a leg up."

"Surely we could just walk?" I offered. "Or take a carriage?"

He shook his head and looked at me dismissively. "You'd hardly see a thing in the carriage and the city is far too large to walk on foot. You act as though you've never been on a horse before."

"I haven't!" I protested before I could think the better of it.

He slapped his face with his hand and rubbed it down to his chin like he was exasperated with my exclamation. "Okay, first thing's first, let's get you *on* the horse. I'll go over how to steer him and if you're still acting as though he'll kill you I'll put you on a lead."

Hot shame raced up my neck into my face. The idea of being put on a leadline like a godsdamned child was far more humiliating than walking around the city on foot because I was too afraid of the damned horse.

"Fine." I grumbled, which seemed to amuse him.

"Are you at least wearing something comfortable under all these skirts?"

"I have a light pair of knickers on if that's what you're asking. It's bloody hot out here."

His smirk was a little too sensual, but I tried not to think about that as he reached down and moved the skirts aside so he could grab my leg to hoist me up. I had to bunch up the damned skirts so I could swing my leg over the horse like he instructed. Before I knew it I was sitting atop the horse and looking down at him. I let the dress fall down and despite being bunched in front of me it mostly covered my legs.

The animal didn't move a muscle. It had a surprising amount of patience, while the horse that I was sure was being held for Andras was stomping its front leg impatiently. The handler swatted at the horse's chest each time it lifted its leg to paw again. He mumbled something under his breath at it but it couldn't have cared less.

41

"Now," Andras started. "You'll hold the reins like this." He held one of the reins in his hand, showing me he had his index, middle, and ring finger around the reins, but his pinky tucked under them with his thumb on top. I mimicked the hold on the other rein and he nodded his approval before handing the one he had in his hand to me.

"To steer you need to look where you want to go and turn your shoulders. Truthfully he will probably just follow my mare, but if for some reason he develops a mind of his own you'll need to know this. To speed up, push in with your heel and calf like this." He pushed my leg against the horse. "To move him over, push with your whole leg." He demonstrated that too and the horse moved away from him.

"Finally, to *stop* you are going to have to stop your hips from moving and squeeze your knees together. If all else fails, just pull on the reins."

"There's no way I'm going to remember all of this." I mumbled and he smiled.

"I can always put you on a–"

"Absolutely not. I can handle this." I snapped, then immediately regretted it when I saw the look on the handler's face for how I snapped at him.

Andras only seemed even more amused. He patted my leg. "I'll bring a lead just in case. Just breathe, relax, follow me, and I promise it will be fun."

He walked over to his own stead and mounted like he'd done it a million times. He urged his horse forward and I attempted to do the same with mine. To my relief, the thing obeyed and lurched forward to follow Andras. Four guards on horseback took up positions in front of us and behind us, two on each side. It made us a very large procession of six horses and riders in total, which would certainly draw attention.

"Wait, what's his name?" I asked quickly when I caught up with Andras. I thanked the gods this horse seemed to do just as Andras said and did everything he could to stay next to him.

"His name is Jake. Quite boring and humanlike, I know, but he's a pretty easy going guy and it seems to fit him well."

I raised a brow. "And yours?"

"Bella." He said simply.

"And you think that suits her?" The mare was a hair shorter than Jake, but she was stunning. Her sleek black coat shimmered in the afternoon sun and her mane was braided like a waterfall down her neck.

"Well, her *full* name is Isabella, and yes, I do believe it suits her."

"Hmm." I hummed and looked forward as we strode out of the gates and into the streets.

He took me through what he considered the nicest part of the city and I had to admit it was far nicer and cleaner than I expected given what I had seen closer to the docks. The people bowed their heads and waved as we passed. It occurred to me then that I wasn't sure that my mother ever did such a thing. My sister didn't either. They spent most of their time within the palace or other estates, but they *never* walked among the people.

I hadn't, but that was because to anyone outside of her inner circle, I did not exist. I was just a resident who lived in the palace. No one ever knew why or what purpose I served, but often they didn't even ask. Most of the staff were human and wouldn't have known me when I'd been born anyway.

There were even a handful of shops we passed that he said were owned and run by mages who had worked their way back up into this side of town. They were healers mostly, but sold other goods too. Healers, it seemed, were still welcome, but any other form of magic was cast out.

By the time we returned to the palace I was exhausted and sore, but I'd learned far more about the political structure of Mytharae, how their people worked, the history *they* remembered, and the prince himself. He seemed far too easy to get close to. Being interested in mages and being interested in *me* are two entirely different things, yet he acted more like the latter and I couldn't for the life of me figure out why.

He once again walked me to the dining hall and had been about to sit down with me when Prince Edward pulled him away–far enough he didn't believe I could hear them.

"You took that mage around our *city*?" His whisper was hardly that and I could only just make out his words. I pretended to be quite interested in my food.

"If we mean to have a good trade arrangement with them, we have to show them what they're supporting. I understand the history we have been told, but she seemed genuinely shocked when I told her. Maybe they aren't all as bad as they were made out to be."

I could feel the glare Edward sent my way. I didn't have to look up to see it for myself when he scoffed.

"They are a power hungry plague of beings that would gladly rule over us once again if the dragons didn't make it damn near impossible. For all you know she's been sent here to learn about our defenses to see if they *can* take this land over again. Are you *really* that naive?"

I looked up now, because it was mind boggling to me that the younger of the two would be so bold as to question the older, but it was not my place to step in. I wasn't even supposed to be overhearing this.

"She hardly seems like she'd have been sent here to evaluate our defenses. She'd never even sat on a horse for gods sake. She's entirely clueless."

I was certain my face turned scarlet.

"That's not what Captain Mercer reported to father this morning."

Andras crossed his arms over his chest. I looked away before Edward could catch me staring, but made sure I could still watch them out of the corner of my eye.

"And what exactly was that?"

"She knows the layout of the palace quite well. Apparently it is almost identical to the one she grew up in."

"Well at least she won't get lost." He quipped.

"Gods Andras, are you that stupid? Has she already enchanted you so deeply that you can't see what's right in front of your face? She knows the palace well enough that she could kill you in your sleep if she wanted."

Andras scoffed. "Oh yes, surely she's plotting my death as we speak." I could see him run a hand over his face in frustration. "She's a fire mage, Edward. If she wanted me dead she wouldn't have to sneak up on me in the night to do that. I looked into it. Fire mages have been lost for centuries, but what history we have of them suggests they could set fire to a whole city block if they wanted with minimal effort."

I had to choke back the laugh that almost bubbled out of me. I'd never felt such a power, though admittedly I was never really permitted to experiment with my magic. Once we discovered it was fire Moira forbade it. Didn't stop me from trying, but she always found out somehow. It was like she had eyes *everywhere*.

"All the more reason she shouldn't be getting a personal tour of the city, brother." Edward said almost too low for me to hear.

"Worry about yourself. I have this handled." Andras snapped and spun on his heel to come back over and sit across from me again.

Edward caught his arm. "I'm just trying to look out for you *and* our people." He urged.

Andras shook him off and didn't look back as he strode over to me.

"Everything alright?" I asked hesitantly.

"Everything's fine." He assured with a tight smile. "Edward is just a little bit of an ass at times, it's nothing to worry about."

We settled into a slightly uncomfortable silence for several minutes after that before he spoke again. "So, Captain Mercer says that you know your way around the palace."

I looked up from my plate and met his gaze. "From what I have seen so far it is nearly identical to the one in Riodian. I can make a few assumptions about where things may be, but I imagine there are differences I have not come across yet."

"Interesting."

I could see him mulling over what Edward had said. I found myself praying to the gods that his little brother wouldn't intervene too much in my plans. I needed Andras to trust me. Needed him to *fall* for me. But if Edward planted doubt in his mind it would make this a lot harder.

Chapter 7

Slade

It took me nearly two weeks to take the detour necessary to sell my story to Leodric. I was irritated, tired, and unreasonably sore from the trek itself, not to mention, the brutal beating that Xavier gave me a week ago to "sell the story". I hated to admit he was right. At least my eye wasn't still swollen shut. The fucker just had to go for my face.

Naomi looked at me like I had six heads when I walked through the foyer of Leodric's manor. I strode straight past her to his office and didn't bother to knock before I kicked the doors open.

Leodric spun around in his chair with wide eyes and a dagger at the ready until he saw me and relaxed.

"Looks like Xavier fought back." His gaze drifted down to my hands, I presume expecting to see a bag with a head. When he realized I didn't have it his eyes snapped back up to meet mine again.

"I asked for his head." He didn't lower the dagger.

"If you'd like his head you're more than welcome to fish his body out of the sea and remove it yourself."

"And why, exactly, would I need to fish him out of the sea?" He narrowed his eyes, but finally sat the dagger down on the stack of papers in front of him.

"He was running to Elkridge. I caught him at the cliffs. As you can see," I gestured to my black eye and split lip, "we fought. I won, but lost one of my favorite daggers in the process."

He raised a brow as if to press me to continue.

I sighed. "He tried to wrestle me off the goddess damned cliffside. I got away from him and threw a dagger. Hit him square in the chest. He stumbled and fell backwards before I could stop him to retrieve the dagger… and his head."

He stared at me in silence for so long I started to question if he'd heard me, or if he was waiting for more. I had nothing more to tell, and hadn't prepared any additional details to make the lie more convincing. I started to run through a million other things to say in my mind when he finally sighed.

"You're certain he's dead?"

"You doubt my aim?"

He considered me for another moment and then looked down at the paperwork on his desk. "Poison is not your style."

I blinked at him. Xavier had spelled Valencia to make her appear to be dead, poisoned, more specifically. It would've looked like she'd been given nightshade. I hadn't even questioned the method.

"It was the most inconspicuous way to do it, and allowed me plenty of time to track down Xavier as you had asked."

He didn't look up, but continued to shuffle the papers around his desk.

"I'll take my payment now."

"Naomi will see to it that the funds are transferred to your account. You're dismissed."

I clenched my fists at my sides, feeling the sudden notion to unsheath a dagger and throw it through his fucking head. No one simply *dismisses* me like I'm nothing more than a fucking errand boy. I bit back my rage, and my retort. It wasn't worth the headache. I turned and stormed out of his manor where I could slip off and shadow myself to my apartment. Perhaps even find a fucking healer for my face.

*

Not even two weeks later Naomi sought me out for a *very* specific high profile request. She wouldn't tell me anything else and demanded I go meet Leodric in person. I followed her back to the manor and stood impatiently just inside his study with the doors closed behind me.

"If this is another 'track down and kill a guild member' task you might as well just try to kill me and get it over with. I'm not interested."

He didn't even look up from whatever letter he was writing. "That's hardly a respectful way to talk to your mentor."

"I don't particularly give a shit."

"You know, if they hadn't specifically requested you, I'd give this to someone else just for your attitude."

"And if you're going to keep grumbling about my attitude like I'm some petulant child I'm going to refuse the job anyway. I was *trying* to enjoy my evening."

That finally got him to look up and roll his eyes. "Yes, I'm sure spending the night in that shit hole tavern is absolutely thrilling. Have a seat."

"No, thanks."

He frowned, put his quill in the inkwell, and leaned back in his seat, steepling his fingers in front of his chest while his elbows rested on the arms of the chair.

"Your target is Prince Andras DuMont."

My jaw nearly hit the floor before I gathered my composure.

"Yes. I thought that would be your reaction, and no it isn't a joke."

"Who in this gods' cursed kingdom would want *him* dead?"

"Does it actually matter?"

No, not really, but in some twisted way, it kind of did. The man was probably the most loved royal I was aware of. Although Queen Nyvara was also fairly well liked.

"I'll take your momentary silence as a no, which is a good thing too because *I* don't know. A hawk brought the message to me and there was no signature on it." He reached into the top drawer of his desk and removed a scroll, neatly rolled with no identifiable seal on it. "This is all of the details. I regret to say that this is another assignment I'm not sure I can give you the option to refuse."

"Attempting to kill him and failing will result in my execution."

He shrugged. "Don't fail."

I stared at the scroll he still held out to me.

"Do I need to reiterate that this is not optional?" He raised a brow.

This time I contemplated killing him far more seriously than I had when he'd told me to take care of Xavier. "No." I grumbled, then stepped forward to take the scroll. It seemed I didn't have to care how I was going to get out of the guild one day. I likely wouldn't make it that long. No one had ever been successful at infiltrating that palace or the one in Emberwyn and it was not for lack of trying.

"Good. The scroll contains the details. Whoever set this up has also set you up with a cover, so I'm going to assume it is someone within their own court. Perhaps even the king himself."

"That wouldn't make any sense." I mumbled while I unrolled the scroll to review it.

He huffed a laugh. "It is far cleaner for the prince to be mysteriously murdered than for the king to revoke his birthright when the people are so in love with him, don't you think?"

I couldn't explain it, but something told me it wasn't the king. It was this weird feeling that I just couldn't shake. The foreboding about the assignment itself was practically eating me alive.

"Follow the instructions on the scroll and I'm certain you'll be back here in under a month and a half with a *very* heavy sack of gold."

I turned and walked out of the room without uttering another word. Torn between having a reputation to uphold and knowing that killing this prince felt like it was going to start a war or be the death of me. Maybe even both.

Chapter 8

Liza

I walked into the library and it looked vaguely similar to what I remembered from when I was a child. Several sections of the books were missing, though. If it were sorted similarly to the library in Riodian, I should be able to find what I was looking for pretty quickly. Assuming, of course, that they didn't destroy *everything* related to magic.

I walked past the end of three rows of shelves before finally turning left down the fourth. My finger traced over the spines that were at about waist height. I was relieved to find that most of the magic related texts were still here. They just destroyed everything historical, by the looks of it.

I stopped on a tome that had a blank spine. I pulled it out to discover it was a book on the history of elemental magic. It looked tattered and incredibly old, like it dated all the way back to the dark times, before Nyvara helped shape the world into what it was today.

I wondered if this was where Andras learned about the history of fire mages. It was a history I had *never* learned. This book belonged on the empty shelves. Those used to hold all of the world history we had. This likely only survived because it was *here* instead of where it belonged.

I spun around to walk back out to the tables that were scattered around the front of the library and nearly walked right into Captain Mercer.

"What do you think you're doing?"

I shot straight up in bed. A dream. It was… a dream? It felt so real, like I'd lived it.

The room was bathed in light, meaning I'd slept through breakfast. I rarely ate more than a pastry, and that was not a luxury they offered here. I didn't think I'd miss Riodian, but at that moment I did.

I drug myself from the bed and dressed quickly. I couldn't stand the thought of staying in this room all day again. What Andras said yesterday about how powerful fire mages were stuck with me. I hadn't ever learned anything about mages like me. However, I hadn't had any reason to look into it either, until now, and my curiosity was getting the best of me.

I assumed there were others. I mean, there had to be. I couldn't exist if there weren't. Magic was genetic, meaning my father must have been gifted with fire for me to inherit it.

The library here had to have *something* about mages in it if Andras had researched it. My dream must have been an unconscious fear that I wouldn't be permitted to go to the library, or would be caught and suspected of something nefarious.

I opened the door to my chambers and found two guards stationed outside as expected. The one on the right turned to face me.

"Can I help you, m'lady?" He was polite, at least. His brown eyes were all that was really visible in the absurd metal armor all the guards seemed to wear. *Except* the captain, of course. I would've found the face shield and helmet quite clunky myself. No such thing was worn by any guard at home.

"I'd like to go to the library, if that's permitted."

He exchanged a glance with the other guard.

"I will die of boredom if I stay in this room for the entire day." I protested, hoping that might at least earn me leniency from these men. I hadn't bothered to pay attention to see if it was always the same set of guards.

"Certainly," he replied abruptly. "Right this way." He turned and started off down the hall to the right, heading back to the main entry. I followed him while the other guard walked less than two steps behind me.

The library was exactly where I expected it would be. Clearly they had not changed much. When I walked in the doors I was struck with the most frustrating sense of deja vu. It looked *identical* to my dream. Lighting and all, including the empty shelves where our historical records would've been kept.

Everything from the lineage of the citizens of Emberwyn down to the actual historical events were logged in thousands of blank and boringly bound brown leather books that looked strikingly like the one I'd seen in my dream. I decided to do exactly what I'd done then.

I walked to the fourth row of shelves, turned left, and ran my finger along the spines of the books until I came across the exact book I pulled out in the dream. I stared at it for several minutes, terrified to pull it out and be correct that this *is* what I dreamt about.

Psychic visions were not normal. Perhaps I was finally losing my mind. So much time spent cooped up would do that to you. Two weeks on a goddess damned boat and four days stuck in a room aside from one meeting with the king, my excursion with Andras, and my meals was rather depressing.

I finally shook my head as though that would shake off my anxiety and pulled the book from the shelf. It felt like a bucket of icy water had been dumped over my head when I turned it and discovered the cover was *exactly* the same as the one I saw.

Elemental Magic - A History of the Arcane Arts

I tucked the book under my arm, spun on my heel to head back out of the library, and walked straight into Captain Mercer. I nearly jumped out of my gods damned skin.

"What do you think you're doing?" His tone was only slightly accusatory and he steadied me so I didn't fall over when I stumbled backward.

"I– Uh–" I stuttered. "I was dying of boredom. I came to look for something to read to pass the time."

He arched a brow at me and tilted his head as his gaze fell on the book I had. "I don't believe that you'll be permitted to take that from the library, but I'm sure that you're welcome to sit at one of the tables and read it if you'd like."

It was my turn to tilt my head. My eyebrows scrunched together in confusion. "Why couldn't I just take this to my chambers?"

He tried to stifle a startled laugh. "You are essentially a foreign operative in our court. You're not going to be trusted with anything that may hold value to us. Keeping the book in this room where the librarians can be sure you're not destroying or stealing it is the only way to protect our interests."

I blinked. While what he said probably should've been obvious, especially after what I overheard with Andras and Edward, the thought had not even crossed my mind.

"Right." I murmured quickly. "Well, then I'll find a seat and read this. Thank you." I made to take a step around him and head toward the front of the library, but he placed his hand on the book and stopped me.

"May I?"

I looked from him, to the book, and back again. "I suppose so." I released my grip on the book and allowed him to take it.

"Elemental Magic?" He questioned while he examined it. "Is this not something you would've had in your own library? You said you were bored but I hardly feel that history books are entertaining."

Embarrassment flushed through me and I was certain he saw it on my face. I wasn't sure what I expected him to say, but that wasn't it. It was like being interrogated without being taken to a private room to do it. Not to mention, the idea of explaining *why* I wanted to read this particular title would make me sound either stupid or insane.

Truth. The best thing was the truth. "Well, actually, this *particular* book was not in the library in Riodian." I reached out to take it back from him. He, thankfully, allowed it. "As a matter of fact," I continued, for no reason other than to try to ease whatever concerns he did have. "I don't believe we had any books at all that contained the history of fire magic. This one seems promising, and I'd like to know more about the history of my kin."

He seemed to accept that. "You are one of the only living fire mages I've ever heard of, so that's not terribly surprising."

"What do you know about them?" The question escaped my lips before I could stop it. I nearly smacked myself in the face trying to halt the words as they left my lips.

That seemed to amuse him, because he smiled slightly. "Not much, admittedly. I didn't know we had this book. Looks like it was on the wrong shelf to me. All I can tell you is that according to the history we were taught, fire mages were wiped out centuries ago. Obviously at least one or two must've survived or you wouldn't be here today. I can't imagine you are *centuries* old."

"Actually, mages are known for living for a few centuries."

His eyebrows shot up his forehead.

I laughed. "Don't worry, I'm only seventy."

He blinked like I'd just said something he was even more flabbergasted by. I patted his shoulder and he let me step around him this time. I finally struck him speechless.

I made my way to a table and sat down to flip through the book. I heard his footsteps trailing me after a few seconds, but he continued walking toward the doors. He mumbled something to the two guards who had come with me, then left.

I opened the book and flipped to the table of contents. *Gods* this book was old. The first "element" listed was blood. We hadn't had blood mages – well, witches, as they were called back then – since before Queen Nyvara ascended the throne. I never learned what happened to them, but those were very dark times. I could make my own guesses.

Spirit was next, and those were usually seers. They weren't much worth reading about. Air, Water, Earth, and then finally fire. The very last portion of the book.

I spent the next couple hours, skipping even lunch, to review the history in that book. Just as Andras had said, fire mages were quite powerful. It was a power I had never known–had never had the chance to, really. I'd played around with it a bit when I thought Moira wouldn't find out, lighting a fire in my palm, occasionally tossing it out and accidentally setting a plant ablaze. Ezra always snuffed it out.

I smiled at the thought of her. I missed her already. She would never give me any helpful instruction or tips, despite that I was certain controlling fire had to be similar to controlling shadows. Fae magic was different was all she would ever say to me.

A thought occurred to me then. Moira had no eyes here. *I* was her eyes. I was to report back to her using the ridiculous code she'd given me, knowing my letters would probably be reviewed before they were sent. I could practice my craft here. I just needed to figure out where it would be safe to do so.

I had a pretty good feeling Captain Mercer could tell me where that might be.

*

Later that evening, I found Captain Mercer in the dining hall. His brows rose as I took a seat across from him at a table where he and several other off duty guards were sitting.

"Please, have a seat." He said sarcastically and took a sip of what I presumed was a very shitty ale. I had yet to have anything here worth writing home about and desperately hoped I could convince one of the ship captains to procure me some wine.

"Thank you, I obviously intended to." I shot back at him.

He smiled. "What can I do for you, Miss Winters?" His tone changed entirely and I was suddenly very aware of the eyes on us.

An audience was *not* what I wanted for this conversation. I cleared my throat and leaned closer to him over the table.

"That book I was reading today…" I started.

He leaned in closer to me with a smirk playing at his lips. "What about it?"

"Well," I whispered. "Truthfully, I wasn't just interested in learning about other fire mages… I was also trying to learn about fire magic in general."

His brow quirked up.

"I was not permitted to use my magic in the palace at Riodian. I was hoping there might be somewhere here that I could… I don't know, practice with it…you know, safely?"

"You're asking if there's somewhere you can't easily light anything on fire?" He leaned back in his chair.

I sighed and sat up straighter. "Essentially, yes."

He looked away for a moment and rubbed his chin while he thought about it. "I may know just the place," he said after what felt like an eternity.

I perked up immediately.

"But–" He gave me a suspicious smile. "I'll only show you where it is on *one* condition."

My shoulders fell. "And what would that be?"

"We have a need for more magic blocking cuffs and shackles. Generally, we don't often have mages who need to be locked up, but it's impossible to keep them contained when we don't have those."

"I can almost promise you that Queen Moira is not going to agree to that."

"I'm not asking Moira. I'm asking *you*."

"I can't–"

"We just need you to get them out of the vault they're in. It was something I'd have asked eventually, but I knew the answer would have been no until I could figure out something to exchange for it."

"What do you mean get them out of the vault?"

"There's a whole room in the dungeon with chains, shackles, and the like that we can't walk into. It's like we're walking into an invisible wall. I assume it was spelled to keep humans out. If you can get in to get us those supplies then I'll give you somewhere to train."

I looked away while my mind spun. There *were* bad mages out there. I knew as much because our dungeon in Emberwyn was never empty. I never knew the crimes they committed, but it was not my business to ask.

"Fine." I finally agreed. "I'll try to get them for you."

He smiled, seeming quite pleased with himself.

"And what happens when I can't?" I raised a brow at him.

"We'll cross that bridge when we come to it. Maybe I'll settle for some exotic imported alcohol instead." He shrugged a shoulder. "There's a whole world full of possibilities."

I didn't like the sound of that at all. I ate my dinner in silence while I listened in on the conversations of the guards around me. They shot me curious glances now and again, but didn't acknowledge my existence otherwise. It felt almost illegal to listen in, but I couldn't bring myself to pick up my plate and move elsewhere. Andras was nowhere to be found, and it was better than eating alone.

When I finished my plate, the captain stood and motioned for me to follow him. I assumed I would have to try to give him what he wanted first. We traversed several hallways and two flights of stairs before the damp smell of earth and mildew started to linger in the air.

It was colder than I expected beneath the castle, and I had never wandered this far on my own. There were certain hallways and stairways that were always guarded, and we'd already gone down three of them. This was entirely unfamiliar to me.

He finally halted in front of a large open archway. I stopped with him and turned to glance inside to find it was just a large open room with a myriad of chains, shackles, and other scary looking weapons and devices that I couldn't possibly name.

He lifted his hand up and touched the invisible barrier he mentioned. "If you can walk through it, just bring the shackles and chains out into the hallway. We'll sort through them and organize them later."

I eyed the opening cautiously. I would've thought it was a trap, were it not for the fact that it was clear the only person who tolerated magic so far was Andras. The captain wouldn't have even been open to paying a mage to put up such a thing.

I stepped forward and walked into the room without running into anything, but a strange tingling sensation did pass over me. It was like walking through a fog. I grabbed a pair of the shackles by the chain holding them together and walked it over to him. The same tingling sensation passed over me as I returned to the hallway.

"Excellent." He smiled. "Move the rest of them and I'll show you the place you'll be least likely to catch anything important on fire, before I escort you back to your chambers for the evening."

I smiled triumphantly. I was one step closer to actually figuring out what my magic was capable of.

Chapter 9

Slade

Nearly a week and a half of hard and fast travel later I was walking into the back side of the palace in Maeus. The absurdity of this assignment only increased when I met the captain of the guard and he looked at me like I was the dirt on the bottom of his shoe. He insisted that I prove my abilities before he'd actually let me take my place on the royal guard.

I had paperwork stating I was more than qualified, but he either didn't read it, or didn't care. He put me into the ring with one other guard first. When I took him down in less than a minute he added four more. They lasted a minute and a half.

I walked up to him at the edge of the sparring ring. He was wide eyed and slack jawed. His men were groaning and slowly climbing back to their feet.

"That good enough for you?" I practically growled. I was exhausted. I desperately wanted to get something to eat, maybe grab some fucking whiskey, and collapse on whatever pitiful cot they set me up with.

"Where did you train again?" He didn't even reach for the paperwork and turned a suspicious look on me.

"I trained with werewolves. As I'm sure you've been informed, I traveled from Elkridge to get here and I would appreciate being shown to wherever it is I'll be staying so I can get a real night's sleep."

"Hmm." He mumbled something under his breath, then gestured for me to follow him as he turned and headed toward the barracks. I picked up my bag and slipped it back over my shoulder. I caught up with him quickly.

He stopped at one of the last doors on the left. "You'll be sharing this room with David. He'll also be on guard with you. There's a fire mage here that we're keeping eyes on around the clock. I assume whoever got this arranged for you informed you that will be your primary task here?"

I nearly stumbled with how quickly my head whipped around at the words 'fire mage.' Fire mages were extinct. One of the long lost magics, much like the mages whose magic came from blood.

He arched a brow at me. "I'll take that as a no." He seemed amused by that. "She's hardly as much of a threat as we thought. Apparently she's not very skilled with her *abilities*." He shrugged. "Report for duty with David tomorrow evening. You'll be on the night shift."

I was about to protest and snap something at him, but he walked away before I had the chance.

Great. Just fucking great. The night shift. Precisely what I hoped for after traveling practically day and night to get here *as soon as possible*. I muttered a string of curses, but dropped my bag and headed off to find something to eat. Surely one of the guards could point me in the right direction.

*

I had just sat down to eat when I caught a glimpse of Prince Andras out of the corner of my eye. I'd need to learn at least a little bit about his daily habits if I was going to have to do this during the day. How I was going to do that *and* sleep was questionable, but I had time to figure it out.

He sat across from a redhead who stood out like a sore thumb. Her clothing was just as lavish and ridiculously pompous as his. Her vibrant and unruly curly hair draped down her back. The deep blue of her gown contrasted it to such a degree I wondered why she'd ever don such a color. The prince seemed absolutely enamored with her.

"She's quite the looker isn't she?" A male voice behind me nearly made me jump. By the goddess I was fucking tired. I didn't even hear him approach and I heard *everything.*

"Can't really say for sure. All I can see from here is her hair and her back." I replied and glanced over at him. He was tall and lanky. I was surprised *he* had the skill or strength to be here, but he was clearly a guard if his leather pants and black tunic were any indication.

"David." He sat his plate of food down next to mine and offered me his hand. He had short light brown hair and hazel eyes. He looked really young, twenty at best.

"John." I took his hand and shook it.

"I assumed as much. We don't often get new guards and you were the only person in here I didn't recognize."

"Right." I went back to eating and tried to be less obvious about staring in the direction of the prince. Watching someone was so much easier when no one could see you. At least the backstory was something I could lean on when I didn't fit in. No one in Mytharae knew much about the culture in Elkridge. I only knew it because of Zephyr.

"I'm convinced Jesse has the hots for her too, but he tries to pretend like he doesn't."

I nearly choked on the overcooked mystery fish on my plate. "The captain?" I clarified when I finally cleared my throat.

"Yup!" He was shamelessly watching the woman interact with the prince.

"And who is she anyway?" I gestured her way.

"Liza Winters. She's a *lady* apparently and it's our responsibility to keep an eye on her overnight. When you're rested up and ready to join me on guard duty for her anyway."

"*She's* the fire mage?"

He nodded while he chewed on the same mystery fish I had. "Gods this is awful." He frowned down at his plate. "We'd probably find something better at the local tavern. They at least know how to cook."

"They have whiskey too?"

"Not sure. I don't drink, but maybe." His attention finally settled on me again. "The captain would be pissed though if he found out you'd had a drink before our shift."

"I don't know that I particularly care what the captain thinks of me."

He shrugged. "You probably *should*. I'll show you around on our next night off. Not all of the taverns within walking distance are worth going out to."

"Noted."

*

The following evening I walked with David just before sundown to relieve her daytime guards. According to what

Jesse had last heard, she'd be in the gardens with the prince, much to his dismay. I was starting to see what David meant.

Having no idea where anything was yet, I was forced to follow his lead. We came across them as they were walking back inside. Liza was hanging off of Andras' arm and the two of them acted like they were far closer than I would have expected. I knew nothing of politics, but I *did* know how much of a big deal it was that the humans ruled this land now. Hooking up with, or at the very least courting a mage seemed asinine to me given the history there, but what did I know.

The two guards trailing them nodded to us, then broke off to head back toward the barracks while we took their place and followed the pair instead. David didn't utter a word, but given the time of day I assumed we were headed to one of their chambers.

This goddess forsaken armor made it impossible to glide along silently behind them. I was used to moving without making a single sound, whereas now I creaked with each movement I made between the chest piece, metal helmet, and other gear we were outfitted with.

If the captain wanted to test my skill, he should've done so in this monstrosity. Perhaps then it wouldn't have been so easy to take down his men. I still could've done it, of course. It just wouldn't have been as efficient.

When they finally came to a stop in front of a single door on our left we halted immediately and got to watch awkwardly as the prince whispered something that I couldn't quite make out into her ear. She laughed the way that all women laugh when being charmed by some insanely corny pickup line. She even went so far as to blush when the prince took and kissed the back of her hand as he bid her goodnight.

I thought I might puke.

He turned and walked away while she turned toward her chambers. That blissful smile stayed plastered to her face until the moment she thought no one could see her. Her face flattened out faster than a head falling from someone's shoulders after I'd cleaved it off with my sword. It was all an act.

That made it much more interesting.

Chapter 10

Liza

I followed Andras up the pathway to the highest point on the palace grounds. He'd insisted he had a surprise for me. I was fairly certain I knew precisely where we were headed, but plastered a smile and look of excitement on my face regardless.

The longer I played this lie, the harder it became to keep myself invested in it. He seemed lovely, sure. I could see myself *liking* him, but the more time I spent around him the more I realized that he was not likely to ever be what *I* wanted. It wouldn't really matter in the grand scheme of things. I would outlive him by, well, several hundred years, so it wouldn't be like I couldn't enjoy other men eventually.

He led me to a clearing at the top of the hill. This area of the grounds was mostly trees and unwieldy brush aside from the pathways we carved into it. It was meant more to be a lookout over the sea, but it was rarely used for that purpose.

When we reached the summit, he stopped, turned to face me, and smiled as he gestured toward the blanket laid out on the ground beyond him. There was a basket placed atop it with a bottle of wine, two glasses, and what looked like a selection of fruit, cheese, and meats.

I smiled, forcing my expression to lighten and an excited chuckle to rise from my throat. "A picnic?"

He shrugged. "A picnic of sorts. My father will never let us escape your escorts, but it's the most private place I could find on the grounds otherwise." He reached down and pulled the cork from the wine bottle, then began to put a generous pour of the maroon liquid into each glass.

I took the glass he offered and followed his lead as he sat down on the blanket. We gazed out over the deep blue sea that stretched from the port as far out as the eye could see. He rested an elbow on his knee and turned to look over at me.

"This is my favorite spot to escape the rest of the residents of the palace, and especially to escape those on the court when they're here." He admitted.

I raised a brow. "Court life is that hard?"

He took a sip of his wine and surveyed me for a moment. "You don't find it exhausting sometimes?"

I stared into my wine like I was considering his words, but I agreed wholeheartedly. I just couldn't decide whether to be truthful or not. I took a sip, savoring the tart taste. There were notes of cherry and a hint of something citrus. I had to thank the gods he hadn't gotten a bottle of fae wine.

"I suppose it can be." A hint of the truth would make some of this more bearable.

He snorted. "Only made worse by my mother's attempt at playing the artful matchmaker."

I was mid-sip when he uttered his response, and I nearly spit out my wine. My escorts lingered close by. Likely far enough that if we spoke softly they wouldn't overhear, but close enough they could intervene if needed. Whether or not they heard his statement, I couldn't tell. They didn't utter a single sound.

"Oh?" I studied him closely as his attention shifted back to the sea. His expression was conflicted, brows drawn together and his lips in a tight line. His gaze didn't return to me, even as I picked through the selection of fruit he'd packed and dug out a strawberry.

"There's a ball next week. She seems to think she's lined up the most eligible maidens for me to peruse. It's dreadful. How on earth am I to pick a wife if I know hardly anything about them?" He looked at me now and whatever emotion now filled his eyes I couldn't quite read, but it made me self conscious all the same.

I had been about to take a bite of the berry, but hesitated with it a breath away from my lips. "I suppose you'll have to make conversation as you dance." I shrugged a single shoulder. "Surely she won't expect you to choose someone without courting them first?"

I bit into the strawberry and his eyes seemed to track the motion. He shook his head and brought his wine to his lips again. A few moments of less than comfortable silence passed before he finally mumbled, "probably. She would likely say that it would be impolite of me to court several at a time."

"Is it really all that urgent for you to find a bride?" I poked about at the other items he brought. "You're quite young, and the king seems in perfect health. Gods, Princess Amelia has been of marrying age for quite some time now and has not been pressured to do anything of the sort."

"I imagine it is different for mages. You live hundreds of years, there's never a rush to continue the royal line."

The wine soured on my tongue as the mention of *continuing the line* reminded me just how much I abhorred the idea of children, or rather, the idea of producing my own anyway. It occurred to me at that moment that perhaps my mother had given me a gift by stripping me of my title. It also removed the inevitable requirement of producing an heir.

It was that thought that spurred my next question. "What *would* happen if you failed to produce an heir?"

He seemed perplexed by the question. "Well, it would entirely depend on the situation of the court at that time. Realistically, there is no requirement for an heir until I've ascended the throne. I suppose if a royal were entirely incapable of producing an heir the crown would transfer to the next person of royal or high ranking blood and their children. If there were no others, it would transfer to another high ranking official as dictated by the current monarch." He tilted his head in question. "Why do you ask?"

I didn't have an explanation prepared, so my look of shock was genuine. I came up with a lie rather quickly this time with a bit of a chuckle. "Forgive me, your suggestion of it just got me thinking of Amelia, and how I could never picture her with a child. She's…" I struggled to find the right words. "A bit too irresponsible, I suppose." I shrugged as if that might help to sell the falsehood.

That earned a half laugh from him and he began to pick through the food as well. "I guess it's a good thing she's got a long time to figure that out. I, on the other hand, might have a few years at best."

I didn't know what to say to him. *If* I succeeded on the mission she sent me on, I doubted my personal opinion on that matter would change, so if he was gauging my interest in it, it was better I kept my mouth shut. I did, however, file away his other suggestions for myself if the day would ever come that I'd find myself upon a throne.

We spent a few minutes in companionable silence before he spoke again. "I do hope I can convince you to join me for at least one dance, even if you are not on my mother's list of eligible women."

He had a playful smile on his lips, and I leaned a bit closer to him and gave him a mischievous smile of my own. "And what exactly could I get in exchange for a dance, your highness?"

"Hmm." He hummed. "Perhaps I could try a bit harder to rid you of your armed escorts?"

I raised a brow. The offer was not entirely awful, but I was hoping for a bit more than that. Still, I smiled a bit wider. "I suppose I'll take that under consideration."

Chapter 11

Slade

Two weeks had passed and I'd managed to explore nearly all of the castle in my off time. Given that it paid to know all of the passage ways, no one questioned that I took extra time before and after my shifts to explore. The damned place was like a maze. I'd nearly gotten lost at least a dozen times, despite my training. Every single hallway looked nearly identical.

Now I stood in a mostly empty courtyard watching Liza desperately attempt to get a grip on the fire magic she'd apparently spent next to no time learning how to wield.

"You would think she'd be a little farther along with it by now, wouldn't you?" David asked far too quietly for her to have heard. The captain stood about five meters from us, watching just as intently as I was.

"Didn't the captain say she was not permitted to practice in Emberwyn?" I mumbled back, watching as she tried again to set fire to the target before her, but control it before it burned through the whole thing. I hadn't ever studied what fire mages were capable of. Destruction, for sure, but what else, I didn't know. They were more a myth at this point than anything.

"Yeah, but it can't be that hard."

"Did you find wielding a sword to be challenging when you started? What about throwing knives, or fighting hand to hand?" I hissed, probably more harshly than I should've, but that struck a nerve. Magic was unruly when you had no idea what you were doing with it.

He jumped, drawing the captain's attention for a half a second before his gaze shifted back to her when he realized there was nothing amiss. "Well, I suppose it was challenging. I hadn't—"

"Exactly. It would stand to reason it is the same with magic. It would be best not to insult her when she could very well just incinerate you where you stand, don't you think?"

She gave the slightest indication she'd heard me, with a quick glance over her shoulder, but then she set to work once more. She set the next target Jesse had set up for her on fire and this time seemed to control the flow of it far better than she had on her last four tries.

Jesse, seemingly satisfied with his observations of her training, walked around us to head back into the palace. He'd been off duty for a few hours by now, so why he had come with us this evening was a mystery to me. He didn't even look our way.

She repeated the same movement several more times, until she could completely put out the fire. She seemed pleased enough to turn and head back into the palace herself.

She made eye contact with me, and it felt like she had a rope tied around my chest and yanked on it. For a few breaths, I couldn't pull my gaze away from hers.

She stumbled like she had a similar feeling. She looked away first, forced to glance down at the ground to lift her skirts and regain her footing. Having been released from whatever spell she put me under, I blinked and shook my head.

I saw David glance between us curiously. If he had asked, I wasn't even sure if I could articulate what had just happened. The strangest urge to follow her took over me. I had to do that anyway, but this felt just like the pull that struck me the moment our eyes met.

"I think she likes you." David whispered to me.

I rolled my eyes. "I think she just tripped over her skirts."

He mumbled something under his breath that was too low for me to catch. We were far enough behind her that she shouldn't have heard either of us. We kept that distance, giving her a modicum of privacy per Andras' request, but we never were far enough that she was out of sight.

When she reached her quarters, she walked in without looking back to see if we followed or took up our posts outside.

*

The next evening I stood in the ballroom, in close proximity to the throne. My shift started early this evening, with the ball for Prince Andras requiring more guards than usual. I was dreadfully bored. Watching the elites of society parade around like pompous pricks was not high on my list of enjoyable activities.

Soft music had been playing for the better part of an hour already when she finally entered the room. I could have sworn the energy shifted entirely as soon as the doors opened. I didn't have to look to know that it was Liza that was entering. I just *knew*, like I could feel her presence wherever she was. It was a frustrating side effect of whatever moment passed between us.

As she strode out onto the balcony to make her way to the stairs, I found myself frustratingly captivated, much like the rest of the crowd from what I could tell. She was stunning. Her fiery red hair was braided back away from her face, but hung down her back in its usual chaotic glory, leaving her shoulders bare. The dress she wore was the deepest maroon I had ever seen, making her emerald eyes shine like the lights themselves. It hugged her curves until it reached her hips, then gently cascaded out and down to the floor.

She walked down the stairs with a slow measured precision that rivaled that of an assassin trailing their mark down a quiet alley in the dead of night. A practiced pace that I could admire. Her eyes trailed the crowd, passing over everyone, but *me* like she was purposely avoiding it. Her gaze landed on Andras and a soft smile rose to her lips. She donned the mask of a starstruck lover so quickly I might've missed it if I hadn't seen her drop it before.

"So you *aren't* gay." David muttered when he stepped up next to me, startling me out of the daze she had left me in.

I scowled at him. "I wasn't aware that was a question."

"Everyone else practically swoons over her, yet you've barely looked at her outside of what is required for your job." He shrugged. "Anyone would start to wonder."

"I'm surrounded by idiots." I mumbled under my breath. He either didn't hear me, or didn't deign to respond.

77

I quickly found her again among the crowd and tracked her movements for the rest of the night. I had to guard her *alone* this evening. It was far too convenient not to have been planned by the person paying me. The additional people in the castle, combined with guards stretched thin, would make it a perfect time to make my move.

When she finally began to make her way toward the doors to leave I fell into step behind her. I didn't miss the disappointed look on her face when she'd never been graced with a dance with Andras. The queen seemed to have made absolutely certain she wouldn't get the chance.

She walked into her chambers without a word and I silently took my place as sentry outside of the door. I knew it would take a while for Andras to return to his chambers for the evening, so I would be standing here for quite a while. I rarely relied on my magic to complete an assignment, but my ability to shadow walk would be useful, and I did not need to get caught.

I heard a few grumbled curses beyond the door behind me, but ignored them. Whatever she was going through was nothing I could be concerned with now, however much her act intrigued me, keeping my focus this evening was most important. I ran through my plan several times again in my head before her quiet question behind me startled me nearly as much as David had in the ballroom.

"Can you help me?"

I glanced over my shoulder to find her still in her gown, one arm twisted behind her back and the other holding the door open. The moment she realized she had my attention she spun around, revealing the knotted mess of corset lace that she was currently struggling with.

I narrowed my eyes and stared long enough that she glanced back over her shoulder at me and scoffed. "I can't get it on my own. I've been trying for the better part of twenty minutes now. I don't know what the maid who helped me did but it will *not* come undone and I desperately would like to breathe again."

I finally turned fully to face her and she looked forward again. I took the laces from her hand and examined it. She'd pulled it so tight in her struggle I was certain it couldn't be undone without some kind of magical intervention.

"I'll have to cut it." I said curtly.

"You could cut the dress and I'm not sure I'd care."

I arched a brow, but pulled my dagger from the sheath concealed at my waist and sliced through the laces. I loosened the stays and she took a deep breath.

"Thank the gods." She mumbled. "Thank you." She tossed over her shoulder before disappearing into her chambers once more.

I stood, stunned and slightly amused as the door slammed in my face. I turned around once more, slipping the dagger back into the sheath.

Around three in the morning I finally slipped from my post like a shadow itself. I stepped out into Andras' chambers, hidden by the shadows cast from his book shelves. The full moon didn't offer much cover when his curtains were open, but it was enough to confirm he was in fact asleep, and alone.

I crept across the floor on silent feet, magic not needing to aid me now. I pulled my dagger from its sheath and slid it across his throat so deeply that he couldn't even utter a scream before the damage was done. He stared up at me in shock for a handful of seconds, clutching at his throat and desperately attempting to make a sound before the life drained from his gaze and he lay motionless.

Something about this one didn't sit right with me. Hadn't, really, the longer I was here. Of the two princes,

Andras would have been a better king, and I couldn't come up with a single reason someone would want him dead. Aside from his possible affections for Liza. Edward was nothing but a spoiled prick. Unfortunately, I had a reputation to uphold, and I'd be damned if I'd let myself get invested in a mark, whether for good reason or not.

I cleaned the dagger on the sheet, tucked it away and shadow walked back to my post. No one had come or gone in the time I'd taken, I was certain. It would take longer than that amount of time to traverse this hallway alone.

They'd find him in the morning. I would likely stay another week so as to not raise suspicion, then follow through with the lie I crafted for my way out.

Chapter 12

Liza

All I saw was his eyes. They were the most brilliant shade of amber I had ever seen. I was transfixed, mesmerized in a way that I hadn't ever experienced. It felt like my world stopped the moment that we made eye contact.

How long had he been guarding me and I had entirely ignored him? I wasn't sure I could say. I didn't look at any of them much. They were a shadow that followed me everywhere. I noticed occasionally when they switched shifts, but beyond that, I never paid them any mind.

I wanted to kick myself for tripping over my skirts. It was humiliating, although he didn't seem to notice, thank the gods. I couldn't get him out of my mind though, and that was frustrating. How could I be so stuck on someone when the only feature I noticed were his eyes?

The thought was shoved from my head in the same way that the breath was forced out of my lungs as the maid pulled the stays on my corset. I was back in the present moment again, looking at myself in the large floor length mirror in my chambers. The gown was a deep maroon, and absolutely stunning.

It was a gift from Andras. I found it in a box on the table just inside the door when I returned to my chambers last night. I should've been excited to see it, but the color was nothing I'd ever considered wearing, and I was sure I would hate it. Looking at it now, it looked like it was made for me. The color complimented my eyes beautifully.

My mind wandered to the guard again, and I shook my head. I couldn't afford any distractions tonight. I *needed* to keep up with Andras. Needed to keep his attention on me and none of the other women his mother planned to parade in front of him.

I thanked the maid as she scurried off. I was already running later than I wanted to be. Being late was intentional, but being this late was not a good look either. There was only one guard at the door when I opened it. He silently followed me down the hallway. I knew for certain that he wasn't the one I had nearly fallen over last night, even without looking at his eyes.

I reached the doors that lead out onto the balcony above the ballroom and the guards opened them up for me. The ballroom was full. Upbeat music echoed through the room and many people were already scattered about the floor dancing.

I could feel his eyes on me like a weight on my chest. For some irritating reason, I knew exactly where he was in the room without having to look. I purposefully avoided making eye contact, or even looking within a few paces of where he stood. It didn't staunch how much I wanted to look at him though.

I found Andras quickly, and tried to keep my focus entirely on him. It was an effort, but I managed. The guard's gaze never left me. It felt like a brand. Despite my best attempts to get close to Andras, I never quite made it. Each time he made eye contact with me, he was torn away by the queen to dance with another woman.

I lost my nerve after two hours and decided I no longer wanted to even be *at* the ball. Plenty of other men tried their hand at dancing with me, but none of them were the one I *needed*. I left through one of the side doors, rather than doing the walk of shame back up the stairs. My shadow followed me out.

*

A loud pounding on my door woke me the next morning. I didn't even have the chance to sit up in bed before the guard came bursting through both doors and into my bed chamber.

"She's coming with us." He declared, and another guard followed swiftly behind him.

The amber eyed guard stood in the doorway. If he was still here, gods, it had to be early. The night guards were never here when I woke normally. It took me far longer than it should have to realize that the very first gray light of dawn was all that lit the room.

"Do you at least intend to tell me *why?*" The guard at the door demanded while the one who came in snarling grabbed my elbow and ripped me up from the bed.

I stumbled into him, barely getting my feet under me as fear gripped me in its clutches far too quickly. I'd never been manhandled like this before. Brutally tortured by Moira with water, yes, but manhandled, no. The second guard grabbed my other elbow and they drug me between them. I couldn't even get my feet to move that quickly.

"The prince is dead. She's being taken for questioning." The first one replied.

I met my guard's gaze as I was hurried past him for the briefest moment, but it was real fear I saw in his eyes. "She's been in her room all–" He started, but we were bounding down the hallway.

"It doesn't matter. Everyone will be questioned."

He didn't speak again after that, and I was too frazzled to even keep track of where we were heading until we reached the dungeons.

I was thrown into a cell like one might throw yesterday's trash out. Surely they were not treating all of the guests this way. That would hardly prove to send out a good message to the people. More importantly, *which* prince. They hadn't specified, and the unnamed amber eyed guard at my door had not asked.

It had to have been shock that prevented him from questioning them further. The same crippling shock that was keeping me silently sitting at the back of this cell clutching my knees to my chest like my life depended on it.

Dead. Andras couldn't be dead. I had just seen him at the ball, and despite not getting the dance I'd hoped for, he was happy and perfectly healthy. They had to mean Edward. He looked just as miserable as he always did, especially when he looked my way.

The cell door swung open and Jesse strode in, followed closely by two other guards. He took in the sight of me and mumbled a curse under his breath.

84

"Did you even consider allowing her a moment to put on something other than a nightdress?" He snarled at the guards behind him.

They didn't respond. He sighed and turned to face me. "We have reason to believe you're involved with the prince's death. Reason to suspect everyone who attended the ball last night, truthfully, but being that you are not a citizen, your name is at the top of the list."

I gaped at him. "What in the world would make you believe I would have had anything to do with it?" I nearly shouted, probably a bit more sternly than I should have despite the fear that didn't seem to ebb. "I don't even know *which* prince. No one has fucking told me."

His head reared back like I'd struck him and he stared at me in disbelief.

"Please, by the gods, tell me it wasn't Andras." I pleaded with him. A desperation I didn't know I had seeping into my voice. "Not that I would have wanted that for either of them, but–"

"Enough." He held his hand up. "Do you know of any plans from Emberwyn, or anyone within Emberwyn to take down Prince Andras?"

A choked sob escaped me and I quickly drew my hand over my mouth to try to stifle it. He was my only way out. The other option was death. Whether that was by their hand or Moira's, it was inevitable now. I had failed–so miserably that I didn't know where to go from here.

He studied me for a few breaths while I began to struggle to breathe. To him, it must've looked more like grief, but it was panic. A panic I wasn't sure I had ever felt before. My life had never felt so finite. This was it. I was sure of it.

I didn't see what he did next, nor what he said. It wasn't until someone was kneeling down in front of me that I had some semblance of clarity. A hand reached out toward me and the person in front of me came into focus between my ragged and rushed breaths.

"Breathe." I read his lips more than I heard the words. "You're alright." He said much louder this time, to where I could hear him over the noise in my head. He took my hand and pulled me to my feet. I don't know when I'd started to shake, but standing was far more of a challenge than I think I had ever had.

He sighed, slipped my arm over his shoulders and urged me to walk with him. He ended up practically carrying me. I couldn't function. Couldn't think straight. It felt like I was paralyzed.

I didn't know where we were going. Didn't know where we'd arrived until he sat me gently on a soft surface and knelt between my knees in front of me. All I knew was it wasn't a cell.

"Look at me." He demanded, but I couldn't. A strong hand clasped my jaw and lifted my face up so I was eye level with him. Amber. His eyes were amber. It was *him*. "Breathe." He urged.

My breath shuddered out of me and he sighed.

"Breathe in." He instructed, and I tried to listen. "And out." He continued. I didn't know why he was trying to help me, but he was surprisingly patient. When my breathing slowly came under my control again he mumbled, "good."

He disappeared for a few seconds and I began to slip into a panic again. He returned with a glass of water, which he held out to me hesitantly. "It'll be alright. The captain has cleared you. I'm needed elsewhere, but keep focusing on your breathing and you'll be just fine."

He waited patiently while I took the glass in one of my shaking hands. He left the moment I had a good grip on it.

*

He hadn't returned like I hoped he might. In fact, no one came to call on me for nearly three days. My meals were delivered at regular intervals and that was the only way I knew time was passing.

I spent the time wondering how the hell I'd ended up in this situation in the first place. My mother had disowned me the first moment I displayed my magic, or lack thereof in her mind. I was never enough, no matter what I did to try to appease her. I was locked away in a godsforsaken castle where no one could find me or even know I existed. Belittled and punished any time I tried to use what little magic I had. Then I was sent off to–

The realization hit me like a ton of bricks. I wasn't sent off to prove myself and regain my stature. I was sent off to die. She thought so little of me she knew I would fail and sent me here so she wouldn't have to do the deed herself. How could I have been so stupid, so naive to think that she actually wanted me to show her I wasn't worthless?

I was a fool. A gods damned fool. And here I sat, wallowing in self pity trying to pull myself together for whenever I returned to the duties that never mattered in the first place. At least I had value here. I had a purpose. Perhaps I could just stay here and she'd never come to call on me.

I laughed at myself then. She'd send Desmond or Azazel to take me out. I was sure of it. She'd said not to bother coming back but I could read between the lines. If I failed, this was my last chance. And I failed miserably.

A knock on the door pulled me from my spiraling thoughts. I rose from the bed and moved to answer it. I was shocked to find the captain standing on the other side, without any other guards. He chuckled when I glanced around like I was missing something.

"Everyone has been reassigned closer to the royal family. It was determined you weren't a risk, so your guards were given duties elsewhere."

I met his gaze and merely raised a brow. This was not at all what I would've expected. I was still wondering when they were going to change their minds, drag me out, and execute me for being involved somehow.

"I'm told you haven't tried to leave your chambers." He continued, looking me over with the slightest hint of concern on his features.

"I was having a bit of an existential crisis, I suppose." I stepped around the door and let it rest against my hip.

The corner of his mouth tilted down in a frown. "I do apologize for how you were treated. If you'll let me, I'd like to make it up to you."

It was my turn to look him up and down, as though I was expecting he was going to present something to me to make it up to me. "And how exactly do you believe you're going to do that?"

He tried to suppress a smile, but failed. "I was hoping to take you out for a drink, if you'd be up for that. They're sending Andras' off this evening and I, for once, am off duty afterward."

The mention of Andras had me looking away and shrinking back into the room a bit, opening the door slightly farther as I withered under his gaze.

"I imagine you'd like to attend that as well." He offered.

"I'm not sure I'd be welcomed there." I mumbled, slipping back around the door once more and holding it in front of me. "I appreciate the offer, but–"

He placed his hand on the door and stopped me from closing it entirely. "I think it would actually be good for you to be there. The king and queen would appreciate it, regardless of how they feel about you personally."

I looked up at him once more and he had a pained smile on his face.

"Let me get you one drink, and if you'd still rather stay cooped up in here after that I promise I will bring you right back."

I thought about it for a moment, glancing back behind me into the room. I had absolutely nothing to wear to a service for the prince. I wasn't sure I owned a single black piece of clothing even if I included my entire wardrobe from the palace at Riodian.

"I'm certain I have nothing appropriate to wear."

He considered that. "Do you have a dark blue or dark green dress? I can let you borrow my cloak."

"I may have something." I relented. "Give me a moment to change?"

He smiled a bit more genuinely at that. "Of course."

I closed the door, leaned my back against it, and blew out a breath. Befriending him was an awful idea. We had a tentative alliance, where I helped him and he helped me, but drinks were… far more than that.

I shook my head and headed for my closet. I dug through to find the darkest dress I owned and slipped that on rather than the sky blue one I'd been wearing. When I slipped back out the door I nearly startled him. He was facing the hallway and turned to offer me his cloak, then his arm. He led me out to catch a ride down to the docks in one of the carriages waiting at the palace entrance.

We spent most of the ride in a slightly uncomfortable silence, neither of us quite sure what to say. That same silence lingered while we each took a flower up to place upon the ship he lay in. It was decorated beautifully, and he was prepared such that no one would know how it was that he had died. I realized I hadn't ever found out, and I wasn't sure I even wanted to know.

The small ship was launched from the dock and floated slowly out into the sea. When it had drifted nearly 50 meters from the dock a flaming arrow arced across the sky and set it ablaze. We watched it burn and continue to drift off until it was nothing more than a flame flickering toward the horizon before people began to leave.

Jesse hooked his arm with mine and guided me back to our carriage. He gave them some directions for where to take us and joined me in the carriage. We were eventually dropped off at a tavern that I would've guessed was two blocks from the palace.

He guided me through the front door and the moment I entered I was seriously reconsidering my life choices. It was loud, far louder than anywhere I had ever been before. A boisterous bard was singing in the corner of the space. It was crowded with people nearly shoulder to shoulder at the bar.

I hadn't experienced anything quite so chaotic before. Jesse didn't react at all, which told me this was likely normal, but I wasn't sure what to make of it all. He kept me close to him and shoved his way in between people at the bar. I was shocked when they moved aside to permit space for me to stand with him.

"What would you like?" He had to lean in so I could hear him.

I gazed at the shelves of liquor behind the bar, unsure what to choose or what the options even *were*. "Uh, wine I guess?"

That earned me an amused smirk. "I'll see what they've got."

He lifted his hand and the barkeep nodded. It took him a few minutes to wander our way.

"What'll it be?" He grumbled, his voice loud and gravelly.

"A glass of William's Reserve and what sort of wine do you have?"

The barkeep huffed a laugh. "I'm sure I've got a bottle of *something* around here. It'll take me a moment to find it."

"We've got all night." Jesse replied and slid a few coins across the counter to the man.

He nodded, swiped the coins into the pocket of his apron and went to work retrieving our drinks.

"A bottle of something?" I muttered, mostly to myself and shook my head.

Jesse laughed. "This isn't the type of place you'll find wine. Whiskey and ale definitely, but wine is harder to come by out here and most people don't bother to drink it."

"I suppose at least it'll be nice and aged." I dared to offer him a smile.

"That's the spirit."

Chapter 13

Slade

When the bastard shoved past me into her chambers, I had to reign in the instinct to cut him down. He hadn't even asked me to move. He'd ignored my question entirely and simply pushed past me like I wasn't even there. There were few things that I had moral codes against. The first was that I would never kill children. The second was that I would never allow someone to manhandle a woman, unless she were a fellow assassin trying to kill me.

Regardless of whatever pull I felt toward her, I would've had the urge to kill them. But with that pull, I was struggling to hold myself back. I stormed after them, and stood guard at her cell door until Jesse came to question her. He, thankfully, was at least upset that they hadn't given her the chance to change, otherwise I may have killed him too.

After I had her settled back into her chambers, I took off in search of the captain. I managed to catch him in the corridor leading to the barracks. I threw my helmet down on the stone floor, grabbed him by the collar when he turned around, and shoved his back against the wall.

He, rightfully, looked concerned. "What the fu–"

"I'll do the talking." I growled. "You *ordered* them to rip her from her bed, drag her down there, and throw her into that cell like she was nothing more than a rabid animal. Last I checked, the King's guard wasn't a bunch of savages, so I'd like a fucking explanation."

"I didn't order them to do *anything*." His voice didn't waiver, despite the hold I kept on him. He glared at me now. "I would never order them to treat someone that way. Even if she *did* kill Andras, that's not how this guard works."

"Then why the *fuck* did it happen? You're their captain."

"Edward was calling the shots before I even woke up to discover what had happened. I am in the process of doing damage control. She wasn't the only one handled that way."

I released him, reluctantly. "If this is the standard the guard is held to, I have no interest in being a part of it. Consider this my formal resignation. I'll be gone by noon."

He rubbed at his chest, and his eyes widened at my statement. "Perhaps you should take a few hours to calm down. It was a long night, surely you're–"

"I don't need time to think this over. I'm *done*."

I spun on my heel and continued toward my room. With any luck, I'd get in, change, and get out before David came back from his shift.

"You can't just leave her unguarded!" Jesse shouted after me.

"That sounds like your problem, *Captain*." I turned into my room and slammed the door behind me.

Whoever hired me was efficient, I'd give them that. A large chest sat on my bed. I opened it to discover the absurd amount of gold that Leodric had promised I would receive. I took a moment to listen for approaching footsteps, before I shadowed the chest and myself to my manor in Larkspire. I took it into my closet, opened the lock on my safe, and dumped it inside. I shadowed back to my room at the palace before anyone could have noticed I left.

I set the chest on the floor and shoved it beneath the bed, changed into my leathers, donned my weapons, and headed to the stables for my horse.

Every single part of me seemed drawn back to her. It was an effort to get to the stables, tack, mount, and ride my horse out into the city. The further I got from her, the easier it got to leave, but the infuriating urge to return to her was almost enough to drive me mad. I didn't understand it. I had no reason to care what happened to her, and yet I couldn't keep my thoughts from wandering back to her. That was going to be a problem.

*

The moment I returned to Edgewood a hawk descended upon me with a message and I found myself called to Leodric's office. I had intended to stop by a tavern, have a few drinks, and call it a day, but there is almost never any rest for any of us where Leodric is concerned.

I brushed past Naomi and her warnings that he was already in a meeting and shoved open his study door. Selene was leaning against his desk and mid-sentence when I walked in. She stopped speaking and scowled at me.

"I'm sure Naomi told you we were in here and *busy*." She growled.

I waved her off. "Yes, I'm well aware. However, *he* summoned me when I would much rather be at home sleeping in my own bed for the first time in what?"

"Two and a half months." Leodric grumbled with a tinge of impatience in his voice.

"I didn't ask for the assignment." I snap back.

"Selene, give us a moment."

She scoffed at him, pushed off his desk and slammed her shoulder into me as she walked past.

"Asshole." She muttered under her breath.

I could've shot an insult back, but I walked up to his desk, placed both hands on it, and leaned down closer to him.

"You *summoned*."

"I have another assignment for you–"

"No." I cut him off before he could continue. "I just spent more than a month masquerading as a goddess damned palace guard. I will not be taking any new assignments for at least a week."

I saw the muscle in his jaw tick in annoyance. I very rarely declined jobs but I just traveled nonstop for days, and I had zero interest in doing anything for him for far longer than just the week I demanded.

"The pay is–"

"I don't give a fuck what the pay is. I will not be taking it. And so help me if you tell me this is not optional *you* will be the next person on my list."

His brows twitched. It was just enough to tell me I'd actually surprised him, which generally was quite hard to do. He studied me for a few breaths, then sighed.

"Fine. I'll give it to Selene."

"Fine." I growled. I shoved off his desk and headed for the door.

"I will be calling on you in a week." He called after me, even as I pulled open the door and stormed out.

Of course he would be. I should've made it two.

*

An hour later I was pacing in the den of my manor in Larkspire. The curtains were drawn and Zephyr sat on the large luxurious couch across from me with a glass of whiskey in hand.

His ruby red eyes tracked my movements and a slight frown sat on his lips. I'd just finished rumbling on about just how much I couldn't stand Leodric lately and caught him up on my most recent assignment.

For all Leodric knew, I was wasting away in a tavern in Edgewood. For all I knew at that moment, I probably should've been. Zephyr sighed heavily and sipped on his drink before finally speaking.

"It seems he's changed." He observed, and it took everything in me not to spin around and growl at him for stating the obvious. The change had been gradual, but these last handful of months had become unbearable. Between getting two assignments that were *not* optional and having him call me into his office the moment I finally returned, I was ready to kill the man.

"You shouldn't have to keep working for him." He said it so plainly that I stopped in my tracks and looked at him. "If you recall, he took you in and trained you because he owed me a life debt. That has long since been paid. Any work you do now is by choice."

I laughed, but there was no humor in it. "You never told me *why* he agreed to take me, so no, I didn't recall that." I ran a hand over my face in exasperation. "He's not just going to let me walk away from the guild now."

"He won't have a choice." His eyes promised murder, but I sincerely doubted he would go do that himself. He seemed to read as much from my face because he smirked. "You're perfectly capable of handling him yourself, if you choose to."

"And then what? I have no desire to run the guild." The deal I made with Xavier came to mind again and I looked away as I thought it through. Faking my own death would probably be easier.

"I'm not sure what ungodly idea is bouncing around your mind right now," I looked his way when he started speaking. "But I can promise you that appointing someone else to take over that disaster would be well within your rights if you did decide to kill him."

"If you felt it was such a disaster, why did you send me there in the first place?" I snapped, maybe a little bit too brazenly.

The outburst only seemed to amuse him. A single fang peeked out when the corner of his mouth curled up in a smile. "It *wasn't* a disaster back then, but what you've told me leads me to believe it has become one now." He shrugged a single shoulder and finished his glass. "Regardless, he owed me a life debt. Raising you and teaching you to defend yourself was my payment. I never expected you to become his prized pupil and be dubbed *Sàmhach Marbhadh*."

I rolled my eyes. "You know precisely how much I despise that name."

"It is creative, I'll give them that." His grin only grew at my discomfort. The bastard enjoyed baiting me. He knew

I'd never kill him and I knew he'd never kill me. It was a vicious cycle we lived in. He needed me far more than I needed him though.

He stood from the couch and wandered over to refill his glass from the decanter on the serving table against the far wall. "What exactly *do* you plan on doing once they begin to notice you've stopped aging? I'd estimate you have maybe five more years before it'll raise suspicion. Have you thought that far ahead?"

"I have." I grumbled.

"And?" He turned and raised an eyebrow at me as he lifted the glass to his lips once more. The bastard could drink the whole decanter before he'd start to slur his words. Fucking vampires.

"*And* that is none of your business."

He snorted. "It will become my business if it gets you killed and I'm forced to find another non-vampire to own this place so no one else can enter."

"Don't worry." I gave him a convincing smile. "It won't."

"Ensure that it doesn't. If he won't let you leave the guild, I'll kill him."

"I should get back before anyone notices I've been missing." I turned my back to him and started to walk toward the door. I stepped through the shadows before he could say another word.

Chapter 14

Liza

I had not intended to follow the captain to his chambers. Nor had I intended to wind up tangled with him in his bed, but a fair amount of whatever passes for wine in that tavern would do that to you. That isn't to say that I didn't enjoy it, but it certainly wasn't the best I'd ever had. Especially when I couldn't get the amber eyed guard out of my head. I didn't even know what he looked like, and he was still haunting my thoughts.

I snuck out quietly, as soon as he drifted off to sleep, and slunk back to my chambers like a washed up harlot. I was thankful to have not run into anyone in the halls, though I shouldn't have been surprised given the early hour of the morning that it was.

When I woke later that morning, I felt more clear headed than I had in a long time. Perhaps this failure was not that at all. Perhaps this was an out. There was a chance that word of Andras' death wouldn't reach Moira if I didn't put it in my reports. Sure, the ship captain or crew could pass along the information, but maybe, just maybe, it wouldn't make it that far.

If it did, she'd probably just let King DuMont take care of me. That would keep her hands clean, and her conscience too, in some twisted way. That left the obvious issue; DuMont wasn't my biggest fan and Edward was even less so. Gods. If anything happened to King DuMont, just by the way Edward looked at me I was certain I would find myself on a chopping block in no time.

I shook my head. I couldn't think of that now. I had to focus on my way out. I needed a plan. The sewers all led to the river and eventually the sea. I didn't know where they all started, and I certainly had no desire to walk amidst waste, but it was an option. I'd research that today.

The library should have records of all of the city's infrastructure, including the sewers and maintenance tunnels. If I could at least make it out of this city, even if everything went to shit, then I could figure it out from there. I would sooner take my chances going through the dragons in the mountains than wait out whatever my fate might be here or in Emberwyn.

That only left the elves, the werewolves, or the vampires. The fae wouldn't harbor someone who was wanted by Moira. Their alliance was far too strong. If given the choice, the werewolves sounded the most appealing. I drug myself out of bed and began to dress for the day.

When my breakfast arrived and was accompanied by a hangover remedy and an herbal fertility suppressant I knew that Jesse must've spoken to the servant and requested it. I asked her to pass along a note to him, letting him know where

I would be for the day. Not that I felt he would care, given that I was no longer guarded. It still seemed pertinent that *someone* knew my whereabouts and it might as well have been him.

I spent several hours digging through every single map I could find within the library until my mind felt like it had turned to mush. I did my best to memorize them, but from what I gathered *any* entrance would get me into the main catacombs of the sewer system. From there I could go a million directions to make my way to the river or the sea.

It looked like even if I got turned around somewhere, I could still find my way out. If I were being pursued, that would be another issue altogether. Pushing thoughts of the sewer out of my mind, I hoped that I could just continue as "trade emissary" and everything would be fine.

I wandered out into the city after lunch. It was easy to find the doorways that led to the tunnels now that I was looking for them. They were surprisingly innocuous looking, but no one paid them any mind. This close to the castle they were just wooden doors built into the stonework of the homes surrounding it.

Once I was satisfied with locating at least a few of them, I made my way to the tavern I'd gone with Jesse to the previous night. With any luck, they'd have more of that wine. Or, if I had no other choice, I would try whatever that whiskey was that Jesse had.

"You drank the last of the wine." The burly barkeep informed me when I reached the only open space along the counter.

I frowned. "I'll try the whiskey then."

"Make that two, and you can add them both to my tab." Jesse's voice behind me startled me, but before I could turn to face him, his arm slipped gently around my waist and he squeezed in next to me at the bar.

I looked at him incredulously, but he just smiled.

"You snuck out *very* early this morning."

"I imagine it isn't a good look for your men to see me with you, don't you think?" It was a shitty excuse. I never stayed with anyone I had sex with. It was a rule I made for myself a very long time ago. It was too complicated otherwise.

He arched a brow and chuckled. "First of all, they know better than to stick their noses in my business, and secondly, the only thing they'd be upset about would be that *they* didn't get to you first."

It was hard to keep the disgust from my face, but I stifled it as best I could. "Right." I mumbled under my breath. The barkeep saved me from muttering anything I might regret by placing the two glasses before us on the counter.

"I didn't expect to find you here." Jesse filled the slightly uncomfortable silence as I picked up and inspected the amber liquid in my glass.

"I didn't plan to end up here, but after wandering around aimlessly I thought it would be nice to finish my day somewhere that was at least slightly familiar." I lifted the glass and sniffed it only to burn my nostrils and almost choke on the wicked bite the alcohol had. "Gods. This has got to taste awful if that's how it *smells*."

I looked over to see amusement lighting his eyes and a knowing grin on his lips. "It's an acquired taste, but generally it will be better to *smell* it if you leave your mouth open."

I narrowed my eyes skeptically.

"Just trust me." He demonstrated by lifting his own glass. "Smells divine to me."

"I have a feeling I'm going to regret this." I mumbled, before attempting once more to smell it. To my surprise though, doing as he suggested was not quite as awful and the notes of vanilla made it seem like I might actually like it.

"When you sip it, take the time to taste it." He took a slow sip from his glass.

I brought the glass to my lips and took a small sip. It felt like I was drinking fire, but I took a few moments to try to identify any flavor in it before I swallowed. The same heat I felt in my mouth filled my chest as I did so. I coughed and cursed, earning me a real laugh from Jesse.

"If you hate it, I'll finish it."

"It's not awful." It wasn't a total lie, but it definitely wasn't something that I thought I would choose for myself if given other options.

"The ale is god awful." A gruff man to my right commented. "Stick with the whiskey, at least you won't have as much of a hangover."

I doubted that he was correct, but I nodded at him all the same.

"What did you get up to today anyway?" Jesse asked and I turned my attention back to him.

I shrugged a shoulder. "I took some time to explore the city by myself. I haven't spent much time outside of a palace, so it was a nice change of pace to walk around among the people."

"You should be careful of where you wander in this city. Not all parts of it are… safe." He hesitated to find the right word. I gave him another skeptical look.

"I assure you I can handle myself."

"With all due respect, you have only just started playing around with your magic, and from what I've seen you aren't going to be able to defend yourself if you get overpowered in a back alley somewhere."

I scowled at him, thoroughly insulted. Starting with 'with all due respect', doesn't lessen the blow of an insult like that. Not to mention, he'd only watched me when I practiced in the training area he gave me. He didn't know what I did in my bathing room where no one could see me.

The ghost of a frown formed on his lips. "I'm not saying that to upset you. It's just the truth. Have you ever actually witnessed the behavior of people who've tossed their morals to the wind?"

I tried to think back to anyone I'd met, and whether they'd fit that category. He continued before I had the chance to reply.

"If you haven't left the castle, you haven't. I can assure you. And you definitely don't want to, so just take my word for it. *Please.*"

I really looked at him now, and the look in his eyes made me want to snap back with a smart ass retort, but the way he said please made me bite my tongue.

"Are you telling me I shouldn't wander on my own at all?"

He gave me a quick once over and sighed. "I'm saying that if you *want* to explore, perhaps you should have someone with you. I can't promise I can spare a guard, but you shouldn't do so alone, regardless of the time of day."

"There are not many people within the palace who will *want* to spend time with me." While he wasn't technically blocking me from leaving, it felt like the walls were closing in on me again, and I *really* didn't like that. I'd finally gotten a taste of what freedom was like, and I didn't want to lose that now.

His lips pursed while he seemed to consider his options. "Just be careful, alright?"

I was sure I could manage that, so I nodded.

Chapter 15

Slade

I was baking beneath my cloak as I walked the streets of Edgewood and made my way to meet with Leodric. Each time I had to make this walk it became increasingly tiresome. Most of the members lived within his manor, so in person meetings were never an issue for anyone but myself and the lucky few who had their own place to live.

The screech of a hawk rang out above my head, which wouldn't normally catch my attention if it weren't for the fluttering of paper that followed. I looked toward the sky to find several dozen pieces of parchment falling to the ground around me. One landed face up at my feet and what I read on it made my heart skip a beat.

THE KING IS DEAD
LONG LIVE THE KING

I picked it up and read it at least three times to confirm I was seeing it correctly. The rest of the paper included a sketch of Edward, the younger of the two princes, being crowned as king and the date of the coronation.

It seemed far too convenient that the king would pass so soon after the prince. The flyer blamed his grief, but that didn't sit quite right with me. I tucked the paper into my satchel and carried on.

When I stepped into Leodric's study he was scribbling something on a piece of parchment. He didn't give me the courtesy of looking up to acknowledge my presence. I waited impatiently for several minutes for him to finally push the document aside and greet me.

"Has your attitude finally improved?" He asked as he steepled his hands together in front of him on his desk.

"Speak to me like that and it will only push your limits with me further." I hadn't intended it to come off as a threat, but it hit its mark all the same.

He raised a single brow. "I have an assignment, if you are open to taking one." His words were selected carefully, like he was acknowledging this fine line we were walking. I rarely questioned him, but he'd pushed too far recently and I was seriously reconsidering our arrangement.

"I'll consider it." I kept my voice icy. "If you'll answer my next question honestly."

This seemed to surprise him, though I doubt anyone else would've noticed the emotion flash across his face. He nodded and waved a hand telling me to go on.

"Do you know anything about this?" I pulled the parchment from my satchel and handed it to him.

He took it and eyed it cautiously. "Surely this is a mistake. A hoax, perhaps?"

"I doubt that hundreds of these would be dropped from the sky via messenger hawks if it was a hoax."

A muscle feathered in his jaw. He folded it over on itself and slid it to the right side of his desk. "I'll look into it."

"So it wasn't an assignment you sent someone else to handle?"

He chuckled, and the sound was a little bit unnerving. "Do you think I'd trust anyone else in this guild with an assignment of that magnitude?"

"I'm not sure what to think with you lately." The words escaped before I could stop them.

My response seemed to amuse him more than irritate him. "Royalty is complicated. Deadly, more times than not." He shrugged. "I'm not sure I would be willing to risk your life on the king, were it not explicitly planned out like the last one was. Your next assignment, should you choose to accept it, is to track down and kill a man wanted for several murders in Cragmore."

"And the payment?"

"Assuming you are successful, half when you accept the task and half when you bring the lord his head. Ten thousand silver."

"No."

He'd gone back to reviewing his paperwork, but his head snapped up and he locked eyes with me. "Excuse me?"

"I said no."

He scoffed. "Is the payment not sufficient?"

"The payment would be fine if I required it, but currently, I don't. You've sent me out on two assignments now that have required several weeks of tracking or travel. If you want me to take an assignment, find one *here*."

I spun on my heel and headed for the door.

"You cannot just refuse every assignment I offer you." He growled.

"I can, and I think that I will, from this point forward, unless it is worth my time or interesting enough for me to consider."

He started shouting something after me that I didn't care to listen to as I strode from his office, through the foyer, and out into the street. I didn't know what I planned for my life when I hung up my hat on this particular profession, but I knew for now that I had no interest wasting my time on assignments that didn't, at the very least, intrigue me.

Chapter 16

Liza

There was a light knock on my door, just as there was every morning when one of the servants brought me my breakfast, except this time when I opened the door it was Jesse. He had a tense expression on his face.

"I need you to come with me."

I eyed him skeptically. "Is everything alright?"

"No." He turned and guided me into the hallway with a hand on the small of my back.

"Are you going to at least tell me what this is about?" I asked, willingly walking with him despite the anxiety welling within me.

"The king is dead. Heart attack, they said. Edward has requested to speak to you, though he hasn't said what for."

I stopped dead in my tracks. Jesse only made it two more steps before he stopped and looked back at me.

"It wasn't a request. It was an order. If you refuse…" His voice trailed off and he looked away as though he was trying to determine how to say whatever it was he was told to do. His throat bobbed as he swallowed, and when his gaze met mine again I knew exactly what he was told to do to me.

I could run. I was sure he could run faster. I wasn't so sure he would disobey a direct order and give me a chance to escape, regardless of our entanglement this past week. It was this thought that forced my feet to move again. I thought I was going to die not long ago. I still thought that someone might show up to kill me. It didn't hurt to hear what Edward had to say.

At least that's what I told myself.

When I walked through the door to the king's study, well, Edward's study now, I found him sitting behind his desk. He looked up as we entered, appearing to be entirely bored with whatever he needed to talk to me about.

I didn't make it more than three steps into the room before something metal was slammed onto my wrist. Jesse jumped at the same moment that I did, which was the only thing that told me he was unaware of this part of the plan.

I couldn't say that I had ever noticed my magic consciously, but the moment that shackle circled my wrist I stumbled from the sudden loss of it. It felt like a part of me had been stripped away, and it made me a bit lightheaded.

Jesse caught my arm to steady me. A guard to my right held a chain that linked to my shiny new adornment.

"Please, have a seat Miss Winters." Edward's voice was surprisingly *kind* given his disinterest and the scowl he always wore when he looked at me. He observed me now with something I'd liken to amusement if someone as miserable as him were capable of such an emotion.

I stepped around one of the arm chairs placed before the desk and sat gently in it. I should have curtseyed, but at that moment, I couldn't find it in me to care. Thankfully, he didn't seem to notice the lack of formality.

"I'm sure you understand, precautions needed to be taken for this conversation." He gestured toward the metal cuff on my wrist. "Now that we've gotten that taken care of, I'd like to discuss your purpose here."

I raised a brow at him.

"You were sent as an emissary, to continue to facilitate trade between Emberwyn and us. I don't intend to change that, however, if you'd like to keep your head, I have a few additional requests."

I swallowed nervously. "And what might those be, your majesty?"

His lips quirked up in the hint of a satisfied grin for a fraction of a second before his expression leveled out once more. "You are going to tell me everything you know about Emberwyn's army, their capital city, and their preparedness for battle."

All the blood drained from my face. I was certain he recognized this by the glint I saw in his eyes, but it didn't stop him from talking.

"And once you've done that, you're going to do anything that I ask of you, or you'll be the first–or next–to die. Because my grandfather had a vision when he freed us from the rule of mages, but once he kicked the pompous pricks out of their places of power he grew complacent. He didn't follow through like he should have and force them into servitude like we were, or exterminate them."

I thanked the gods that I was sitting. I was certain that my knees would have buckled at his words if I had not been.

Perhaps he knew that. Or, perhaps he thought I'd react with rage. The chain would suggest that. My mind spiraled.

He studied me for a few uncomfortable moments. "I'm waiting." He tapped his fingers impatiently on the desk in front of him.

My mouth opened as though I could speak, but no words formed. I knew nothing of Emberwyn's armies. Nothing of their battle strategy or preparedness. I barely knew what was necessary for keeping our trade agreement moving. That was all I had been prepared for.

"Your majesty," Jesse began. "As I have told your father several times, she has no knowledge of any of the inner working–"

"I did not ask you, Captain." Edward snapped. His eyes turned to ice now as they peered over my shoulder at him. When that cold gaze fell to me I felt frozen in place.

"I– I don't know anything of the sort. I was never permitted to leave the palace. Only interacted with the guard, and even that was minimal." I was rambling now. I didn't know what to tell him. "I would tell you if I did. I swear it, but I–"

"Useless." He grumbled and ran a hand down his face. "Fine. I'll have other uses for you. What *do* you know?"

I opened my mouth, but shut it. Opened it again, and drew a blank. "I– Uhm." I was stuttering, grasping at the archives of my mind for something useful. Maybe I could get out of this still. The chain and shackle suggested otherwise, but surely they wouldn't throw me in a cell. Right?

I shook my head. "Her spymaster's name is Desmond. He is a dark fae."

"Tell me something I wouldn't already know." He snarled. "We do still have all of the records from her ruling here."

"I– I'm not sure that–"

"Take her back to her chambers." He shouted. "Your first task is tomorrow. Do not disappoint me."

I didn't get the chance to ask what exactly that was before the guard who held my chain was beside me and yanking me up from the chair. His grip on my arm was sure to leave a bruise. He practically dragged me out of the room.

Jesse refused to look my way. The look on his face was one of frustration and betrayal. His gaze was fixed on the ground behind the chair I had been sitting in.

"Captain, please sit. We have much to discuss…" The king's words were cut off by the door shutting behind us. I scrambled to keep up with the guard beside me and prayed that whatever my first task was, I could do it.

*

When I was pulled from my chambers the following evening, I assumed I would be headed back to Edward's study. I had no idea what to think when they took me out the front doors of the castle, down the stairs, and beyond the front gates. I was met by a hastily constructed wooden platform, upon which Edward, Jesse, and a handful of nobles had already gathered.

To the left of that were three tall wooden poles surrounded by firewood and straw. Three men were tied to the poles, their hands bound in a set of shackles in front of them. I nearly tripped up the stairs because I was too focused on figuring out what in the world their purpose was.

Edward's booming voice brought my attention back to him. The crowd that was gathering quieted as he began speaking. "Good Evening. I am sure that the news of my father's passing has reached you by now."

He was interrupted by the people simultaneously saying, "King DuMont may he rest in peace."

Edward nodded his head. "While my coronation is not for two more days, we're not going to take his death or my brother's death lightly. My grandfather had a vision when he overthrew the tyrant queen. It was our freedom, first and foremost, but he didn't follow through like he should have."

The crowd began to murmur, but that did not stop his speech.

"You see, before the vampire queen rewrote history it was humans who ruled this world. Their kingdoms were small, and the original borders were lost to time but they were proud and strong. They realized that they could use the power the mages held. They tried to determine where their magic came from and how they might harness it themselves.

"They failed at obtaining that power of course, but they did *not* fail at keeping them under their control. It is time we reclaimed that level of power and put them to use."

My stomach bottomed out. I glanced around at the crowd hoping to see they were just as horrified as me, but they looked hopeful. Some even looked excited.

"I have already managed to secure one, who Queen Moira delivered willingly to our doorstep." He gestured to me now, with a proud smile on his face. I could *feel* the glares from the men tied to the posts. While I did not understand what was happening, I was certain they had not agreed to work with him, and I was about to witness their punishment.

"I'm sure that Moira had no idea what would transpire here to lead her emissary to agree to do my bidding, but I am grateful to her for that nonetheless. Because, you see, not only did she deliver me a mage, but she delivered me the *last* surviving fire mage."

Gasps rang out around us. I was unsure if they were shock or horror. Perhaps both. I knew I was feeling the horror myself.

"From this point forward, any mage or magical being of any sort will be taken into custody, questioned, and either put to work for us or put to death. We will be kind and give them the choice."

I failed to see how that was a kindness.

"And now, our fire mage is going to exterminate the first group who have refused to work for us. "

I looked at Jesse, as though that would level my pitching stomach. He was not looking at me. His gaze was pinned on the platform in front of him and his arms were tucked behind his back. Every bit the dutiful captain of the guard he was supposed to be in that moment.

I shifted to face Edward, who was smiling at me from ear to ear like he'd just won an award and I was his prize. The shackle I had been stuck wearing for the last day and a half was unlocked and removed from my wrist.

The rush of power that hit me would've felt incredible were it not for the task I'd been given. The piles of firewood and straw made sense now. He meant for me to burn them. *I was to burn them to death.* My lunch threatened to spill on the wood in front of me as I stood frozen in place.

"Any time now, Miss Winters." Edward whispered, just loud enough for me to hear.

I turned toward men. The scowls and disgust in their faces burned through me like a fire itself. I wasn't even sure if I was capable of producing so much fire. Perhaps the additional fuel around them had been Jesse's suggestion. He had watched me practice.

I studied the poles, the distance between them and the crowd. I scanned my eyes out toward the city. Toward the escape routes I had planned for myself. I imagined having to get to the sewer from the palace, but I had never been more thankful for having listened to my gut about finding *every* route possible.

I could do this. I was certain. They were bound with rope, not metal. I just needed to find a way to get to them quickly. I was certain I could jump off the platform. I hoped anyway. Maybe I could get to them and–

"Miss Winters." Edward snarled under his breath.

I took a deep breath and lifted my hand to point toward the prisoners. I could do this. I was sure of it. I didn't have a choice but to try. I *couldn't* kill them. It went against everything I stood for.

An explosion erupted to my right. Stone and debris rained down on the crowd and flew toward us. The wood beneath my feet shook and rattled. I stumbled and was knocked on the shoulder by something, though I did not see what.

Chaos ensued. My ears rang, but I could still hear the screams. Another explosion echoed through the street before I finally got my bearings. I was on my hands and knees. The men tied to the posts were furiously fighting against the rope binding them.

I threw fire behind me blindly, shoved to my feet, and moved faster than I'd ever run before. When my feet hit the cobblestone beneath the platform I stumbled and cursed. My ankle twisted, but the pain was numbed by the adrenaline coursing through me.

When I reached the first man he snarled something at me I couldn't hear. I set fire to his bindings and he was free in seconds. I patted out the flames on his shirt and turned toward the next. I yelled for him to follow me, but I didn't look back to see if he obeyed.

I freed the next two men the same way. It was a relief when the others came to aid my attempts to put out the fire on the last one. Then I was running and yelling at them to follow. Once again, I did not look back.

The pain in my ankle began to register as I dodged through the crowds toward a street I was hoping had an entrance to the sewers. My hearing came back slowly, and by the gods did my fucking head hurt. I threw fire toward buildings, carts along the road, anything that would burn on its own and offer a distraction.

I had to feel along the walls as the smoke from the explosions and the fires I had set began to fill the street. I had never been more relieved when I felt the metal handle of the door beneath my palms. I yanked on it, but it felt stuck.

"Move!" A male voice behind me shouted just before I was shoved out of the way. Two of the men I freed yanked twice before the door finally budged and cracked open. I slipped through and the three of them followed. The last to slide in with us pulled it shut behind him.

Smoke billowed in between the bars of the window at the top of the door.

"This way." I yelled loudly enough that I hoped they heard me. I descended the steps and the stench burned my nose. I tried to force myself to breathe through my mouth, but it was so poignant I could almost taste it and I didn't want to puke.

As the ringing in my ears finally stopped I began to be able to hear their steps behind me. I hadn't ever known darkness like this before. I felt my way along the walls. I didn't think I could see my hand in front of my face if I tried.

When I was sure we weren't followed, I let fire rise to my hand.

"Thank the fucking gods." One of the men breathed. "A fire mage." He chuckled. "You're not supposed to exist."

I turned to face them and they crowded into the space before me. They were filthy even before the soot from the smoke covered their faces. I assumed the one who spoke was the one who had a sly grin on his face. He had dark brown hair, if it wasn't just that dirty, and deep brown eyes to match.

"Damian." His grin grew to the point where a dimple appeared.

"Laslow." The man next to him offered. He was an inch shorter than Damian with blond hair and grey eyes.

"Ian." The final one spoke now. He was older than the other two. His dark hair had begun to gray just a bit, and if he was a mage, that easily had to make him a couple hundred years old.

"Liza." I looked down at their still bound hands. "I could try to at least melt the chain…"

"Nevermind that." Ian shook his head. "How do we get *out* of here?"

"The sewers all lead to the river. We should be able to find our way to an opening and then figure a way to cross it."

"We could just swim." Laslow suggested.

The look on my face must've given me away, because Damian was who said. "I'm guessing *she* doesn't know how or that would've been her first suggestion."

"We'll figure it out." Ian mumbled. "Let's just focus on finding the end of one of these tunnels before they find us."

The other two nodded in agreement and I was back to leading us through the dark again.

We finally reached the river by the time night had fallen. I thanked the gods that it wasn't a full moon. At least that would give us some cover.

There was a significant drop to the water, and nothing but rocks leading up to the city above. We either had to jump in and swim, or we weren't going to make it out.

"Looks like you're going to have to try to melt the chain afterall." I turned to find Damien holding his hands out to me. "If you think you can melt the cuffs without burning my wrists beyond recognition, I can make this swim much easier for us."

"Don't even try it." Ian grumbled. "We'll get them off once we're far enough away from here."

I didn't even protest and suggest I could do it, because quite frankly, I wasn't sure I could melt the chain between them without burning their wrists either. I stepped up to Damian's outstretched arms and used the fire I was holding to give us light to start the lengthy task of melting the chain.

"It just needs to get hot enough that we can manipulate it. We can probably just break it." Laslow stepped up to watch while I worked.

I tried to put as much focus and energy into the flame, making it as hot as I could manage. Judging by the grimace on Damian's face, the heat was traveling up the metal chains to his wrists, but he didn't pull away until the center chain was glowing bright red.

I shifted to do the same to Laslow's chain while Damian tried to pull his wrists apart until it eventually gave and broke. It took nearly an hour to get them all separated, but it worked.

"Hold onto me." Damian instructed.

I eyed him skeptically.

"Just wrap your arms around my waist." He rolled his eyes. "I promise not to let you drown if you promise not to panic and let go."

I wasn't sure I trusted him, but I also had no other choice. The other two jumped first and he waited until they resurfaced to look at me and ask if I was ready.

"As ready as I'll ever be." I mumbled. He wrapped an arm around me and we jumped off the ledge together. The frigid water was a shock to my system, nearly making me let go all on its own before the icy grip of panic took hold. I held onto Damian like my life depended on it, and in this moment, it did.

By the time our heads broke the surface I was sure I was going to drown. The current was pushing us down river, but he did his best to swim around my clumsy limp form to get us to the far shoreline. I couldn't have guessed the width if I tried, but it took an eternity to get there.

By the time my feet could touch the murky bottom of the shoreline I was practically frozen. My teeth were chattering despite the warm air that hit me the moment my shoulders and torso rose above the water.

"We need to keep moving." Ian quietly instructed. "No fire until we know they can't see us from the city."

The idea of a fire sounded splendid, but I did as he asked and withheld that until we'd been walking for nearly three hours. We made camp in the thickest part of the trees we could find, hoping that the copious amount of foliage would keep us hidden until the three of them could use their magic again.

Damian and Laslow took to trying to break off their shackles with rocks. The clang of the rock against metal grated against my still aching head. I assisted Ian with collecting sticks and branches for a fire, then lit it once we were satisfied with our pyre.

The metal clangs halted with a whoop of triumph from Damian. He lifted his now freed wrist into the air in excitement. Ian mumbled something under his breath and didn't move from the fire.

"Don't you want to get yours off?" I asked, studying the way he seemed to be losing himself watching the fire dance between us.

"Not enough to beat at it all night with a gods damned rock."

I couldn't argue with that.

"Once Damian can use his magic, he can freeze it. It might break easier that way." Ian shrugged a shoulder. "How *are* you alive anyway? Fire mages were wiped out centuries ago."

I couldn't tell him the truth, and I hadn't come up with a good lie for that particular question yet.

"Couldn't tell you." I mumbled. "I'm not so sure of the answer myself." It was a selective truth.

His huff of amusement told me he had accepted it.

"So what do we do now?" I looked at the fire. "I can't go back to Emberwyn."

"Going back to Emberwyn would be the best decision, though I don't know how we'll get there. Crossing the mountains is not a good idea."

I thought about it for a few moments, then finally looked up to meet his gaze. "I know all of the captains of the trade ships from Emberwyn. Perhaps we could sneak into the port and I could get you all a ride on one of their ships?"

"And you think that will be possible given that all four of us will surely have a bounty on our heads now?"

I frowned and looked down at my hands. "It's worth a try isn't it?"

"Do they dock anywhere other than the port?"

"No. Not in Mytharae anyway."

"What about a messenger hawk?" Damian asked as he approached the fire. I glanced over at him. His wrists had large welts from the shackles where they burned him when I tried to melt the chain.

"Brilliant idea, asshole." Laslow commented, walking around to my other side to sit close to the fire. "I'll just pull a hawk out of thin air."

"Fuck off." Damian sniped. "We can't be far from Cragmore now. They have Messenger hawks you can just pay to send messages. Surely we could *borrow* one."

"You mean steal." Ian cut in.

"As if that will be the least of our charges." Damian grumbled.

"He's not wrong." Laslow added.

"*We* can blend in easily." I looked over at Daman as he spoke. "But *you* will be easily recognized. Your hair will damn you from a mile away."

I pulled the still drying mess that was my hair over my shoulder. It was nearly to my waist, and was definitely not easily hidden. The idea of cutting it made me want to cry, but worse than that was the idea of being caught and killed. Worse yet, by the very thing that I was just learning to control myself.

"I have nothing to cut it with."

"You'd have to do more than cut it." Laslow pointed out. "Dying it somehow would be far more practical."

"Cutting it is easier." Ian reasoned. "But… we should find something to dye it with."

"Why would you help me?" The question escaped my lips before I could stop it. Though I didn't look up from the mop of hair I was preparing myself to lose.

"You helped us." Damian said it like it was just that simple. Kindness was not something I was used to without a

122

price. Having only had one real friend, I wasn't sure what to make of it. Even she wouldn't have helped me with something like this.

"Would you cut it?" I looked at him now, desperate for someone else to do it, because I wasn't sure I could bring myself to.

He nodded solemnly and stood to walk over to me. A water mage could make ice sharp enough to slice through a person, surely he could slice off my hair with little effort. I pulled my hair back behind me and held all of it in a ponytail at the base of my neck.

"Are you sure about this?" He took hold of it and I lowered my hand into my lap.

I closed my eyes. "Just do it before I change my mind."

He didn't waste a second. I heard the ice cut through it. When he released what was left of my hair it hung to my shoulders and I felt lighter than I had in decades. I let out a shaky breath.

"It's not exactly even, but–"

"It's fine." I insisted. "Burn it."

He walked around me and I watched as he tossed the curly mess of still slightly wet hair into the fire. It sizzled and hissed as the flames took it. It felt like starting over. I could be whoever I wanted. There were no expectations now. I was *free*.

"How do I dye it?"

Chapter 17

Slade

I sat at the bar at a tavern I visited quite regularly. The barkeep refilled my glass without even asking.

"Any interesting assignments lately?" She asked with a knowing smile.

"You know that I wouldn't tell you even if I had one." I raised the glass to my lips, but then my curiosity got the best of me. She almost never asked me about work, even though she deduced pretty quickly what I did. "Why do you ask?"

I took a sip and sat the glass back down. She glanced around and leaned across the bar so she could whisper. I braced my elbows on the bar and shifted closer to her.

"Well, there's been some whispering about Prince Andras. He didn't die of natural causes, but no one knows who killed him." She straightened just enough that she could look me in the eye. "You were gone for a while. When you got back, the prince was already dead."

I frowned. "I wasn't aware you paid that much attention to when I came in here and when I didn't."

She looked insulted. "I take pride in paying attention to the people who tip me well. I know your drink, and I know precisely what time of the day to expect you. If you don't show up, I can assume you're off on an assignment."

I silently cursed myself for being so predictable. I hadn't even noticed I slipped into any kind of routine when I wasn't working. I knew better than that, but this was the only goddess damned tavern in this city that stocked the whiskey I preferred.

"If you have a question, just ask it."

"I have two, actually. Though I'm not sure you're going to answer either of them."

I snorted, but took another sip of my drink. Depending on the question, she was probably right.

"Are you Sàmhach Marbhadh?"

I raised a brow. "You think that highly of me? I'm flattered."

"That's not an answer." She stood up straight and crossed her arms over her chest.

"What's your other question?"

"Was it you?"

"Do you think I'm stupid enough to even attempt something like that?" I picked up the glass and swirled what was left in it.

"I think you're certainly cocky enough."

I chuckled, but put my hand over my heart in feigned hurt. "Ouch. I didn't know you could be so cold Fiona."

She grumbled something under her breath. "You're an asshole."

"No, darling. I can be quite the gentleman, but you'll never get me to talk shop with you, so you should give up trying."

She rolled her eyes and walked off to help the man who walked up to the bar while we were chatting.

The front door slammed open suddenly and everyone in the building turned to look at the disruption. Two men in partial armor stood in the doorway. They glanced around the space until their eyes landed on whoever it was they were looking for.

They moved quickly, each walking around the table the brunette woman sat at and standing on either side of her.

"Amelia Whitefern?" One of them questioned.

"Y–Yes," she stammered.

"You've been summoned for an audience with the Duke of Edgewood." He grabbed her arm and yanked her up from the table. The other man slapped a set of cuffs on her wrists. They drug her along with them as they made their way back to the front door.

The man holding her continued outside without hesitation. The second one turned around and addressed the spectators.

"King Edward is collecting any and all citizens who have magic. If you know someone who possesses any kind of abilities, you will be heavily rewarded for turning them in. Please make your reports to the Duke."

My brows rose nearly to my hairline. Whispers quickly filled the silence. The guard slipped out and shut the door behind him. I downed the rest of my glass, set far more coins on the counter than were required to pay my tab and stood to leave. If *anyone* at the guild other than Xavier knew about my magic, I was well and truly fucked.

Chapter 18

Liza

We realized quickly that getting a messenger hawk when our faces were plastered all over Cragmore was not going to be possible. That meant we'd have to find a way to sneak onto the ships ourselves and pray we could stow away, or we'd have to find somewhere else to run to.

Valehaven was out of the question. Mages and humans were *not* welcome among the elves. We didn't dare attempt to cross the Beithir mountains lest we be burned or eaten by the dragons who called the mountains and their valleys home.

That only left Elkridge, which would take nearly three weeks to reach if we tried to travel by roads that were not commonly used; according to Ian anyway. He was far more adept at navigation than I realized, and thankfully for me, was able to steal a map from one of the carts in the market.

Damian helped me collect enough walnuts to dye my hair. He said it *should* make it black, but I wasn't sure I believed that just looking at the color of the nuts we ground down and boiled in the kettle Laslow stole from an abandoned home. Either way, anything other than the vibrant red I had would make me far harder to find.

I didn't appreciate all the theft. It felt like we were stealing from people who hardly had anything already. I couldn't argue against it though when all we had were the clothes on our backs. We did our best to stop and clean ourselves up in the streams we passed, but realistically, we smelled awful and needed the clothing they stole so we had the chance to really clean ourselves off.

As I sat with my hair soaking in the dark liquid, I couldn't stop myself from thinking of all the other mages that were being carted off to Maeus. There had to be *something* I could do.

"Don't think too hard. You'll hurt yourself." Laslow joked, and I craned my head to try to look in the direction his voice came from. I hadn't realized he'd come back already.

"Did you manage to actually *catch* anything?" He'd claimed to be quite the fisherman, but for some reason I didn't have any faith in his abilities.

The wet smack of what I presumed to be fish carcasses hit the ground. "Yes."

I made a face that suggested I was slightly impressed. "How's the hair coming?"

Damian leaned over and fished a few strands out of the pot behind me. "Probably dark enough that you can sit up and let it dry now. It'll need to be redone as it fades, but it'll do for now."

I sat up slowly and grabbed my hair to ring it out before it could stain the dress I had on. It was still odd having so little to wring out. It would be dry in no time compared to how long it would have taken before it was cut.

When I glanced at it, it was startling. It had turned a dark brown. I could still catch notes of red in the light, but it was subdued and barely noticeable unless you looked for it. I must have been gawking at it for longer than I realized, because Ian chuckled.

"It suits you." He commented, with an amused smirk.

Somehow, I doubted he was right, but it made a small smile rise to my lips all the same. "So what *are* we going to do now?"

I watched Ian lay out the map, trying to keep my focus on that and *not* the fish that Laslow was currently cutting up near the fire.

"Well, the safest bet would be to go to Elkridge. I can't say I'll be thrilled to live with werewolves, but I would rather that than chance the dragons. We might even be able to catch a ship from one of their docks to Emberwyn."

Damian knelt down next to him and looked at the map. "That'll take three weeks at least if we want to avoid the main roads. Otherwise we'll be walking aimlessly through the woods on the border with the elves and I'd rather keep my head."

"I'm with Damian on this one." Laslow called out.

"So we're not going to talk about how he's going to round up all the mages and either make them serve him or kill them?"

Both Damian and Laslow looked up at me like I'd grown two extra heads.

"I'm not sure what that has to do with us." Damian mumbled.

"We can't just let him *take* them." I insisted.

Laslow frowned. Damian shook his head and ran a hand down his face. Ian, on the other hand, seemed to don a look of understanding.

"We barely got out of that alive and you're just going to suggest we become some kind of band of heroes? By the gods woman, you're more naive than I thought."

I almost snapped at him, *almost*. I would've said something I regretted though, so I bit my tongue. "I never said you had to help me." I finally grumbled.

"Like you'd make it on your own."

He meant it to be under his breath, as though I wouldn't hear him. Unfortunately for him I had better hearing than most.

"Oh fuck you!" I shouted. "Had it not been for me you wouldn't have even made it off those posts you were tied to."

"She has–" Ian started, but Damian cut him off.

"Listen, you may have enough of your *honor* from your days in the army to feed into her delusion and want to help her but *I* am not interested in risking myself to save anyone else." He growled at him.

"And if he succeeds in taking down Moira?" I asked, standing up now and glaring down at him. "If he does what he promised and returns us to whatever history he claims that Nyvara destroyed?"

"Lies, the lot of it." Laslow called over. "I've never heard of anything before the vampires."

"Have you ever thought to ask?" Ian queried.

"Well, it's never been relevant, so no."

"What did you have in mind, Liza?" Ian asked, and I turned my attention back to him.

"Well, I imagine they're being carted to the capital somehow. We could ambush that transport and turn them loose. Or find out where they're being held as we travel by towns and figure out how to release them there. We've got magic. Surely we can take them."

"Bold talk for someone who barely seems to have a grasp on her magic." Damian quipped.

Ian elbowed him in the ribs. "It's not much of a plan, but maybe we can work something out." The corner of his mouth quirked up. "It wouldn't hurt to help the lady if it's on the way, would it?"

Damian shook his head, but seemed to relent his inevitable retort when Ian suggested that it would be on our way.

"If it looks like it's going to be a real fight, you can count me out of it, but if it seems like we can help them escape without risking ourselves, then I've got you." He gave me a stern look. "But if you think for one second, I'm going to save your ass if you get into trouble, you do not know me very well."

I rolled my eyes. "I just met you two days ago. I hardly know you at all." What I had managed to figure out though, was that Ian was probably the only one I could really rely on *or* trust. Damian and Laslow's kindness only stretched so far.

*

On our journey northward, we stuck to the routes that Ian assured us were less traveled. It surprised me when we came across a small group of soldiers traveling on foot with a horse drawn wagon that held about a dozen men and women who were obviously prisoners.

Two men in full armor sat in the back with the prisoners, two sat in the driver's seat, and there was a pair on foot in front of and behind the setup. It seemed absurd that the soldiers on the ground were without horses. Surely horses weren't that much of a limited commodity that they couldn't have spared some for them.

Damian commented on as much, but begrudgingly agreed that we could try to help them. Damian planned to cut through the harnesses that attached the horses to the wagon with his magic, while Laslow would blow the soldiers at the back over with a gust of wind. Ian apparently was a water mage as well, and he decided he would freeze the two walking at the front in place so that the frantic horses could take them out.

They were sure they'd be spooked with all the clatter of the armor as the drivers fell. I was responsible for fighting off the two in the back. I wasn't entirely sure how to do that without burning them. I wanted to save these people, but I didn't want to hurt anyone in the process. Even if they were our enemies.

They all sent their magic out at exactly the same moment. Just as they'd said, the horses took off and barreled into the soldiers who'd been frozen in place. They sprung into action after that. Damian and Laslow threw themselves at the startled men, while I ran to the back of the wagon. I didn't look to see where Ian went.

The prisoners, noticing the commotion, stood up and began to fight back on their own. Swords were drawn and swung, but caught mid-swing by the ice Damian put in their path. I was useless. All I could do was watch in horror as Damian, sword now in hand, cut down one man while Laslow went for the other.

Some of the women jumped off the wagon and put some distance between themselves and the chaos, while the men armed themselves with the soldier's weapons.

"You were supposed to handle them." Damian shouted at me. "Have you ever fought *anyone*?" He advanced on me until only two paces separated us.

"I–"

"Give her a break, Damian." Ian scolded. "You should've known giving her that task wasn't going to work. She lived in the palace. I doubt she's had to fight for anything a day in her life."

I should've been insulted, but he was right.

"It was *her* idea."

"Yes, and you could've let her set something on fire to spook the horses, or even burn their harnesses off. Play on her skills rather than expecting her to fight off assailants."

Metal clinked as shackles began to hit the ground. Someone must've found the keys. I, however, felt entirely useless to this effort.

Laslow approached from the left and offered something to me. When I looked his way and found it was a dagger, I hesitated to grab the hilt.

"Take it. Whether you've been taught how to fight or not, I'm sure you can figure out how to stab with it, can't you?"

"I suppose I could." I took it reluctantly, but had no idea where to put it.

"Good." He smiled. He turned to the gathered group of people. "The safest place to go is Elkridge. Do you know how to get there on your own?"

Indistinct chatter erupted among them.

"You can also brave the mountains if you want to run to Emberwyn." Damian almost laughed. "But do so at your own risk."

"We're just going to leave them?" I asked.

"What, you want to add more to our group, little firefly?" Damian mused. "Trying to compensate for your uselessness?"

Fire formed in my hand before I had the chance to think the better of it. I might've thrown it at him if it weren't for the collective gasps of the group behind him.

He glanced over his shoulder. "Yes, it's a fire mage. I'm sure it's thrilling to see." He shook his head. "Get moving before more of them get here and have the chance to arrest you again."

Ian grumbled something under his breath and headed off in the direction they'd been traveling from. "We should also keep moving." He called back to us. "Leave the supplies to them. We can manage without it."

I followed him, unwilling to stand and be gawked at and furious that Damian found it so fun to taunt me. If he called me 'firefly' again, I might just use the damned dagger Laslow gave me on him, even if the sight of the blood they spilled behind me made me queasy.

Chapter 19

Slade

Fiona had just sat my glass down and slid it across the counter when the room suddenly went eerily silent. My hand was on the hilt of the dagger strapped to my chest before the cause of the silence spoke.

"Leave the money on the table for your food and drink, and get out." It was a voice I recognized, though I failed to remember who it was until I turned to glance over my shoulder.

Captain Mercer stood a few paces inside the door, with a group of six guards behind him. Their armor glinted in the candlelight. I scowled at him when his gaze fell on me.

"Except you."

"Excellent." I muttered while everyone quickly did as the captain demanded. Fiona eyed me wearily. "I'm sure he expects you to leave as well." I gestured toward the back room with a tilt of my head and she darted out as well.

"It's been a few weeks, Smith." The captain mused. "Or should I call you Sàmhach Marbhadh? It's so unclear."

I let go of the dagger and took a sip of the whiskey instead. In all that armor, I would hardly break a sweat if I had to fight them off. The captain *might* put up more of a fight, but I doubted it. I might as well enjoy my drink.

"Call me whatever you like, Captain." I stood from my stool and turned to face him, waving the glass unceremoniously. "If you've come to demand I reenlist, I would have to politely decline."

He frowned, then pulled a piece of rolled up parchment from his vest pocket. "I'd never want the likes of you on my guard, especially now that I know who you *really* are. I'm here to deliver a message." He walked over and offered it to me.

"And what exactly is this *message*?" I didn't take it from him.

"Read it for yourself."

I scoffed and took another sip of my drink. "You're the captain of the king's guard, not an errand boy. You know damned well what that piece of parchment reads, so don't waste my time with reading it and tell me what the fuck it is that has you here ruining my otherwise perfect evening."

He glanced around us with a grimace and a shake of his head. "You're going to track down Liza Winters and deliver her to King Edward. This piece of parchment has the details on where we *think* she's run off to, along with a description of the other escapees who may be with her. If you find her with them, you've been ordered to kill all three of them on sight."

I looked between him and the parchment, then back again. "I'll pass. Thanks." I turned to sit back on my stool and he grabbed my shoulder.

I spun out of his grip, took the arm he grabbed me with and had it twisted behind his back with my dagger at his throat before he could register what had happened. Every guard in the tavern with us had their weapons drawn on me then. They made a half circle around us.

"Just give me an excuse, Mercer. I have no issue killing you where you stand."

"You either find her and deliver her to the King." He forced out through gritted teeth. "Or your assassination will be the next one he orders." He turned his head as much as he dared so he could glare sideways at me. "Surely even you are not so invincible that the entire guild of assassins can't kill you."

I would give him credit. He didn't fight against my hold, nor did he seem to be concerned that it would just take a bit more pressure on his neck to end him. The threat though, that irritated me.

"Are you so foolish to think that I don't know precisely how to hide?"

"You'll have nowhere to hide when he reveals that it was you who killed Andras."

So that was why they needed the bar empty.

"I may not know how you managed to do it," Mercer grumbled. "But right now, you're a loose end. One he's eager to be rid of, unless you can be useful to him."

"I am not a bounty hunter." I released him and shoved him away. "If he sends me after her, I'll be bringing him her head."

He shoved the parchment into my chest. I took it, begrudgingly. "You will deliver her *alive* and you'll be heavily compensated. Your treason will be forgiven and you'll be allowed to return to this shithole of a city at your leisure. If any harm comes to her, he will not hesitate to announce what you've done *and* place a bounty on your head that no one in your guild could resist."

"Fine." I growled. "Now get the fuck out of this bar and let me enjoy my evening in peace."

"You have one month." He unhooked a chain from his belt and tossed it my way. "You might want that." He turned on his heel and walked toward the door. Once he stepped through it the guards lowered and sheathed their weapons, then followed him.

"Fuck me." I walked around the bar to help myself to a new glass of whiskey. After that, I might need the whole fucking bottle.

I unrolled the parchment and reviewed it. They were cutting a path northwest, no doubt to follow the dirt roads to Elkridge – if they had any kind of self preservation anyway.

Fiona walked back in. "So it was you."

It wasn't a question, and I had the sudden inkling to kill her. The name they gave me was common knowledge, but the face behind it was a mystery, and I wanted to keep it that way. *Someone* would die for letting that slip.

"Bold of you to admit you were spying on the entire conversation when you know my reputation."

She stopped walking. I glanced her way to find her staring at me in disbelief.

"You're not going to…"

"What?" I asked, advancing on her slowly. "Kill you? I *should*. Knowing *what* I do is one thing. Knowing who I am makes you nothing more than a liability."

Her eyes widened and she searched my face for any sign that I might spare her. "I won't say anything. I swear it. I've never even told anyone that I suspected. I–"

"Enough." I put up a hand to silence her. "I'm not going to kill you... yet. But if I find out you spoke a single word of what you overheard today, I can promise you that I'll be back, and you won't be breathing long enough to beg me for mercy. Do you understand?"

She swallowed nervously and nodded slowly.

"Good." I stepped around her, walked back along the other side of the bar, and grabbed the bottle. "I'll be taking this." I tucked the parchment into the small satchel on my belt and tossed a few more coins on the counter. "Enjoy your evening."

Chapter 20

Liza

I was increasingly reminded of my uselessness by Damian the farther we traveled and the more times we tried to free the mages we encountered. However, dying and cutting my hair had made me nearly unrecognizable when compared to the sketch on the wanted posters that were distributed, so I was one of the few of us who could walk around town without drawing attention.

I was wearing the cloak that Ian stole for me. Despite being less recognizable and *useless* I was not an idiot. It would be stupid to wander into a town without anything to hide my face.

We reached Ravencroft today, and while they went on their usual thieving missions, I decided to wander through the city and see what I could find out about the king's efforts to collect mages. If I'd learned anything from my time in Maeus, it was that bars were the best place to linger and listen.

Thanks to Laslow, I did at least have enough money to buy myself something to eat, rather than surviving one more gods damn day on his awful cooking. I might even afford a drink too.

I made it to the nicer part of the city before I found a tavern that looked like it might get me the information I was seeking. It was just fancy enough that I was sure the food would be good, but just seedy enough that guards probably went there too.

It was nearly sundown, so the bar was almost full. The inside was bustling with activity on both floors. I didn't even see an empty table. I wove my way through the gathered patrons and found an opening to order at the bar. The barkeep rattled off what they had available as well as the price. I had just enough for a warm meal and a drink.

I took the stew he brought to me as well as a single glass of whiskey to a quiet spot in the back of the tavern. Wine this far from the port would've been far too expensive, if they even had it.

A man in a black cloak slid into the seat across from me. I nearly jumped at his sudden arrival. I hadn't even heard him approach. I silently scolded myself for not being aware of my surroundings. I was far too distracted by my first *real* meal in days.

"You don't strike me as the type to drink whiskey." He observed. His voice was familiar, but I couldn't place it. Between his hood and the shadow it cast, all I could see of him was the bottom half of his face. He had scruff from a few days' growth of a beard and a chiseled jawline that might've made me swoon if I weren't currently concerned about his intentions.

"It's an acquired taste." I mumbled and sat my spoon down. "I don't recall inviting you to sit with me."

"I don't recall asking." His lips twitched up into a smirk. "And you seem to be alone."

I cleared my throat and took a moment to look around at the rest of the patrons. I couldn't find a way out of the situation, aside from rushing off and leaving. I still wanted to try to see what I could overhear, and he didn't seem like he would leave me alone if I didn't just *leave.* Something at the back of my mind didn't really want him to either.

"I'm actually waiting on someone." I tried to make it look like I was looking for them.

"Shame on them for keeping a woman like you waiting." He mused, and my head spun back toward him so quickly that my hood nearly slipped down.

I adjusted it awkwardly and reached for my glass. I took a sip and hesitated with it in front of my lips. "What is that supposed to mean?"

"Well, it's given me an opportunity to talk to you. I wouldn't give anyone else the chance if you were mine."

Gods why couldn't I place his voice. It couldn't have been anyone from Riodian. I knew them all too well to ever mistake them for someone else. This man was *flirting* with me, and I was certain I knew him somehow. Worse yet, the longer I sat this close to him the more I wanted to stay right where I was and *not* run away.

I took the final sip of the whiskey and sat the glass down. "What makes you think I would ever *be* yours?" I didn't know why I was playing along, but maybe if I could fight him off with my words he'd get the point and leave before I lost my better judgement.

"It's rare that I don't end up getting what I want."

I snorted. "Wow, you think quite highly of yourself."

He gave me a cocky grin. "So I've been told."

"I–" A sudden wave of dizziness hit me out of nowhere and I placed both my hands on the table to steady myself. "Woah." I breathed. This *wasn't* normal. I had whiskey before but it never did this to me. "Excuse me, I– I think I need to go." I tried to quickly move from the table and stand, but I swayed on my feet.

He caught me without hesitation and slipped an arm under my cloak and around my back to steady me. "I've got you." He said softly. "Had a little too much to drink?"

"I'm fine…" I wasn't though. The room was spinning and I was struggling to keep my eyes open. "I just had… the one."

He slipped my arm over his shoulders. "It's alright. I've got you."

"No, I…" I didn't finish my final reply before I faded into oblivion.

Chapter 21

Slade

I would've recognized those emerald eyes anywhere. Her hair was cropped at her shoulders. It was uneven, and a bit of a mess. The dark color was new, but it was fading and hints of red peaked through in the sunlight.

They had left enough bodies in their wake that figuring out where she might go next was far easier than I expected. If they were trying to be inconspicuous, they were failing at it. Although *she* hardly seemed like the type to harm anyone. I was left to assume it was the three men with her.

Whatever pull I felt toward her at the palace seemed to reappear when I got closer to her. I still didn't understand it. I started to think it was some kind of charm she put on me. It didn't make a whole lot of sense, but *everyone* at the palace had been infatuated with her so it was the only explanation I could come up with.

Regardless, it was a convenient tool for tracking her down. Thankfully, she was alone when I caught up with her in Ravencroft. I followed her into the tavern and waited until I was sure no one was joining her. I couldn't make a scene, and truthfully, I didn't feel like fighting her companions just so I could take her. I sifted through my satchel beneath my cloak until I found the tincture I was looking for. With any luck, I could dump it in her drink.

I slid into the seat across from her and she visibly tensed. I enhanced the shadow from my cloak to hide my eyes. That was the only feature I worried she might remember. There was still a chance she would recognize my voice, but it was a chance I had to take. I'd rather take her quietly than draw attention to us.

I couldn't bring myself to look her in the eye, relying on the hood to cut off her face above her nose. I remembered how it affected me in the palace, and if it would have an effect on me now I couldn't take the risk. I couldn't afford any distractions.

I just needed to figure out what to say to her.

"You don't strike me as the type to drink whiskey." It was the most ridiculous way to start the conversation, but I found myself entirely speechless. As though this were my first time ever talking to a woman in a tavern. I could've kicked myself for how stupid it probably sounded.

She studied me closely for several breaths, like she was desperate to try to figure out how she knew me. She *definitely* recognized my voice, but I thanked the goddess that she couldn't seem to place it.

"It's an acquired taste." She sat down her spoon. "I don't recall inviting you to sit with me."

"I don't recall asking." I couldn't stop the smirk that rose to my lips at her smart ass response. "And you seem to be alone."

She cleared her throat and looked around nervously. I took the opportunity to pop the cork on the vial and empty the contents into the whiskey.

"I'm actually waiting on someone." She was still looking around the bar like they might walk in at any moment. She was a terrible liar though.

"Shame on them for keeping a woman like you waiting." I continued to play the part. She turned to look at me so quickly that her hood nearly slipped off. She adjusted it and reached right for the drink. Thank the gods.

"What is that supposed to mean?"

"Well, it's given me an opportunity to talk to you. I wouldn't give anyone else the chance if you were mine." I surprised myself with the words that came out of my mouth. Where the *fuck* had that come from? I wasn't ever that possessive with a woman.

She finished her whiskey. "What makes you think I would ever *be* yours?"

It seemed to keep her interested. "It's rare that I don't end up getting what I want." And *that* wasn't a lie.

She snorted. "Wow, you think quite highly of yourself."

I shot her a cocky grin. "So I've been told."

"I–" She clutched the table like it might hold her up and she swayed a little. "Woah." She squeezed her eyes shut. "Excuse me, I– I think I need to go."

She swayed on her feet when she tried to stand. I was right there to catch her. "I've got you. Had a little too much to drink?"

"I'm fine…" She wasn't. "I just had… the one."

I pulled her arm up over my shoulder. "It's alright. I've got you."

"No, I…" She collapsed against me. I turned and headed straight for the back door. It led into an alley. I had visited Ravencroft plenty of times. Enough that I knew precisely how to get out of this part of the city without anyone noticing that she was unconscious.

I made my way back to the hitching post I left the horses at and tossed her up over my horse's shoulders. I needed to get the cuff the captain gave me onto her wrist, but I didn't want to waste time doing that until I was out of view of anyone in this city. I didn't need them asking any questions or assuming I was taking her in for a bounty and trying to fight me for her. More importantly, I couldn't risk the men who were traveling with her noticing that she was on *my* horse.

I untied my horse and the horse I brought for her. I tied the other horse's lead to my saddle, and mounted my horse behind her. I guided both horses toward the road that took us over the northern side of Aelearon Lake. It would be the fastest route to the Maeus and it was very unlikely we'd run into anyone else on the way. I just hoped I had enough packed to get us that far without having to slow down to hunt for food.

Chapter 22

Liza

When I came to, I was slung over the shoulders of a horse, with someone sitting in the saddle and holding me in place with one arm over my back. My shackled wrist hung below me, bouncing as the horse walked, and my head was absolutely killing me.

He must've noticed the change in my body, and that I was awake because the horse suddenly stopped. "Welcome back." He said with no small amount of amusement.

He swung himself off the horse, nearly smashing me with his body weight briefly as he did so, and then he hauled me down to the ground with him. I swayed when my feet hit the ground and muttered a curse. He caught me before I fell down completely. I shot him a glare, but froze the moment I met his eyes.

He seemed caught off guard that I would do such a thing, and quickly broke eye contact. "Do you think you can handle riding on your own, or would you rather remain slung over my horse's shoulders for the ride?"

I sputtered, not knowing what the fuck to say to him. My mind spun in a million directions. I realized why I recognized his voice now, and my throbbing head was not helping me organize my thoughts. He was a palace guard, but he certainly didn't look that way now without the armor.

It didn't take me long to realize this was the same cuff they had around my wrist at the palace. Part of how I was feeling was the lack of magic, not just whatever drug that was– *Wait.*

"You drugged me!"

"Yes." He still wouldn't meet my gaze.

I scoffed and swung at him with everything I had. He caught my fist in his hand and pushed me back against his horse. The animal swung its head around at us like it meant to bite us, but he didn't even flinch.

"Do *not* fight me. It won't end well for you." He met my gaze now, and the violence in his eyes should've stopped me.

I brought my knee up between his legs. He didn't see that coming, and didn't have the chance to block it. He muttered a curse and doubled over, but his grip on my hand only loosened a little. I yanked my hand away from him, grabbed the dagger from my belt and swung. I sliced his leather armor, and didn't wait around to see if it went through to his arm.

I turned and tried to slip my foot into the stirrup to climb up on the horse. I only made it halfway. He grabbed my cloak and yanked me down. I coughed and choked as a result of the clasp catching me in the throat *hard*. His free hand gripped my wrist so tight I was forced to drop the dagger.

"You bitch." He spat.

I took that as a compliment. For someone as incompetent and useless as Damian always made me out to be, I was at least putting up a decent fight against a palace guard. I threw my elbow back at him and he grunted.

"Don't make me hurt you." He growled in my ear.

"Then let me go." I shouted. I tried to shake off his grip on my cloak. He released me, to my surprise, but then had me spun around with my arm twisted up behind my back. He pulled it so high and tight that I shrieked in pain.

"I *don't* want to hurt you." His lips brushed my ear, which distracted me enough that I stilled. "You have two options. If you'll be cooperative and come with me, you can ride your own horse. If you're going to fight me like this the whole goddess damned way back to Maeus then I'm going to tie you up so tight you won't have a choice but to be slung over my fucking horse for the next several days. And I can promise you, this beast is not going to appreciate it."

"I'm not going *anywhere* with you. Least of all fucking Maeus." I ground out. "So you might as well fucking tie me up if that's your plan."

"Gods above." He sounded like he'd rather be anywhere but here. "I am not getting paid enough for this." He yanked me around so viciously that I whimpered. I wasn't sure how my shoulder hadn't dislocated.

His grip loosened as we neared the other horse. The long set of reins it wore were tied to the saddle and a rope connected it to his horse. "Get on the fucking horse."

"No."

He muttered a few more curses as he let go of me, but before I could turn around and swing on him again he grabbed my leg and shoved me up onto the horse. It jolted forward a step, but he moved us both with it. He shoved my leg over its back and grabbed the chain hanging from the cuff on my wrist.

"I'm not riding with you in front of me for days. If I have to tie you to *this* horse somehow, I will." He gestured to the rope hanging off of his saddle.

"I am not–"

"Going anywhere with me. Yeah, I heard you the first time. Unfortunately for you, you don't get a say in the matter. Unfortunately for me, I get to listen to you bitch and complain about this for days. Will you *please* just shut the fuck up and ride the horse? You aren't going to get away from me, if that wasn't obvious, and I am in no mood to argue."

"You wouldn't have to listen to me if you just let me *go*."

He glared up at me. "Believe me, I had no interest in this *assignment*, but I don't have a choice either."

He walked back to his horse, lifting the chain over it until he mounted and started walking forward again. I was stunned into silence and didn't have a retort for that.

My horse followed him without question. I didn't even have to pick up the reins. The moment there was pressure on the rope that connected it to his horse, it moved. The stirrups, oddly enough, were the correct length for me to reach them. I didn't know how he'd managed to guess that, but I was thankful I wouldn't have to try to ride it without them.

"Why did they send *you*?" I asked after a few minutes passed. He ignored me. I reached up and grabbed the reins so I could pull on them and make my horse stop. It obeyed, but protested when the rope pulled forward. His horse came to a halt reluctantly as mine pulled back against it and got increasingly agitated.

He looked back at me. "Do you have to be so goddess damned stubborn?"

I would've slapped him if I were close enough. "I asked you a question." If I wasn't getting out of this situation, I was at least going to make it miserable for him.

"Fuck me." He breathed. "They sent me because they knew I'd find you *and* deliver you within the timeframe they requested. Now can we *please* go? I have a deadline to keep."

"What experience would a palace guard have with tracking someone down and bringing them in?"

"I'm not a palace guard." He snarled, like the fact that I believed that to be true about him was utterly insulting.

"Oh, I'm sorry, last I checked you *are* the guard who stood outside of my bed chambers every night for the gods knew how long, how was I supposed to know any different?"

He sighed and pinched the bridge of his nose. "I'm not going to explain this all to you. I already have far too many people who apparently know the truth and you're probably the biggest liability of them all."

"What the fuck is that supposed to mean?" I nearly shouted.

He muttered something under his breath, backed his horse up until he was almost next to me, and reached for the reins. I pulled them out of his reach.

"If you make me get off this fucking horse…" He threatened, and reached for them again.

"You'll what?" I mocked him. "Tie me up? Is that the best threat you can come up with?"

"I'm starting to think being a fugitive would've been a *lot* easier than dealing with you." He grumbled. He leaned over into a single stirrup, grabbed the reins and yanked them from my hands. He undid the knot holding them to the horn so quickly I didn't have the chance to catch that part of the reins before he had them over the horse's head and tied up with the rope.

"If you're quite finished, I'd like to get moving now."

"I'm not."

"I don't care." He kicked his horse on and mine followed willingly.

The thought crossed my mind to simply throw myself off the horse. I didn't see how the chain was attached. Perhaps I could try to run. He could probably catch up with the horse before I got too far…

"Whatever gods awful ideas are running through your mind right now, please don't do it." He sounded genuinely exhausted now, rather than annoyed.

"Fine." I rested my hands on the pommel of the saddle. "Will you at least tell me what I'm supposed to call you? Or am I just supposed to yell 'hey asshole' when I need something?"

He was silent for long enough that I wondered if he'd deign to respond at all. He finally glanced over his shoulder and muttered, "Slade."

"If you're not a palace guard, why were you *my* guard?"

"You were far less annoying when you were unconscious."

"You were much less of an asshole when you were simply my guard."

"If you think insulting me will get you answers, I hate to tell you that you're not going to get anywhere with that."

"If you were a bounty hunter, you wouldn't have taken a job at the palace." I guessed. At this point, I was having more fun irritating him than I was really concerned about getting an answer.

"Wow, I didn't think you'd be able to put that together."

"I'm not a fucking idiot." I snapped.

A dark chuckle rumbled out of him. "You certainly act like it at times."

"Fuck you!" I spat.

"No, I'm good, thanks."

I growled in frustration.

"I was there on an assignment." He finally relented and answered me, likely just to shut me up. He seemed to regret the words as soon as he said them, because he muttered a curse. All it did was pique my interest.

"What kind of assignment?" I studied him a little closer, but there wasn't much I could see. He was wearing a thick black cloak. I wasn't sure how he wasn't roasting in it. The fall weather had set in, but it was still hot at this time of day.

"It's none of your concern."

"I'll decide what is and is not of my concern. If I'm stuck with you for *days* I'd like to know the kind of person I'm chained to."

"I can assure you, you'll be far happier if you don't know."

He didn't look back at me. His eyes stayed trained on the path ahead. It irked me more than I should have let it.

"I can assure you, I'm not going to shut up until you tell me."

"And I can promise you that I have plenty more of the drug you drank yesterday to keep you unconscious until we get to Maeus if that's what it will take to get a moment of peace."

I laughed, which finally got him to look my way. "First you threaten to tie me up, then tie me to the horse, and now you're going to threaten to drug me *again*? Answering my questions will get me to shut up faster than threatening me."

His face contorted in a scowl. "Right, because that's worked so far." He looked ahead again.

"Will you just tell me what the fuck you are? Then I'll *finally* give you the peace you crave so badly."

That seemed to snap the thin patience I had been wearing down, because he halted his horse abruptly and turned it so he could look at me fully. My horse, thankfully, stopped before we ran into them.

"If you must know, then make sure you listen closely and understand. My *assignments* would be a head dangling in a bag off the back of this horse by now if I had not been blackmailed into keeping you alive until I turn you in. And each question you insist I answer is pushing me further toward disobeying that order and killing you anyway."

The last few words didn't quite have the bite I think he intended them to. The rest left me speechless though. I searched his face for a few moments before he finally turned back to the road ahead and urged his horse into a walk.

"You're an assassin." I eventually mumbled. He didn't say anything. He didn't really have to. I tried to piece everything together in my mind, and when it clicked it left me hollow. "You killed Andras." The words left my lips as nothing more than a whisper.

"It was my greatest achievement yet." He didn't say the words with pride though. They were flat and emotionless. Dare I say laced with a bit of regret.

"You were why they came for me." I snarled at him.

He barely spared me a glance. "No. I don't know why they came for you. You're a fire mage. If you wanted to kill someone you'd have set them on fire and they'd have found a pile of ash in his bed."

"I wouldn't ever harm anyone!"

A small smile played at his lips when he glanced back at me. "Funny, you had no problem swinging that dagger at me earlier."

"You drugged me and put me in chains. How did you expect me to react?"

"I didn't have expectations, but I didn't expect *this*." He motioned toward me in annoyance.

I scoffed, but for once, I didn't have anything else to say to him. *He* was the reason I was in this mess. *He* was the reason that I failed at the mission Moira sent me to accomplish. The reason I would lose my throne. The reason I would likely find myself dead before the Solstice.

And if I had to spend the next several days chained to him. I was going to make him miserable until he was rid of me.

Chapter 23

Slade

This woman was going to be the death of me, I was sure of it. She annoyed me to no end. While it did offer at least a bit of entertainment, it made me remember why I preferred to travel alone.

It started raining in the late afternoon and the temperature dropped. It was a welcome reprieve from the heat of the day. By the time I finally guided my horse off of the narrow path the rain had stopped for a little over an hour and night had fallen.

I dismounted and started to unpack my sleeping roll and other supplies to set up a camp. I pulled the hobbles out of my pack and placed them on my horse's legs.

It took me a few moments to realize that she had yet to dismount. When I pulled down my hood and glanced her way she was shaking life a leaf, and uncharacteristically quiet.

Her cloak was soaked clean through, and I imagined her clothing beneath it was the same. She hadn't uttered a single complaint, or if she had it wasn't loud enough to hear over the rain.

"You can get off now."

She looked around like she couldn't determine the best way to get down from the horse. I sighed, left everything I had unpacked on the ground next to my horse, and walked over to pull her off myself after I secured the second set of hobbles around her horse's legs.

She shrieked when I pulled her down, and nearly collapsed when her feet hit the ground. I unclasped her sopping cloak and let it fall to the ground. I removed my own cloak and draped it around her shoulders.

"You could have mentioned your cloak wasn't waterproof."

She scoffed through her chattering teeth. "As though you would have cared."

"I'll make a fire." I turned and walked back toward my pile of supplies, then carried them to the most open space in the trees around us. I was forced to stop when the chain between us pulled against my belt.

I turned and looked back at her. She was clutching my cloak close, and she glared in my direction.

"You're going to have to walk *with* me if you want me to build a fire."

She scowled. "I could just *make* a fire."

"I am not stupid enough to remove that shackle and give you the chance to burn me to a crisp."

"You know all too well that I won't do that. I may have fought you earlier, but I don't *kill* people."

I surveyed her for a moment, giving her the idea that I was considering it. I wouldn't, of course, but this was a game

I didn't intend to lose. I could annoy her just as much as she would try to annoy me.

"No." I said simply, grabbed the chain, and yanked it. She stumbled forward, nearly falling on her face.

"You bastard!"

I smiled. "I've been called far worse, Firestorm." The nickname rolled off my tongue far too easily, and I didn't know where it came from, but it seemed to fit her all the same.

Her face flushed red, though I wasn't sure if it was a blush or rage. The glare suggested rage. She gathered up the chain in her hands and yanked at me, but I saw it coming so I didn't budge.

"The longer we play this game, the longer it takes for you to quit shivering. But please, do continue to refuse to cooperate. I am perfectly content to skip a fire."

It was definitely rage that burned in the depths of those emerald eyes as she stomped her way toward me, warmed by the fury bubbling within her.

"Has anyone ever told you you're an absolute prick?"

It was hard to hide the smirk that threatened to rise to my lips. "Oh many times." She paused next to me and glared up at me. "Has anyone ever told you you're an irritating little brat?"

She tried to punch me, but I caught her fist. "No." She grumbled. "You get to be the first arrogant prick to do so."

"What an honor." I mused and released her fist. "Why don't you help me find some kindling?"

She looked at me like she'd want to swing that fist again, but muttered something under her breath and turned to look for it like I asked. At least she was beginning to realize she wasn't going to win with me.

By the time we gathered enough wood for a fire her shivering had almost stopped. I still got the fire going anyway, then prepped both of the cots I brought along so that we could get a decent rest before we set off again in the morning. She didn't say a word when I handed her a small portion of the jerky, bread, and cheese.

She stared into the fire while she picked at the food. It was almost like she could *feel* the way it moved and breathed. It was a little unnerving, if I was honest. She didn't have a propensity for violence, but I could see the monster underneath if she were ever brave enough to let it out.

Something about her was different–ethereal, in a way I couldn't quite place. I hadn't ever encountered a mage with the presence she had about herself. Perhaps that was just how fire mages were. I had never known one to be able to confirm that other than her.

"What does the king want with me, anyway?" She finally asked, looking up and locking eyes with me.

It was like her gaze froze me in place. The intensity behind her eyes was mesmerizing. I couldn't think beyond it. I could've stared for an eternity, but she finally looked away. I blinked and shifted my own gaze back down to the bread I was picking apart.

"I wasn't informed what they wanted. I was just ordered to bring you alive and unharmed."

"And if you're taking me to my death?" I glanced up at her. Her expression held a quiet rage. "What then?"

I thought about it for a moment, my gaze flicking to the fire before returning to her. "I'll be a little bit pissed that I had to waste my time to deliver you if all they intended to do was kill you."

I watched the fire dance in her eyes. "I'll meet an untimely death whether it's by your hand, theirs, or someone else's, I'm sure. I'm surprised I've made it this far."

It was such an odd thing to say, especially from someone who I'd come to think was too naive and optimistic to believe such a thing. And for some irritating reason I found myself wanting to save her from that fate. She had to have charmed me. I hadn't ever cared about anyone other than myself. This was the same confusing feeling I felt in the palace when they drug her away. It was going to drive me mad.

Chapter 24

Liza

I was thankful for his cloak, even if it became too hot not long after the fire was lit. I hadn't expected him to care, let alone give me something to warm myself up with. When I woke the following morning he was already packing up his things and preparing the horses, who hadn't wandered far.

He had, much to my surprise, detached the chain from his belt, at some point. The fleeting idea of running crossed my mind, but I recognized that I wouldn't get very far and I had absolutely no idea where we even were. Instead, I used the opportunity to relieve myself.

When I returned, he had begun rolling up and packing the cot I'd been sleeping on. He didn't even acknowledge my presence. My entire body ached from sleeping on the shitty cot on the ground, and spending the entire day in the saddle. I wasn't sure I could handle much more. He'd said it would take days, and I desperately prayed we might move faster.

By now I was sure Damian, Ian, and Laslow had realized I wasn't coming back and probably moved on without me. Which meant that I was doomed to this fate regardless of what I did. He knew I was not skilled or fast enough to escape.

He walked over to retrieve the chain and attach it to his belt again. "What level of defiance should I prepare for today?"

"You didn't seem all that concerned that I would run off."

"You *were* sleeping and you're also not an idiot. Naive and a bit daft at times, but not an idiot."

My hands balled into fists at my sides, a motion he didn't miss.

A smirk rose to his lips. "Oh, did I hit a nerve?"

"No, but I'd like to."

He chuckled, the sound as grating as it was endearing. "All bark and no bite. Your cloak is dry." He motioned toward the branch he hung it on last night. "I'd like mine back. Wear yours or don't, I don't care either way, but we need to get moving."

I mumbled just how much I couldn't stand him under my breath, unclasped his cloak, and shoved it at him. He waited patiently while I retrieved my cloak and tossed it over my shoulders before he headed back toward the horses and I begrudgingly followed. I managed to mount mine on my own, thank the gods. The last thing I needed was for him to have an excuse to put his hands on me again.

*

I stayed quiet throughout the day. My curiosity got the better of me when we stopped for the night. "What made you decide to become an assassin?"

The question seemed to startle him, as though he'd forgotten that I was sitting a few feet away, or perhaps that he forgot I could speak.

"What kind of question is that?" He gave me a look that suggested it was as dumb as he was trying to make it sound. It was a rather interesting life choice, in my mind.

"The kind that *has* an answer, if you weren't so good at trying to avoid giving them." I pointed out and popped another piece of cheese in my mouth.

"It wasn't a decision I made on my own, nor is it something I plan to discuss." He dismissed me so quickly that it sparked my anger again. Only Damian had ever annoyed me to the point where I threatened or considered violence, but even that was fleeting. This man did so consistently, to a point where it was driving me nuts. A small part of me was thrilled by it, but I tried to ignore that bit.

"Fine." I grumbled. "How many people have you… assassinated?"

This question had his face twisting in disbelief that I would even ask. "I'm failing to understand how any of this is relevant or something you need to know."

"I'm failing to understand why you are refusing to hold a conversation with me."

"Says the one who has been a functioning mute for most of the day." He laid back on his cot so he was looking up at the treetops rather than at me.

"You've not given me any reason to think you'll answer me when we're moving. What was the point in asking during the day other than to test your patience?"

164

He didn't respond. He tucked one arm behind his head. I finally took the time to really look at him. There were daggers strapped to every part of him. He didn't take them off even while he slept. The only weapon he *did* sit to the side was his sword, which lay right next to his cot.

"You still haven't answered my question." I laid down on my side and propped my head on my elbow.

He sighed, but didn't look at me. "Would you believe me if I told you I didn't remember the number?"

"No." This earned me a glance. "An arrogant bastard like you is far too cocky not to keep a tally."

I didn't miss the smirk he tried to hide before he turned his gaze to the sky again. "Why don't you guess then? Make it interesting."

I thought about it. "Thirty?"

He sat up and propped himself on his elbow. A look of actual disdain crumpled his features. "That's just insulting."

I smiled. For some reason, while the thought of that many people dying didn't actually amuse me, his reaction certainly did. "Too low then?"

"Substantially."

I made a show of looking around while I considered another number. "Seventy eight."

He raised a brow, but shook his head. "By the gods this is going to take all night."

"More, or less?"

"For the sake of eventually getting some sleep," he mumbled. "More."

"By the fucking gods." I gasped. "Alright, a hundred and thirty."

"I'm sure you'll guess it by the time I'm long dead." He laid back down on his cot as though he'd grown bored with our exchange already.

"Two hundred?" I sincerely hoped that I was wrong.

"One hundred and ninety eight, to be specific." He shrugged a shoulder and rolled his head to the side to look my way. "Would've been two hundred and one if I caught you with the men you were traveling with, but thankfully, you walked into the bar alone."

I blinked, the only sign of my surprise, but he chuckled all the same.

"What?" He mused. "You didn't think that they'd assume you were with the men who escaped with you? The men who left all of those bodies in your wake each time you freed mages bound for whatever Edward had in store for them?"

I wasn't quite sure what to say to that. As if sensing my internal crisis he sighed once more. "I'm sure there was another question. Might as well get them all over with."

I swallowed, gathering my scattered thoughts. The only question I had thought of before he said that was how old he was when he killed his first mark. It was a macabre detail I desperately needed to know.

"How old were you when you succeeded in getting your first kill?"

Any amusement in his face disappeared quickly when his expression darkened into something I couldn't read. "I was eight. The details are not something I'd like to explain, so you'll just have to accept the age and move on."

Something told me not to push the issue, so I dropped it. I had intended to make him miserable, but I didn't think that the answer to my question would do it for me. As much as I hated him for putting me in this situation in the first place, I suddenly felt guilty for asking.

*

I was only half asleep when rustling in the bushes nearby caught my attention. I didn't get the chance to look before I was being yanked up from the ground.

"Well, what do we have here?" A male voice mused.

I looked around, panicked. A burly man with a beard held my arm so tightly I was sure there'd be a bruise. At least seven other men had wandered into our camp. Four of them had their weapons drawn and surrounded Slade, while the other three were with me.

"A bounty hunter and his prize." One of the others said, looking between where Slade laid with a scowl on his face, hands at the ready to grab at his weapons, and where I was standing in the grip of the dark haired man. He was looking at me with a hunger in his eyes that made me extremely uncomfortable.

"Our prize now." The man holding me replied. "And a pretty one at that. Just think of the fun we can have with her before we turn her in."

I thought I might be sick.

"You'll regret laying a single fucking hand on her." Slade snarled.

The man chuckled. "And what are you going to do? There's seven of us and *one* of you. Don't be foolish, boy. Tell us where we'll need to deliver her for the bounty and we'll let you go."

Slade laughed. It was somehow deadly and maniacal at the same time. It was like he slipped into a persona I had yet to see. When I looked at him, I swore I saw death in his eyes.

"And if I refuse?" Each word was laced with violence, and I was very certain that he would be the one to draw first blood.

The man pulled my cloak back with his free hand and gave me an appraising once over. "We'll just kill you." When his gaze met mine, the lust in his eyes made my stomach twist.

"I'd love to see you try."

The man smiled. "Unhook that chain from his belt and kill him. Whoever deals the final blow can have her when I'm done with her." He started to back me away from my cot.

I didn't move but two steps before metal clanged with metal and I could see the chaos around Slade out of the corner of my eye. A chorus of grunts, curses, and other horrifying sounds rang out from them while I tried to figure my way out of the situation.

I bumped into another body, and I was trapped between them. The man in front of me smiled, and I brought my knee up into his groin.

His grip on my arm dropped as he shouted a curse and fell to his knees. "You little bitch."

I was grabbed by the man behind me and a knife was at my throat. It wasn't till I looked up and met Slade's furious amber eyes that I realized why.

He was breathing heavily. Blood poured from a wound on his side and trickled down the side of his face. All four of the men who'd been standing over him laid motionless, or nearly so, on the ground around his cot. Their blood pooled beneath them and was splattered all over his black leather clothing.

"Release her and I *might* let you live." He snarled. He wasn't totally steady on his feet though, and I saw him struggle to focus on the one holding me.

The man on the ground before me managed to breathe, "kill him," again, as though the two men behind me stood any chance if the four that tried the first time failed.

"Take one more step toward us and I'll slit her pretty little throat." The man holding me threatened.

Slade smiled and I had never seen anything more terrifying. "Go ahead and try."

The blade pressed harder into my neck, and I whimpered, leaning back into him as far as I could to get away from it. The sound must've snapped some bit of self restraint within Slade, because he moved like a shadow.

The pressure at my neck disappeared, as did the man behind me. I heard two sickening cracks. When I turned around, I found the man that had been holding me on his knees, choking as the knife he held against my throat was shoved through his neck by Slade. Shadows wreathed around him, like they were at his beck and call.

I gasped and backed away, nearly tripping over the body of the bearded man who'd threatened me first.

"You're—" I couldn't even say the words. A mage. *He* was a mage. And he'd hidden it.

He was in front of me in the blink of an eye with one of his own knives at my throat. One hand gripped my hair and held me still. "You will not speak of what you saw here tonight or I *will* kill you, deliver your body to the king, and blame these men."

I stared at him in shock. How he'd gone from protecting me to threatening me I didn't understand. "I– I promise I won't speak of it. I swear." I searched his face hoping he would accept it.

He glared at me for a few more of my panicked breaths before finally releasing me and sheathing his knife. He cursed under his breath and held his hand over the wound on his side.

"Gather up your things. We're moving." He ordered, then walked back toward the mess that was his cot.

I fumbled with my cot, rolling it haphazardly thanks to my shaking hands. The adrenaline was not helping me now.

I looked over when Slade hissed in pain. He was leaning against a tree for support and pouring something on his side. By the smell of it, it was whiskey. A few mumbled curses fell from his lips. He held a bundle of cloth against it, but it bled through the fabric.

"Get. Over. Here." He demanded. I dropped the cot and obeyed without a second thought. He fumbled with the keys on his belt. He was losing a lot of blood. I could try to run. He wasn't in a state where he would be able to catch up to me quickly. He was likely to bleed out before he could.

This was probably my only chance to escape.

"If I take that shackle off," his voice shook, which was surprisingly sobering for me. "Are you going to fry me?" He looked at me then, and I realized he was both desperate *and* asking a very genuine question.

I hesitated to answer.

"For the love of the gods, woman, answer the fucking question. If I don't do *something* to stop this bleeding I'm going to die anyway."

"N–No." I stuttered, still trying to decide if I could leave him here and just run. I was close enough to steal the keys and undo it myself. But for some reason, I couldn't make my body obey. Because another part of me wanted to stay and help him. I didn't want him to *die*.

I reached down and placed my hand over his where he was holding the cloth to his side. I tried to ignore the feel of his blood slipping through my fingers.

"What do you need me to do?" I was surprised by the steadiness in my own voice.

He slipped his hand from underneath mine, grabbed the cuff around my wrist and unlocked it. "I need to cauterize it. I need fire."

I opened my free hand and a flame flickered to life in it. He dropped the cuff and the keys, and undid his belt.

"What the fuck are you…"

He folded the belt over on itself and stuck it between his teeth. It was then that I noticed it almost looked like he had fangs. I wondered for a moment if I was just seeing things. He pressed my hand harder into his side, and grabbed a dagger with the other.

He held the dagger in the fire that hovered over my hand until it glowed red. He pulled my hand and the cloth away and instead pressed the flat end of the dagger over part of the wound.

I wasn't sure I would ever forget the way he growled in pain, or the smell of burning flesh that reached my nose. I had to turn my head away when he held the dagger over the fire again. I couldn't watch him do that another time. I might puke.

Another growl and then the clinking of the belt buckle against a rock on the ground was what told me it was safe to look at him again. The bleeding had stopped, replaced by a burn that looked awful. He locked the cuff around my wrist less than a second later and the fire winked out.

"You thought about leaving me here to die. I saw it on your face." He said simply while he retrieved his belt from the ground and attached both the chain and the keys to it. "Why didn't you?"

I couldn't look at him while I tried to come up with a reason. I didn't have one. It was stupid to have stayed. I *should* have run. I didn't know which direction to run of course, but I should've done so anyway. I could've blamed it on the shock, or even tried to lie and say I hadn't thought about it, but I had.

"I don't know." I finally admitted. "But…" I looked him over again. "You're a mage. Couldn't you have just healed yourself? Isn't that a trait all mages have?"

"I've never been capable of healing." He walked over to pull the daggers he used out of the bodies scattered around his cot. "I don't know what other mages are capable of."

"You weren't trained to use your magic?" I watched him wipe each blade off on their clothing before he placed them back in their respective sheaths.

He paused, his grip on the hilt of a dagger that looked like it had ended up directly in the one man's heart. "I was trained."

"Wouldn't your mentor have told you how to do that?"

He pulled the dagger out and cleaned it just like the rest. "Vampires can't heal with their magic."

"Wait, you're–"

"Do I look like a vampire to you?"

"I've never seen one so I wouldn't know." I snapped at him.

He started to gather up his other supplies. "They've got blood red eyes and fangs that you absolutely can't miss. In case you haven't noticed, I possess neither of those traits."

I thought back to the fangs I thought I saw. It must've been a trick of the light. His features did remind me more of Ezra and Azazel. Perhaps he was half fae. I hadn't ever heard of a shadow mage before. Shadow magic was dark, and to my knowledge, it was only something the fae and the vampires shared.

"Was it the vampire who trained you to be an assassin?" I walked over to my cot once more and picked it up. I was halfway to my horse when he grumbled his response.

"No, but he sent me to the man who did."

Chapter 25

Slade

My head was throbbing nearly as much as my side. It was almost midday. I glanced over at her. She had been silent since I told her that a vampire sent me to the guild. I didn't know if it was because I finally managed to make her speechless, or if she were trying to find a million more questions to ask me just to annoy me. From what I gathered so far, her mission from the moment she woke up was to do exactly that. It only got worse when she realized I killed Andras.

She stared straight ahead, even though she had no idea where we were headed. Her eyes were distant, like she was lost in thought. I thanked the gods that she hadn't fought me. She could've run last night. Eventually, I would've bled out. It wouldn't have stopped me from trying to stop her, but she had a way out. Why she didn't try was beyond me.

I should have killed her. Ten years ago I wouldn't have hesitated. I looked ahead again. There was no sense trying to figure it out. I would get her to Maeus, leave her there, and never look back. That's what I kept telling myself anyway. The closer we got, the less I wanted to follow through with that.

"So I guess that makes two hundred and five then."

I looked over to find her watching me intently.

"Is your magic why you have killed so many?"

"No." I urged my horse a bit faster, entirely uninterested in wherever this conversation was headed.

She pushed hers faster too. "The way it looked to me, you wouldn't have been able to kill the rest of them if you hadn't used it."

"I didn't exactly start from a good position." I shot her a glare. "You certainly didn't help much."

"Oh, I'm sorry," She sarcastically quipped. "I was chained to you *and* I had no magic. What was I supposed to do?"

I ignored her and stared ahead. I wasn't going to take the bait.

"How many times *have* you used your magic to complete your *assignments?*" The disdain with which she said assignments made me want to shove her off the damned horse.

"Three times."

"Andras was one of them, wasn't he?"

I could feel her piercing glare. There was no sense in lying. "Yes."

"How *did* you kill him? No one ever told me."

I sighed and glanced her way. "Do you really want to know? I know how much you pretended to court him."

She looked rightfully insulted. *"Pretended?"*

"For someone like you, the act wasn't too bad actually."

"Someone like *me*?" She scowled. "You're avoiding my question."

"Your question doesn't require an answer."

"Gods." She ran a hand over her face. "I haven't met a single person who makes me crave violence as much as you do."

"Why were you pretending?"

"I wasn't pretending." She insisted, but she looked away.

"You're a terrible liar."

"And you're a terrible person." She spat. "You kill people for a *living*."

For some reason, that struck a chord within me. I must not have masked my reaction quick enough, because I saw the split second of regret that passed over her features before she turned her face away from me.

"I didn't choose this life for myself." I muttered. "And, if you absolutely must know, I slit his throat. He died in seconds."

"As though making it quick makes it any better." She mumbled bitterly.

"Hate me if you need to. I wasn't given a choice in the matter. When you accept an assignment, it is kill or be killed. Those are the rules."

"You realize you just contradicted yourself. If you *accepted* the assignment, you were given a choice."

"We are usually given a choice whether or not to accept. That assignment was accepted *for* me. The person who set it all up selected me by name, or rather, the name that has been *given* to me. They created a position at the palace for another guard, orchestrated a fake identity, and gave me the perfect opportunity to kill him when there were hundreds of suspects within the castle walls."

"Who gave you *this* assignment?"

When I looked at her now, she had a fresh hatred in her eyes, like she'd figured out who paid for me to kill Andras on her own.

"Captain Mercer." I gave her a quick once over. "But I know it wasn't him who set me up for Andras."

"No." She clenched her fists. "It was Edward who paid for you to kill Andras."

"And what makes you think that?"

She let out a bitter laugh, and it was so out of character for her that it was startling, yet somehow, frustratingly sexy. "He basically admitted it, but he didn't know I could hear him. In my first few days at the palace, he said 'She knows the palace well enough that she could kill you in your sleep if she wanted.' He paid you, and he planned to punish me for it."

"What was Andras to you anyway?" I don't know why I needed to know, but I did.

"It doesn't matter now." She looked over at me dismissively. "He's dead."

*

"Are you alright?" Her question startled me. I'd nearly fallen asleep atop my horse.

"I wasn't aware that you cared." My voice reflected my exhaustion. The sun was setting. We had been riding for at least eighteen hours by now.

"You look like shit, and if I'm not mistaken, you just almost fell asleep on top of your horse. We abandoned the road and I haven't the slightest clue where we're headed so if you *do* fall off and knock yourself out we're completely fucked."

"Sounds like that would be good for you. You'd get another opportunity to escape."

"I wouldn't even know what direction to run."

I shrugged.

"Gods, you're such an asshole. Has anyone ever told you that?" I glanced her way and she shook her head. "Forgive me for worrying that maybe you needed to rest."

"How do you go from looking at me with blatant hatred, determined to make this trek as miserable as you can for me, to asking if I'm *okay?*"

She mumbled something I couldn't make out under her breath. I halted my horse and hers stopped a pace or two ahead. She glanced back at me.

"We'll make camp here, since you're *so* concerned." I leaned forward, which stretched the burn on my side and had me hissing a breath through my teeth as I swung my leg over to dismount.

She continued to mutter things under her breath as she did the same. She walked around the back of my horse, dragging the chain over it with her as she went. I had a dagger in my hand and at her throat before she could get any closer to me.

"What the fuck do you think you're doing?"

She was reaching toward my side. Her hands stopped the moment the flat of the blade touched her skin. Her eyes lifted to mine.

"Let me see your side." She demanded.

"And why in the world would I allow you to do that?"

"Because I may be useless when it comes to fighting anyone, but I know a little bit about treating burns. You didn't put anything on it before we started moving. It's going to scar

178

for sure, but more importantly it could get infected." She calmly lifted her hand and grabbed my wrist. "So lower the knife and let me see it."

I searched her face for any sign that she was trying to take advantage of my current state, but there was nothing but concern and a hint of frustration on her face. I let her push my arm away and I put the blade back in its sheath.

She leaned over and pulled at the tear in my leathers with her fingers. She muttered a curse and sighed. "I can't see it very well. You're going to have to take this off."

I chuckled. "You know, if I didn't know any better I'd say you were just doing this to get me to strip for you."

She straightened, leaned her face far too close to mine, and yanked my leathers and tunic up, aggravating the burn in the process. I let out another hiss in pain and grabbed her wrist.

"You can either remove this on your own, or I'll do it for you, but I promise if you make me do it, it's going to hurt." I must have been more delirious than I realized, because for some reason, that threat was far hotter than it should've been and I actually *wanted* her to pull it off for me.

She stepped back and crossed her arms. "Or, I can just leave it alone. It'll get infected, and you'll be fucked because there aren't any healers to help you."

It felt like a bucket of icy water had been dumped on my head. That snapped me back to reality pretty quickly. "And you call me an asshole." I grumbled.

"What was that?" She said innocently. "You want me to let it get infected?" She started to turn to walk away. "That's really not a problem. I–"

I caught her by the arm. "Fine. I'll take off my shirt and you can look at it."

She glanced over her shoulder back at me. "Apologize."

"For what?" I looked at her incredulously.

"For calling me an asshole."

"I didn't–"

"*Implying* that I was an asshole."

I scowled at her, and the hint of an amused smile rose to her lips. "I'm waiting."

"You're enjoying this."

She shrugged. "A little." She shook off my hold on her and turned back to face me. "I'm waiting. It's just two little words."

I sighed, unclasped my cloak, and let it fall to the ground behind me. She watched intently as I untucked the rest of my tunic. I pulled it and my leathers over my head.

"I'm sorry I *implied* that you were an asshole, little Firestorm. *Please* attend to my wounds."

She tried to bite back her amusement and turned her face away from me. I had to fight the urge to catch her chin and lift it so I could look at her. *What the fuck was wrong with me?*

She cleared her throat, looked me up and down for a breath, and then went back to examining my side. "I'll need to see if I can find some herbs." She glanced up at me. "Can you unhook the chain so I can look while you set up camp?"

"Can I trust you not to just run off?"

"I have nowhere to run to."

I unbuckled my belt, pulled the chain off, and handed the end of it to her. "If you're not back within five minutes I'll be coming for you."

"Yes, yes, I know."

She wandered off while I unpacked both of our cots. She returned surprisingly quickly with a handful of plants.

She set them down next to her cot, found two rocks, and got to work crushing them into a disgusting looking paste.

"Get over here and lay down." She didn't even look up at me when she made the demand. When I didn't move, she finally stopped messing with the paste and looked up at me. "Don't make me repeat myself."

I raised a brow, but walked over and did as she asked. I laid on my uninjured side and watched as she scooped up some of the paste with her fingers and hesitated over the burn.

"Sorry." She offered before she began to smear it on. I ground my teeth to prevent myself from grumbling a curse. She used every last bit of it before she sat back and surveyed her work. "Now don't touch it. I should probably refresh it tomorrow."

"You hated me. I could see it in your eyes. What changed?"

She locked eyes with me. "What makes you think anything has changed?"

"You don't help people you hate."

She sighed and handed me the end of the chain. "You were easier to hate before I knew you didn't have a choice but to kill Andras."

She started to push herself to her feet but I caught her arm before she could. "How did you learn how to treat burns?"

She offered me a sad smile. "When you've spent most of your life locked away in a palace, you have to find something to pass the time. I've learned pretty much everything you can think of *except* how to use my magic."

Chapter 26

Liza

We would reach the halfway point, according to Slade, when we found Aelearon Lake. I lost all sense of direction when he decided to stray from the main road and head straight for it. It was a precaution, I was sure, because of the ambush we found ourselves in two nights ago. I was having a hard time coming to terms with what I was feeling since then.

I wanted so desperately to hate him. I had at the beginning, but the more he revealed to me, and the more I figured out on my own, the less I could. He was as much a product of his environment as I was. He was trained in violence and I was trained in court. The only difference was that he was wildly successful at his craft, and I was a miserable failure at the one and only task I was ever given.

It was a welcome relief to see the lake through the trees ahead. It was enough to stop my spiraling self loathing. I had rarely gone more than a day without bathing while living in either palace, and life on the run was not what I was made for.

He halted his horse a few meters from the shoreline, dismounted, and promptly put on the hobbles he'd been using overnight. He walked over to do the same to my horse, who halted almost too close to his. I dismounted stiffly, and was surprised when he was there to assist me.

"I imagine you'll be just as relieved to bathe as me." He gestured toward the lake. "I'm going to allow you to do so *without* this," he gestured toward the cuff, "so you can heat the water if you'd like, but do understand that if you run, you won't get far. And if you try to burn me–"

I cut him off. "We've established at this point that I am not going to burn you." I held up my wrist and gestured toward it impatiently.

For once, he didn't hide his amusement. He pulled the keys out of his satchel and unlocked it. It clattered to the ground between us. The familiar wave of power returned to me and I'd never been more relieved.

He tucked the keys away and turned to walk toward the water himself. I watched as he stripped off his cloak, the leather he wore over his tunic, and then the dark tunic itself. There was not much light from the moon, being that we were nearing the new moon, but my eyes adjusted enough that I could make out some of the scars on his back.

The new burn on his side still looked red and tender, but did not appear nearly as bad as it had before I put the herbs on it. He was already an imposing figure in his armor, but without it I could see every single muscle. And by the gods, he was easily the most incredible man I think I'd ever laid eyes on.

I shook my head, trying desperately to pull my eyes away from him, but he continued to undress, until he was in absolutely nothing. He didn't look back, didn't pay any attention to me, but I could not avert my gaze until he was almost entirely submerged in the water.

The only change of clothes I had was a dress, which was not a good choice if I was riding a horse. I desperately needed to wash what I was wearing so I could wear it again tomorrow. I could sleep in the dress if I needed to.

I removed my cloak and hung it on a nearby branch. I lifted the tunic I wore over my head and removed my pants as well. When I turned to walk toward the water, clothing in hand, I caught Slade's gaze sliding up my body, only looking away when his eyes met mine.

I was sure I turned scarlet, but I wasn't sure why. Many men had seen me nude. I wasn't ashamed of my body, though I rarely witnessed someone so visibly appreciating it.

The water was absolutely frigid, which I guess was to be expected given the weather was turning colder by the day. I hadn't ever swam in a lake before, so I had nothing to compare it to. I used my magic to warm the water around me. That would've been a nice trick to have done when we all jumped in the river, if I had known it was possible and hadn't panicked.

I washed out my tunic and pants as best I could without any soap, then tossed them onto the shore. My bra and panties followed. I waded farther into the water, warming it as I did, until it was up to my shoulders. I wasn't sure how Slade wasn't absolutely freezing. He was further out in the water than I dared to venture. I would never go beyond where my feet could touch.

He walked my way and passed the soap I hadn't even realized he'd brought in with him. It smelled like cedar. He moved to continue to the shore, but I caught his wrist. I surprised myself with my brazenness. He stopped and turned to look back at me, the unasked question clear on his face.

"If you had been given the choice, would you still have taken the assignment to kill Andras?"

He was taken aback by the question. "Why is this something you're wondering about now?"

"Would you just answer the question?"

He studied me like it might unravel the puzzle in his mind for why I cared, or why I asked *now*. "No."

"Why?"

A muscle in his jaw feathered, while he deliberated whether or not to answer me. "The risk was too high. Regardless of the pay and precautions."

I frowned and let go of him.

"Were you hoping I had some kind of moral reason for it?"

I couldn't look at him. "You haven't given me any reason to think you have a moral code at all."

"I don't kill children. If I have to kill a woman, it's always quick and I make sure they don't see it coming. That'll have to be enough for you."

I heard him start walking away again. I turned to face him. "You said Captain Mercer gave you this assignment. Does that mean this wasn't something assigned to you by your guild?"

The water was at his waist. He stopped and looked over his shoulder at me. "Ask me what you're really wondering, Liza. Don't dance around it."

"If the guild didn't give you this assignment. What is the harm in not completing it?"

"If I don't turn you in, Edward will hire the guild to kill me."

That surprised me enough that I stared at him in disbelief for a few seconds before I could form my next thought. "Wouldn't they refuse such an ask?"

He laughed coldly. "Leodric never turns down money. He'd either come for me himself, or send several of the other members after me just to see who survives. We're required to swear our loyalty to the guild and to him, but that doesn't mean he won't turn on us if he's offered enough money."

Every single hope I had of talking him out of turning me in crumbled. I don't know when I even began to believe such a thing was possible, but if what he said was true it wouldn't matter what I could offer him. It was him or me, and I couldn't really blame him for choosing me.

*

We had been riding for most of the following day in silence. There was still not a road in sight, so I had no idea how he was figuring out which direction to go.

"Can I ask you a question?"

Slade sighed. "You just did."

"Asshole." I muttered under my breath.

"I heard that." There was a hint of amusement in his tone.

I kicked my horse to urge it to move faster until it was walking right next to his. He glanced my way, though I couldn't make out his face beneath the hood.

"Did you actually happen to stumble upon me while I was alone, or did you wait until I was alone?"

"Still trying to find a redeeming quality in me, I see."

"Just answer the question."

"I got lucky and you were alone."

Firestorm

"If I hadn't been alone, would you have waited until I was to take me in, or would you have just done as Jesse asked and killed all three of them?"

His head whipped my way, like I'd just well and truly shocked him. *"Jesse?"*

My face scrunched up in confusion as I studied him for a moment. Was that jealousy in his voice? No. That was ridiculous. I cleared my throat. "Uhm, I meant the captain."

"Right…" The way he said it only furthered my confusion. "That would entirely depend on how much time I had. His explicit instructions were to kill your companions if I found you with them, *but* seeing as I didn't want this assignment in the first place I would have at least observed for a while before I did anything."

"That didn't answer my question."

He sighed again. "It is far easier and cleaner to just take you. If I could have done so without having to fight and kill three people, then that would've been my preference."

"Fine." I rolled my eyes and looked forward.

"Go on then." He muttered.

"What?"

"There are more questions rattling around in that head of yours. I can see them written all over your face."

"How can you even *see* my face beneath that godsforsaken hood of yours?"

He reached up and removed it. The faintest smirk rose to his lips. "Happy now, Firestorm?"

"No."

He snickered. "What's the next question?"

He was actually enjoying this. I eyed him suspiciously for a few steps, before I gave in and asked my question. "If, hypothetically, you were one of my *companions* and I asked

187

you to help me free the mages that Edward was rounding up, would you kill every soldier you came across?"

He looked genuinely perplexed by the question. "I'm going to need a bit more context for this hypothetical question."

"You know that Edward is rounding up mages and anyone with magic right?"

He nodded.

"Do you know what he's *doing* with them?"

"No, but I get the feeling that you do."

"He's giving them the choice to work for him or die."

He arched a dark brow. "And the men you were with…" He trailed off while he put the pieces together.

"The men I was with refused to work for him."

He gave me a long look, like he was trying to figure out the answer to a question he didn't want to voice. "Alright, fine. You've intrigued me. I don't want to get called an asshole again, but I know you're not skilled enough to break out of a dungeon without magic, so how *did* you escape with them?"

I looked down at my horse's neck. I couldn't even be angry at his observation, because it was painfully true. "I agreed to work with him. It seemed like the only option I had."

"And then what?"

"My first *task* was to burn them. He had them tied to poles in front of the palace with kindling spread around them like some sick and twisted bonfire. I really don't know where the explosions came from, but it was enough of a distraction that I was able to burn off the rope that held them and get us to the sewers. We just stuck together after that."

When I looked over at him again he was staring straight ahead again.

"So you asked them to help you free the mages on the way to the palace so that they wouldn't have to face the same choice." He chewed on his lip while he mulled that over for a few moments.

"No. I wouldn't have killed the soldiers unless it was absolutely necessary. I would have knocked them out. They're following orders. Contrary to what you might think about me, I don't *enjoy* killing people. It's just a job."

"They killed them all."

"If they killed them all, then no one would have known it was you. So either they missed one, or one of the mages you freed was recaptured and tortured for information."

I cringed at the thought of the second option.

"What is Edward's master plan?"

"He wants to go back to the way things were in the dark ages. Before Nyvara became queen. I don't know much about that, but it sounded like humans ruled *everywhere* and mages were used for their benefit."

He frowned, but neither of us spoke again after that. For once, I was actually thankful for the silence. It gave me time to think. Time to process the fact that he wasn't just a killing machine like I thought. And that made it impossible to hate him. In fact, I was actually starting to *like* him. And that scared the fuck out of me.

Chapter 27

Slade

We were almost to Branwen. We returned to the road an hour ago. If my estimation of where we were was accurate, we could reach Branwen tonight, it would just be a much longer day than usual.

"Slade!" Liza shouted from behind me. I turned to glance her way at the same moment that I heard the snap of a bowstring. I barely had time to react to the arrow flying at me. I blocked my head with my arm, and even that almost wasn't enough to stop it.

I grumbled a curse. The arrow pierced my forearm, but didn't make it all the way through. I grabbed Liza's reins and urged both horses into a gallop. My arm throbbed around the arrow, but I didn't want to wait for our assailant to get the chance to draw another.

I didn't know how she saw it, but I owed her my life. Twice now, she'd saved me.

*

We reached Branwen not long after dark. By then I had gotten used to the ache of the arrow in my arm. I had yet to ask her how she saw it coming, or if she saw *who* had taken the shot. I slowed both horses to a trot and headed toward the south side of town.

I could've kept going straight through to Maeus, but I didn't trust showing up to the palace when I wasn't able to fight properly. Nor did I want to do so in the middle of the night.

I could feel her eyes on me. The chain nearly reached the ground where it hung between us. She gathered it up when we began to walk down a road in town. I halted our horses outside of Poppy's Tavern. I'd been there many times on my assignments. They always had a healer.

I dismounted as best I could without disturbing the arrow. The chain rattled as it stretched between us. She dismounted and came around to me.

"What can I–"

"Hood up. Don't speak. Follow me." I unhooked the chain from my belt and shoved it at her. "And hold onto this."

She took it, and did as I asked, but the worry was clear in her face. She could have just let them take the shot. Should have. I still couldn't figure out why she didn't.

I tied the horses at the hitching post, strapped my sword to my back, collected our bags, and walked toward the door. She followed less than a step behind me. When I walked into the bar, conversations stopped and heads turned. My cloak was tossed back over my shoulders, revealing all of my weapons.

The barkeep stopped pouring a drink and looked our way. I walked up to where she stood.

"I need a healer." I slammed a few coins down on the counter with my uninjured arm.

She looked me over appraisingly. "Perhaps you are unaware but they've all been conscripted to the crown. There are no healers here."

"A room then." I growled.

She glanced behind me, the slightest smirk rising to her lips before she looked at me once more. "I have one left." She swiped the coins off the counter. "This will cover the room and a meal. This way."

She pocketed the coins, ducked under the bar to retrieve a key, and headed toward the stairs. We followed her until she stopped at a room on the right.

"I'll bring your meals to you. There's a bathing room attached. Please try not to bleed on everything." She gave me a slightly disapproving glance and handed me the key.

"Our horses will also need to be tended to. I've tied them outside."

She nodded. "I'll see to it that they're stalled for the night. That'll be—"

I shoved more coins into her hand. "I know." I stepped to the side and gestured for her to move around me. I pushed open the door and Liza walked in first. I didn't look back to see if the barkeep left before I closed the door behind me and locked it.

I headed into the bathing room. I needed to get the damned arrow out, at the very least. I drew one of my daggers, sat on the edge of the tub and braced my injured arm against the sink basin so I could work on cutting through the shaft.

"What can I do to help?" I looked over to find Liza standing in the threshold, without her cloak, and the chain still coiled on her arm.

"Nothing." I turned my attention back to the task at hand, grumbling and cursing each time my sawing at the damned thing moved it in my arm. It was no easy task with one hand, let alone my non-dominant one.

She grabbed hold of the arrow as well as a knife from the strap across my chest. She held it to my throat. I froze and lifted my gaze up to meet hers.

"You will let me help you." She pressed the blade harder against my throat. "Or I'll give you another wound to tend to."

Something about that demand was far too hot and I found a smirk rising to my lips. "Alright, Firestorm. I'll hold the arrow while you cut it."

"Fine." She removed the knife from my throat and knelt down next to me.

I sat down the dagger I had and grabbed the half with the fletching. Between her hold and mine, the arrow hardly moved as she worked. When she'd finally gotten through it she sat the half she was holding down on the counter.

"Now what?"

I pulled the other half out of my arm with a hiss. "Now I can pull it out." I gave her a half hearted smile as blood dripped from the wound into the sink. "I need to clean it and wrap it."

I was about to roll up my sleeve when she reached over to unclasp my cloak. "What are you doing?" I raised a brow at her.

She met my gaze with a look of confusion. "You're filthy and you're just going to roll up your sleeve to clean it?" She shook her head. "Do you want it to get infected?"

I blinked in surprise. She shoved the cloak off of my shoulders "And what is your plan then, Firestorm, to undress me?"

As if she just realized what she was doing, her cheeks flushed red and she stepped back. "I– uh–" She cleared her throat. "The barkeep requested you didn't bleed all over everything. I was just–"

"Undressing me." I smirked. I unbuckled my bandolier with my other hand and let it fall to the ground. Then pulled my tunic up over my shoulders and tossed it to the side.

Her cheeks flushed an even deeper shade of crimson and she took a few steps back. "I can see that you're perfectly capable of handling that yourself without making a bloody mess. I'll leave you to it." She turned to leave, but I grabbed her arm and stopped her.

"Why did you yell?"

She looked back at me. "What do you mean?"

"You saw the attack coming. Why did you try to bring it to my attention?"

She turned fully back around now and gave me a confused look. "Why wouldn't I have pointed it out?"

"If I die, you'd be free to run again."

She considered that, looking away for a few breaths. "In case you haven't noticed, I'm not a fan of violence."

"Says the woman who just held a knife to my throat for refusing to allow her to help me."

Her eyes narrowed when she looked my way again. "That was because you were a stubborn prick. Yes, letting him kill you would've let me go free, but you saved me from the gods only know what if those other men took me. Consider it my way of thanking you for that."

"I might very well be delivering you to your death. And, need I remind you, I killed seven men."

"You've killed two hundred and five, actually." The hint of a smirk appeared on her features. "But that doesn't mean I want to watch you die. I can promise you that you won't be the last to come for me. Letting you die just so I could gain a little more time is not something I want on my conscience."

There was a light knock at the door.

"I have food and bandages." The barkeep called through the door.

Liza raised a brow at me and I nodded. She walked toward the door, unlocked it, and directed the woman to place the tray on the dresser just inside the door. She locked the door again when the barkeep left. When she returned to me she presented me with the gauze and fabric to wrap my arm with.

"There's a little bit of whiskey left in my bag."

She moved immediately, running out to where I'd dropped the bags as we walked in and returning with the flask. She'd also retrieved the bar of soap.

Without being asked, she turned on the faucet in the sink basin and began to clean the wound. When she unscrewed the top of the flask and poured the whiskey over it, I hissed, despite my attempt to hide the reaction.

"Sorry," she muttered under her breath, then quickly began to dress and wrap it. "I'll leave you to bathe then." She scurried out of the bathing room and pulled the door almost shut behind her.

The strangest urge to stop her hit me before she disappeared into the room. I didn't know where it came from, but I'd never had a woman *threaten* me before, aside from the other members of the guild. From them it was expected. From her it was... intriguing. I shook my head and went about bathing. It was not worth spending much time thinking over.

When I finally returned to the bedroom she was picking at her food. Her gaze lifted just long enough to note my return, for her face to flush bright red when she took in me in a towel, and then she looked back down at her food.

"You act as though you weren't watching me at the lake." I commented, walking over to the bags I'd dropped when we walked in and rummaging to grab a pair of loose pants and a shirt.

She nearly choked. "Says the one who couldn't seem to stop watching *me*."

"It was my responsibility to make sure you didn't run off."

She hummed, collected the chain, and rose from the bed. "If you'll excuse me, I'd like to get cleaned up as well." She hurried into the bathing room after collecting something from her bag.

I rummaged through my bags to find something clean and more comfortable to sleep in. By the time she came back out I had finished my food and was lounging on the bed tossing a dagger into the air above me. She wore a loose cotton dress that had seen better days. The very same one she wore the night we spent at the lake.

She let out an amused snort. "You know, if you drop that you're going to stab yourself and I'm going to laugh."

"I won't." I didn't even need to look at it to catch it.

She shook her head and then glanced around the room. "Wait." Her face tightened in what I could only describe as horror or dread. "There's only one bed."

"Really?" I caught the dagger again and gestured around with it. "I had no idea."

"You are *not* making me sleep on the floor." She cocked her hip out and crossed her arms over her chest. The chain rattled with the movement.

"*I'm* not sleeping on the floor, if that's what you're getting at." I had already spent far too many nights sleeping on the ground. She'd been a thorn in my side for at least half of those days. Sure, the gentlemanly thing to do would be to let her have the bed, but that was never a term I would use to describe myself *and* she was my prisoner.

"Well *I* am not sleeping in a bed with *you*."

I sat up, letting one leg hang off the edge of the bed while bending the other up to rest my elbow on my knee. "Most women would fight for a place in my bed." I was walking a dangerous line, but I was finding irritating her to be quite amusing.

She turned her nose up, but I saw the fire in her eyes. "Well, they'd have to be fools to fight over such a thing. No man is worth that."

"Then why did the mention of other women fighting for a place in *my* bed make you so angry?"

"I wasn't– Ugh, gods you are such a self centered prick." She mumbled.

I chuckled and shrugged. "Sleep on the floor or sleep on the bed. I don't particularly care." I blew out the candles on the bedside table and only the light of the moon filtering in through the window lit the space. I got up, took the end of the chain from her, and attached it to my belt. Just in case she decided she could run now that she knew where we were.

"But please, if you do choose the bed, do us both a favor and keep your hands to yourself."

Chapter 28

Liza

I woke curled into a warm body and it took me far too long to remember where I was and *who* I was curled up into. His arm rested around me, but he most definitely was not consciously aware of that. I was sure that I couldn't untangle myself without waking him.

I started to try to move slowly, lifting my arm off of his stomach and retreating. As expected, it didn't work.

He woke with a start, and he was on top of me on the bed, pinning me down with a dagger to my throat before I could even register what was happening. His amber eyes were wild, and took a moment for him to realize it was *me* he had pinned. He glared down at me.

"What the *fuck* were you doing?" He pressed the flat side of the knife harder against my neck. "I *warned* you to keep your hands to yourself."

I should've been scared, horrified even, but my body had a far different reaction to this than my head. His knees bracketed my hips and he held my arm up over my head. I frantically searched his face for a few breaths while I tried to remember how to form words.

"Answer me." He seethed.

Did he really not realize how tangled up we were upon waking? I couldn't figure out how we ended up like that without him reacting this way in the first place if he was always such a light sleeper.

"N– Nothing." I stammered. "I must've rolled into you in my sleep but I just woke up."

He surveyed me for a few seconds, as if trying to find a lie. He finally relaxed, rolled back to his side of the bed, and laid back down. I stayed where I was, frozen and staring at the ceiling. The sense seemed to return to my body while my mind caught up.

He sat up and rose from the bed. "Get yourself ready. I'll get breakfast and then we're heading for the palace." He didn't bother to grab his weapons, leaving the dagger he held to my throat on the bedside table, and headed out the door. He did, however, take the keys and lock the door behind him.

I had to assume that was for my safety rather than to keep me in, because I could unlock the door myself and leave if I wanted to. He would find me though. Of that much I was certain. If his magic was anything like Ezra and Azazel, finding me wouldn't take much effort at all.

I got up from the bed and wandered into the bathing room. I pulled on my still damp clothes. I don't know why I had bothered to wash them. Surely I would either meet the gods today or be thrown in a cell and cleanliness would be the least of my concerns.

By the time I emerged from the bathing room Slade had returned and a tray of food sat on the bed. He brushed by me to go in and freshen up himself.

The keys to my cuff were in his pile of things. I could unlock it myself and run. If he caught up to me, I would at least have my magic to fight him off. I couldn't ever see myself using my magic on him though. The idea of it just felt wrong, impossible even. If I had access to it when we were ambushed in the woods, I may have used it on the men who found us. But not on him. Never on him.

I picked at the food he brought, and ate a few grapes. My appetite was almost nonexistent. After he had his fill of our shared breakfast he directed me to put on my cloak as he strapped his weapons on. A moment later he ushered me out the door.

He held the chain now, guiding me through the streets of Branwen until we reached the bridge that connected it to Maeus. The walk went by surprisingly quickly.

The guards stopped us before we could step onto the bridge.

"State your business." The man on the right demanded.

"I'm here to deliver this mage to the king." Slade replied, but did not lower the hood of his cloak.

"Name?" The guard stepped closer and demanded.

"Sàmhach Marbhadh." The name rolled off his tongue like he'd used it for years, but I didn't miss the way his shoulders twitched in irritation at having to say it. *Silent Killer* - it was fitting, I suppose, for the name of an assassin.

The guard's expression turned from irritation to a hint of fear. "Of course, sir. We've been expecting you. We'll provide an escort."

"I can assure you that won't be necessary." He tried to grumble and walk past them.

"We've been directed to give you an escort upon arrival. I will not disobey a direct order." The man stood up a bit straighter. The guards seemed to come to an understanding silently, because the one who spoke to us and one of the others turned and led the way across the bridge.

By the time we began walking the streets of Maeus we had a six person escort. People watched from their porches and windows. I felt like I was being paraded for all to see, but thank the gods, my hood was up.

When we reached the palace gates, it felt like my heart dropped to the ground. It took an immense amount of effort to walk through them, and the stairs at the entrance felt like a mountain to climb. I looked up to find Jesse standing at the top of them with a grim look on his face.

Of course he would be here waiting. I wasn't sure why I didn't expect to see him. I was only slightly relieved that I didn't see any visible injuries on him from the chaos that happened when I escaped. They probably would've healed by now though.

"I was starting to wonder if you'd failed to find her." He grumbled at Slade.

"You know my reputation, *Captain*." The title was said with a sneer. "Surely you knew better than to assume I would do anything but deliver her as you asked."

Jesse stepped forward and reached for me, but Slade stepped in his way. He turned and pulled my hood down, revealing my face. A hint of surprise ghosted Jesse's face as he took me in, coupled with a look of relief.

"As I'm sure you can imagine, it was harder than expected to track her down with her change in appearance."

Jesse jolted as though he'd forgotten we were not alone. He cleared his throat and muttered, "Of course. This way." Then turned on his heel and led us, along with our six guard escort, to the throne room.

When the heavy wooden doors opened and we walked in it felt like my world was imploding on itself. Edward sat upon the throne at the far end with a pleased smile on his lips. Slade stopped two steps before the steps that led up to the dais and dropped into a bow but did not wait to be told to rise before righting himself.

Edward didn't seem to notice. His eyes were locked on me. The captain walked up to him, muttered something in his ear and then turned to face us.

I glared at him. I didn't plan to give him the pleasure of watching me curtsey or bow to him. If I was going to die today, I was going to die with my dignity, at least.

"You should bow before your king." A male voice behind me growled.

"He is not my king." I grumbled defiantly, earning a glance from Slade, though I could not make out his features beneath his hood.

My knees were suddenly knocked out and I landed on them, hard, but the assault stopped there when I heard the distinct sound of a sword leaving its sheath. I looked up to find Slade holding the blade to the guard's throat.

"She is my prisoner until I hand her over to you. Lay a single hand on her, until she is no longer *mine* and your head will hit the floor before you have the chance to notice I've moved." I stared up at him in shock. He was playing a dangerous game.

"That's quite enough." The king snapped. "Your task is complete." He handed a sealed piece of parchment to Jesse, who started to descend the steps. "The Captain will see you out and ensure you've received your payment. Hand the chain over to the guard at the end of your sword and be on your way."

From this angle, I could see Slade's face. He gave me an apologetic look before lowering his weapon and doing as he was told.

Jesse handed him the parchment. "Your pardon," he whispered, only loud enough for Slade and myself to hear. He motioned for him to turn and follow him out. I watched helplessly as he walked away and left me to my fate.

"We have much to talk about." Edward mused, and my attention flew back to him. "I believe I've tracked down the rebels responsible for the little show that aided in your escape. I realize now that asking such a monumental task for your first act as one of my servants was too much for you. I do hope that you'll come to find working for me will help you far more than you think."

"I doubt that." The words were muttered under my breath, but the guard behind me clearly heard them, because he landed a kick to my ribs.

"That's enough, Simmons." I looked up to see Edward glare at the guard. "I'm trying to have a polite conversation with our prisoner." His gaze returned to me. "We're not all that different, you and I."

"You're a monster."

This seemed to amuse him. "Moira is a monster. Tell me, love, which monster would you rather serve? A mage who wiped out all of your kin, or a man who recognizes your power and can give you purpose?"

I narrowed my eyes at him. "I would choose neither."

He shrugged. "A few days in a cell might change your mind." His gaze shifted up, to the guards behind me. "Toss her in a cell. No water or food for three days. If she's still alive when you go to retrieve her, we'll have another chat."

My eyes went wide and the grin on his face only widened. Hands closed around both of my elbows and yanked me from the floor with little effort. I fought against them, snarling, kicking, and screaming. It was no use. Their grip was iron tight and they lifted me to the point my feet didn't have any hope of touching the ground.

I had been so, so wrong. I thought he'd kill me or just toss me in a cell. I had never imagined that he would starve me to try and convince me to work with him *again*.

Chapter 29

Slade

I followed the captain down the same pathway we had walked to enter the throne room.

"What will they do with her?" I asked, unable to hold the question in for any longer. I needed to know that she wasn't going to just be killed. My plan would be useless otherwise.

"Why would that matter to you?" The hint of jealousy in his voice didn't go unnoticed.

"If I've collected her for him to kill, I will be quite upset that you wasted my time and efforts bringing her all the way here." I did my best to sound as cold and irritated as I always did when talking with Leodric.

The captain chuckled. "Of course, why would we waste such an esteemed assassin's valuable time." He mocked. "She will not be killed. Not right away anyway. Though I am not at liberty to discuss the king's plans for her."

"So I brought her back here for him to... What? Throw her in a cell until he decides to toss her on the chopping block?"

"Something like that." There was a dangerous edge to his voice that told me he knew exactly what his plan was and a part of him didn't agree with it.

We were met by another set of guards at the front steps. They shoved a heavy sack of coins at me. I accepted it, nodded, and descended the steps. No one followed. In fact, they seemed to clear extra space for me as I passed through the front gates and headed out into the city.

I took the same path they brought us in on, keeping the pouch of gold tucked beneath my cloak. I knew the moment I crossed into Branwen her cohorts would catch up with me. I noticed the three of them trailing us until we reached the bridge, but they had no way to get into the city.

They were wanted men. They were lucky to have made it this far without being caught. I crossed over the same bridge and turned down a side street where the guards wouldn't be able to track my movements. I could sense them in the shadows.

I didn't even flinch when one of them appeared in front of me with a sword pointed at my throat. The other two lurked a few paces behind me.

"Give me one good reason I shouldn't remove your head." The man growled. I could see him even beneath his cloak. He was older, clearly the leader. Ian, I believe the details for this assignment had said.

"You must be Ian." I didn't move. "Which means that it's Laslow and Damien behind me, if I'm not mistaken." This seemed to waver his conviction just a bit. "You can certainly remove my head if that's what would make you happy, but do that and you'll never see Liza again."

I saw the thought cross his mind. It was visible in his expression. The sword pressed the slightest bit closer to me, actually putting pressure on the cloak where it clasped together on my chest.

"You've already made sure of that."

"Have I?" I asked. "All I've done is take her into Maeus."

"Liar. You were escorted by guards. You took her straight to the king." One of the men behind me snarled.

"I would advise you to keep your voices down. I don't believe any guards are trailing me, but you're certainly not doing yourselves any favors by ambushing me in this alley. Perhaps we could find somewhere a bit more *private* to discuss this."

"So you can kill us there?" Another male voice behind me asked.

"I have completed my assignment. I have no reason to kill you now."

"You left seven bodies in your wake in the woods." Ian spoke again.

"They threatened my mark." I shrugged. "And me. I don't take kindly to that sort of thing. If you don't want the same thing to happen to you, I would advise lowering your sword and following me. Or, you can *try* to kill me. It's your choice."

Ian glanced between the men behind me.

"This is your last chance."

The sword was removed from my chest and sheathed. "Fine."

"Excellent." I smiled even though he couldn't see my face. "This way." I stepped around Ian and continued down the alley. I knew the back entrance to Poppy's Tavern, as well as a back way to get there, which meant none of them would be seen with me and I wouldn't have to worry about the gold I was carrying under my cloak.

I ushered them in the back door. "Go ahead and get yourself some drinks. I'll be back down in a moment."

"We don't have the money for that." One of the younger ones snapped.

"I'll pay." It wasn't like I needed all this goddess damned gold anyway. They muttered something but headed in the direction of the bar while I made my way up the stairs to deposit the bag in the room. Wisely, none of them took off their hoods.

When I returned and walked to the bar myself the barkeep handed me a letter. "Messenger hawk delivered this for you this morning. Seems important. It's got a fancy seal on it."

I took it and ordered myself a glass of whiskey. She retrieved it quickly, I paid the tab, and joined the men at the table in the darkest corner of the room.

I popped the wax seal and skimmed the letter. It was a stroke of luck that Murdock was in port with his ship. If he hadn't been, I'd be stuck trying to figure out how to shadow them all out and into Emberwyn without any of them knowing that it was *me* that did it.

Liza knew of course, but for some stupid reason I trusted her to keep that secret.

"Good news, gentlemen. I have a one way ticket for the four of you to get to Emberwyn."

"The four of us?" Laslow questioned.

"Yes, the four of you."

"For all we know Liza is already dead." Damien growled.

"She's not. I can't speak to what shape she is in currently, but I at least know that she's alive."

"And why should we trust you? You're the one who delivered her there in the first place." Ian eyed me cautiously. I still had yet to lower my hood.

"I'm not sure you have much choice, but if you don't believe me, perhaps this will ease your mind." I tossed the letter their way. "He owes me a favor. A favor, mind you, that I'm feeling generous enough to call in for Liza. The three of you I could care less about."

They leaned over one another to read the letter at the same time. When they finished, they looked up at me.

"Why?" Ian asked.

I took a sip of my whiskey before I answered. "Perhaps because I don't agree with anyone being forced into choosing between working for someone or dying." I shrugged. "But you've met her."

Damien chuckled. "Oh good, she's charmed you too."

"I'm not so easily swayed. But despite my line of work, I do have morals."

Laslow scoffed. "Right, of course. A bounty hunter with morals."

"An assassin." I snapped.

"What would an assassin be doing collecting someone for the king?" Ian looked more skeptical now, and I couldn't say I blamed him.

"Blackmail. And that's all I'm willing to share."

I saw the realization light up Damien's gaze. "It was you."

"I'm not sure to what you're referring." I deflected. "You either accept this, make your way to the docks along the river here in Branwen and board the vessel listed on that letter, or you don't. That's up to you. Regardless, *she* will be delivered there tonight."

"And how exactly will you get her out of the palace dungeons?" Damien crooned.

"That's none of your business." I took another long sip of my whiskey. "Now, are you going to be on that ship, or can I let Murdock know that he'll only have one stowaway?"

"We'll board it." Ian answered for everyone.

"Great. She'll be delivered to the ship by a shadow mage. She'll be unconscious, so she doesn't fight me or him when he delivers her to you. If I find out any of you harmed her while she is indisposed, I will find you and I *will* kill you, even if there's no bounty on your head. Do you understand?"

I didn't miss the smirk on Damien's lips, but they nodded all the same. I rose from the table and headed toward the stairs. I would need to change and prepare before I shadow walked into the dungeons. As much as I hated to admit it, I'd grown to enjoy her company, and I felt a little hollow without her. The room felt frustratingly empty when I returned to it as well.

*

I shadow walked to the darkest part of the dungeons, where I knew I wouldn't need my magic to hide me. Finding her would be the first problem, and shadowing her away the second, if she was chained to the floor or walls.

It was late, but I wanted to be sure I didn't come at a shift change. There would be too many people wandering around for that. I walked silently through the corridors, clinging to the shadows and shadow walking where necessary.

This was probably the most I had relied on my magic in years. When I finally saw a familiar head of hair laying on the floor of a cell I shadow walked into the space behind her. She was sleeping and not chained beyond the set of shackles on her wrists. An upgrade from what I left her in.

I pulled the cloth from my pocket, silently poured the herbal mixture I prepared to knock her out long enough for them to leave port onto it, and gave the corridor one last look before I placed it over her mouth and nose.

She jolted awake and tried to fight me off. I muffled the noise she made as best I could. She only struggled for a few breaths before she fell limp in my arms. I shadowed us away before anyone could round the corner to see me.

I arrived in the cargo hold of the ship. It was almost too dark to see were it not for the single candle the men had burning where they laid out their cots. I placed her on the wood floor before me. A part of me wanted to take her back to Edgewood with me, but I was *not* what she wanted, nor what she deserved. I may have grown to appreciate her company, but I was certain I hadn't earned any favor by turning her in.

I slammed my fist into the side of a wooden crate in a practiced pattern, hard enough to signal to the men a few paces away that she was there, but also to signal to Murdock to set sail. I shadow walked back to my room in the tavern.

Chapter 30

Liza

I woke up laying on something much softer than the dungeon floor. It felt like the world was swaying beneath me and I thought I might be sick. I hadn't felt like that since I traveled to Mytharae.

I cracked my eyes open enough to try to see what was around me without alerting anyone that I was awake. It took me a moment to realize I had no shackles on my wrists, and Damian sat on a crate across from where I was laying.

I shot upright. "Damian?" I breathed. "Where? What the fuck?" I looked around then and spotted Laslow and Ian sitting on cots laid out not far from mine.

Damian chuckled. "Seems you managed to charm the assassin and he arranged for someone to break you out of the dungeons. Arranged us this ride too." He gestured around us with a smirk. "That pirate is an interesting character, but I'm not one to look a gift horse in the mouth."

Pirate? Slade *arranged* for someone to break me out? That was a lie. A cover, I was sure. He had boasted enough about his skills, and he had the knowledge of the layout of the palace to be able to pull a stunt like that. I hadn't expected him to care at all, let alone care enough to get me *out*.

It was the perfect move though. He completed his task. What he did after that was not defined. But, wait–I charmed him?

"What in the world do you mean *charmed* the assassin?"

A playful grin spread across his lips. "Well, he was *very* clear that if anything happened to you while you were… 'indisposed' because of whatever they used to drug you to get you to be cooperative, he said he'd track each of us down and kill us." He shrugged. "That's not a threat someone makes for another person if they don't have some kind of feeling about them, if you catch my drift."

I scoffed. "He most certainly didn't give a rat's ass what happened to me."

"You sure about that?" Ian asked.

I looked his way. "I mean, he didn't care beyond keeping me alive to complete his mission."

"And yet here you are." Damian mused. "Alive, well, and headed back home."

"And how in the gods' names did you all end up here?"

"Damian thought it would be a good idea to threaten and kill your captor." Laslow grumbled. "I advised against it, seeing as my arrow didn't even seem to bother him, but Ian agreed."

"He knew we were following him, somehow." Ian added. "He wasn't even remotely surprised when we jumped him."

That might've meant he knew they were in the woods. It felt like the world fell away beneath me. If he knew they were there, was he going to *let* him take the shot?

"I think she's just realized something and she looks like she's going to faint." Laslow mumbled.

I shook my head. "I can't go back to Emberwyn."

"Well you certainly couldn't stay in Mytharae." Damian pointed out.

I couldn't tell him the truth, even now. If she hadn't sent anyone to kill me yet, telling them who I was *would* land me on the chopping block with Moira I was sure.

"I can't just let them round up mages and kill them."

"Many of them agreed to work for him. They're not *all* being burned." I looked over at where Ian sat watching me thoughtfully. "And you're certainly not going to be able to free them on your own."

"He's going to try to go to war with Emberwyn. You heard him. This is just the beginning." I insisted. It was something I was worried about too, so it wasn't entirely a lie that it would motivate me to return to Mytharae.

"I hate to be captain *obvious*," Damian started, "but you're not going to be able to do anything to stop that so you might as well go back to your cushy place in the palace with the Queen and just tell her about it."

I got up like I might run above deck and demand the ship be turned around. The rocking of it told me we were already out at sea. Damian caught my arm.

"I don't know what you're thinking, but Captain Questionable up there is on the same strict orders we're on. You are to get to Emberwyn alive and unharmed, and there is no way that he's going to take you back to Mytharae with him. Not without payment."

"We'll see about that!" I yanked my arm out of his grip and headed toward the stairs that led to the higher decks. I heard footsteps following behind me. I guess they didn't expect me to know how to find the captains quarters. If this was anything like the ship I rode to Mytharae, I was sure I would figure it out.

I pushed up the hatch and climbed out. The space was wide open, with hammocks hanging on either side of it. I could hear one man snoring while he swayed with the movement of the ship. Ian climbed out of the hatch behind me. He motioned toward the stairs that led to the next deck.

We walked in silence until we traversed those stairs and found ourselves on the weapons deck. Four cannons lined either side of the ship, anchored in place by heavy ropes.

"By the gods, we really are on a pirate ship." I breathed. The cargo ship I traveled on didn't have any weapons that I could see.

"Did you think Damian was lying?" Ian asked while he guided me to the final set of stairs that I hoped would bring us to the main deck.

"I… well, I guess a pirate *does* make sense given that Sl– uh, the assassin is who procured it."

Ian glanced back at me with an arched brow. "You got pretty close with him if you learned his name."

"The alternative to getting him to give me his name was to call him '*asshole*' the entire time." I shot back.

Ian chuckled and pushed open the door that led to the main deck. "Either way, he gave you a name. They aren't usually so casual with people. I doubt that Captain Murdock even knows his name."

I looked out over the edges of the deck railing. I could see the cliffs of Mytharae in the distance. We were *definitely* out of the port. The seas were calm, thank the gods, and a steady wind filled the massive black sails. I couldn't picture a ship like this sitting in the port. Surely pirates weren't welcome there.

"What is your plan?" Ian queried. "Are you going to beat down his door and demand he turn around?"

I gave him a calculating once over. "I'm figuring it out as I go. Maybe if I could charm an assassin, I can do the same to a pirate."

His lips pulled into a tight smile. "Charm away." He gestured his arm toward the wooden door beneath the deck that held the steering wheel.

I took a deep breath and headed that way. I only had to knock twice before the door swung open. The man that greeted me was younger than I expected. He had dark brown hair that fell beyond his shoulders and a well groomed beard. His eyes were the color of the sea. His black waistcoat was well kept and the gray shirt he wore beneath it was open at the collar, leaving half of his chest visible.

He had a belt that rested on his hips laden with pouches, a set of keys, and a single cutlass. His black pants were clean and tucked into mostly unscuffed boots. His hat, adorned with feathers that reminded me of a raven, sat slightly crooked. It was the only thing disheveled about his overall appearance.

"Well," he proclaimed with a whistle. "I can see why he went to all the trouble." He contemplatively looked me over. "Although, I don't understand why he didn't just take you for himself."

I blinked furiously, while my face flushed. "Uh, I beg your pardon?"

He gave me a suggestive grin. "Did he owe you a life debt, or were you just an exceptional lay? He didn't give me any specifics."

My jaw dropped and I stared at him like he'd grown an extra head.

He huffed a laugh and put his head in his hand as he leaned against the door. "Gods forgive me." He breathed, then looked up at me again. "I've forgotten my manners. Captain Ravik Murdock. It's a pleasure to have you aboard the Black Dagger. What can I do for you Miss Winters?"

I stood a little taller. "I'd like a word."

He arched his brow.

"*Alone.*"

He smiled in a way that sent a shiver down my spine. "Of course, come on in." He waved his arm back into his quarters.

I slipped past him into the surprisingly well lit room. A large window spanned the back wall and gave me a stunning view out the back of the ship. Beneath it sat a large and luxurious looking bed that was an absolute mess, like he hadn't bothered to make it this morning. Directly in front of me, sat a large mahogany desk with a high backed chair behind it. Maps and papers were strewn about haphazardly. The only thing the captain seemed to care about was his appearance. This room was a disaster.

"The lady said she wanted to talk *alone.*" Murdock reminded Ian. I turned around to see he had drawn his cutlass and blocked the doorway with it. "I'll make sure she finds her way back to the cargo hold when we're finished."

Ian looked like he was about to protest, but the door was slammed in his face and promptly locked. He slipped the blade back into the scabbard on his belt and walked around me to take a seat at his desk.

"You've got me alone. Although I am sure your companions were given the same threat as me, so please get to the point quickly. I don't need him coming after me for *anything*."

"What exactly did he ask you to do?"

"I owed him a favor. He cashed in on that favor to grant you safe passage back to Emberwyn. He didn't specify *where* in Emberwyn, so we'll be dropping you off at the point where the northern most branch of the Tlaloc River meets the sea. I'm not welcome in Emberwyn's ports, or their waters for that matter." He reached into his desk and pulled out a massive canvas bag that jingled like it was filled with coins. "He also brought me this and said to give it to you to split among your companions as you saw fit."

I stared at the bag like it might kill me. "Is that…?"

"His entire reward for capturing you? Yes. So tell me what, other than a life debt, would have him call in his favor with *me*?"

I looked down at my hands while I desperately tried to think through every single interaction we had. Aside from him blatantly staring at me when I was basically nude, he seemed like he couldn't have cared less about me. His frustratingly limited morals didn't give me any clues either.

"I don't know." I looked up at him again. "But what I can tell you is that I am not welcome in Emberwyn either. I came in here to ask you to take me back to Mytharae."

He barked out a laugh. "Ah, wanted in Emberwyn too. Gods, he picked a winner. Sorry, lass, the best I can offer you is to take you with me to Runelheim. I won't be going back to Mytharae until the spring. Surely you're not wanted there too?"

"You misunderstand me. I *have* to go back to Mytharae." I insisted. "I'll pay you whatever you want, but I need to find a way to stop Edward–"

"Let me stop you right there." His face shifted from amusement to something stone cold and serious so quickly that it was a little unnerving. "No single person can stop the war that's brewing between these two countries. It's been building up for a long time on both sides. If you think you'll be able to do anything, you're nothing but a fool. My orders were to drop you in Emberwyn and continue on my way. If you choose to leave once we've dumped you on their shores that's your business, but I swore a blood oath to him and I have no intention of finding out what happens to me if I don't follow through with getting you somewhere safe."

"And Runelheim would be safe?" I nearly shouted.

"By the time we dock in Runelheim, I'm sure that Slade will have arrived there himself. He spends his winters down there somewhere. I'm sure you could find him."

"If the vampires don't kill me first." I mumbled, mostly to myself while I stared at the intricate carvings of sea creatures that went down the front of his desk. Surely I could find a way back to Mytharae if the most he would do was drop me on the shore.

"There are strict laws in Runelheim that prevent vampires from feeding from any being without consent. If they're found to have fed without it, they get thrown in the palace dungeons for a hundred years. If they *kill* a human, they're executed. I can assure you, it won't be the vampires you'd need to worry about."

That caught my attention, and I surveyed him a little closer.

"So what'll it be, lass? Am I dumping you on the shores of Emberwyn like he requested, or are you continuing

219

on with me to Runelheim?" He was leaning back in his chair now, surveying me just as closely as I was doing to him.

"Leave me on the shore with the rest of them. I'll find my own way."

His jaw tensed, but he nodded. I stood up and walked toward the door.

"Don't forget your gold." He called after me.

"Give it to me when we're headed for the shore."

*

Less than two days later we boarded a dingy and got dropped off on the shoreline. Murdock gave me the sack of gold and plenty of supplies to get us to the nearest village. It was almost dusk, so we made our way away from the water to set up camp.

"Well this is just shit." Damian commented, examining what they had and what we were given. "I don't even have a gods damned map of Emberwyn."

"There are little villages and farms all over the place. I'm sure that we can find somewhere to stop and get more food if we need it."

"I thought you'd never been outside of the palace?" Damian unrolled his cot.

"I've traveled *between* Riodian and Maeus before. I've seen the villages along the river. They're small, but we've got plenty of money. They won't turn us away."

"Yeah, how did you get all that gold anyway? Surely that assassin isn't just that kind." Laslow glanced my way while he set out his cot as well.

"I don't know. Murdock didn't say why he left it for us, and I couldn't tell you what I would've done to earn his kindness. All I did was annoy him."

"That's no surprise." Damian quipped.

"Oh would you just fuck off." I snapped, and he stared at me blankly. "I've had enough of your shit already."

"Easy firefly." He cooed.

Before I was consciously aware of what I'd done, I threw a massive fireball at him. Hot steam exploded over him when he blocked it with water. "Fuck, I'm sorry. Alright?" He raised his hands in surrender. "I'll stop. I was just trying to get you to laugh."

"No." I growled. "You were just about to remind me how useless and annoying I am. You didn't have to come back for me. You could've carried on your merry way to Elkridge and left me with *him*, but you didn't. You *chose* to come back for me and now you're here, with a pile of gold that *I,* the annoying and useless one, somehow managed to secure for us all. I'm not fucking useless, and I'm sure as shit not annoying unless I'm actually choosing to be."

He blinked at me. "Listen, Liza I–"

"Just shut *the fuck* up, Damian."

He listened, thank the gods, and laid down on his cot. Laslow looked at me like I might turn on him, but wisely laid down on his as well. It was only Ian who looked at me with the tiniest flicker of pride.

I sat down the sack of gold next to where I placed my cot. I didn't trust letting any of them have it until I got what I needed, and I'd make sure of that when they were all sleeping.

The moon was high in the sky by the time I finally prepared to make my escape. I rolled up my cot silently, tied it up, and slung it over my back. I packed myself a single bag of cheese, bread, and cured meats. Pulling out the gold and putting it in a separate bag was the most tedious part. I couldn't make a sound. Satisfied with my work, I stood and turned to head off toward the mountains.

"Where do you think you're going?" Ian whispered.

I jumped. I hadn't realized he was awake. He was only two steps behind me. "I– uh–"

"You're going to need this, princess." He handed me a large rolled up piece of parchment.

I searched his face for some kind of clue as to what it was he was giving me, or why he suddenly decided to nickname me *princess.* He didn't offer me an explanation, so I unrolled it to discover it was a full world map. It marked the larger villages, towns, and cities, as well as the rivers and bodies of water. It wasn't the best, but it was something.

"They gave us a map. Why didn't you say anything?"

"I stole it, actually, but I had a feeling. I knew you wouldn't want anyone to come with you, so I thought if you at least had a map that *maybe* you'd make it through the mountains and actually make a difference."

I rolled the map back up and tucked it into the bag with the rest of my supplies. "Captain Murdock seemed to think that one person can't stop the war that's coming."

"You might surprise yourself." He offered me a small smile. "You're stronger than you think. I don't know what changed while you were with that assassin, but whatever it is, I'm glad for it."

I shook my head. "You've known me for maybe three weeks in total. You can't believe in me that much, if at all."

"That's where you're wrong, princess. I've known you for far longer than that. You wouldn't recognize me, because you paid the guards no mind, but I served your family long before Moira wiped out the fire mages. You were a refreshing beacon of light and hope before she destroyed you."

My world tilted on its edge. He'd recognized me and known this *whole time.*

"I might've been sworn to secrecy about you where anyone else is concerned, but by the gods I hope you give her what she deserves one day. She left us defenseless. She sent no aid. Many good men died the day that the DuMont's and their resistance took Maeus. I've never forgiven her. I can promise you the rest of her guard haven't forgotten that either."

I swallowed thickly. "Have you ever crossed the mountains? Since the dragons arrived, I mean?"

"There were always dragons in the mountains, Liza. That's how they got their name, but they multiplied nearly twenty times overnight. We don't know where they came from, but I can tell you to avoid the valleys as much as you can. They nest there, and it's the females that'll kill you." He smiled. "You've got the fire power though so I'm sure you'll make it through."

I laughed nervously. "I'll keep that in mind."

Chapter 31

Slade

I packed up my things as soon as I returned to the tavern. There was no way I was sleeping, so I laid on the bed staring at the ceiling in the hours before dawn. Murdock had been right about one thing. I was a gods damned fool. Breaking her out was probably the stupidest thing I could have done. Worse than that though, was that I sent her off with those three idiots.

She had a home to return to though. A nice one. In a palace where she'd never have to worry about a thing. The way she watched me leave I knew she would have killed me if I broke her out and then took her home with me. This was all a goddess damned trick. A charm she placed on me like everyone else she was around. It *had* to wear off eventually.

That was what I told myself repeatedly as I rode away. I thought it had worn off before until I was near her again. My only saving grace was that this time I would *never* see her again. It was that reassurance that kept me from turning around and trying to catch up with the damned ship.

It was almost noon when the thunder of several sets of hoofbeats drew closer to me. The horse she had been riding shook its head and bucked, while mine pranced anxiously beneath me. I didn't have to look back to know it would be several of the king's guards. It certainly took them long enough to notice she was gone.

They circled around me and Captain Mercer blocked my path with his horse. I halted both horses.

"Can I help you, captain?"

"She's gone."

I cocked my head to one side. "What do you mean *she's gone?*"

"She wasn't in her bloody cell this morning, you fucking idiot. That's what I mean."

"Seems to me that your guards aren't doing very well at their jobs. As you can see, she's not with me. I don't know why you would have wasted your time finding me when you should be looking for *her*, but here we are."

"What do you know about it?"

"What makes you think I would know anything about how she slipped through your fingers?"

He drew his sword and turned his horse to face mine. "Damnit, do not test me. I don't have the patience for it today."

I shrugged. "I don't know anything, and if you don't lower that blade and get the fuck out of my way, you'll find out how little patience I have right now as well."

"You need to find her." He demanded.

"I'm not wasting more of my time finding a woman I couldn't care less about." I maneuvered my horses to pass him on his left. "Good day, captain."

He held his sword out so that it blocked my path, hovering just in front of my chest. "You threatened to cleave the head off of a guard just yesterday for kicking her to her knees."

I pushed the blade up and over my head at the same moment that I urged my horse forward again. "I have two rules, captain. The first is that I don't kill children. The second is that I don't believe in hitting a woman, unless she's another member of the guild who's decided to kill me. Your guard crossed that line. He should count himself lucky he still has his head."

He didn't move to follow me.

Chapter 32

Liza

The days began to blur together as I traveled. I walked until I physically couldn't anymore, then collapsed, unrolled my cot, and slept. I wasn't sure how far I went, but I knew for certain that I needed to cross the mountains *before* the first river I encountered. Otherwise, I would be getting far too close to Valehaven.

My options were Cragmore, which felt far too close to the capitol, or Edgewood. I knew we encountered smaller villages when we traveled that route, but they were not on the map. I ventured into the mountains two days ago. I tried to avoid the valleys, but it was almost impossible. Winter was creeping in, and even in the valleys it was frigid. I prayed to any gods that would listen that I'd come across a town before I froze to death.

I was slinking through the trees, the sounds of nature around me the only thing keeping me calm. I heard dragons flying overhead many times during the day, but I had yet to see one. I hoped that traveling alone would give me a bit of an advantage. A group would be easier to spot and could seem like a threat, but one person traveling *should* be pretty innocuous to a beast like a dragon.

My breath froze in my lungs as I stepped beyond the underbrush and into a large clearing. It wasn't the scenery that halted me, but the large golden dragon sleeping in the grass ahead of me. Its scales glimmered in the moonlight, like stars themselves. Its chest rose and fell with deep even breaths.

I hadn't woken it. I just had to retreat, make my way around quietly, and–

A branch cracked under my foot as I stepped back. The beast's eyes snapped open and zeroed in on me immediately.

Shit. Shit. Shit. Shit.

Panic rose in my chest, and even though logically I knew I needed to run, I couldn't move. It was like every single muscle just refused to cooperate.

It lifted its head and sniffed. Its movement was bizarre enough to make me tilt my head and evaluate it as much as it evaluated me. I expected it to breathe fire and end me immediately. Like everyone *thought* they did to anyone who ventured into their space, but it just watched me. I found myself marveling at the giant spikes along its spine. Large membranous wings rose from its back and they pitched higher behind it as it sat up on its haunches.

It blinked once, slowly, as it lowered its head once more and breathed in my scent. I blinked, and it was gone.

"Gods." I breathed and looked around frantically like it might reappear. I would have thought I'd hallucinated were it not for the indent in the grass where its body had been.

"What the *fuck* was that?" I said aloud, then shook my head. Dragons weren't capable of invisibility, right? Surely that would've been documented somewhere.

I trudged on. That was not something I needed to contemplate right now. I needed to focus on getting to a village or a town. Getting myself more food and a real night's rest in an inn.

*

By the time I came across the first village, I was almost delirious with hunger and exhaustion. I stumbled into the first tavern I found, hood up over my head, and tucked myself into a room for the night. The barkeep brought my food to my room, and never once questioned why I hadn't removed my hood.

Perhaps this was the type of company they always expected. Travelers who kept to themselves. Hiding their identities. All they cared about was payment, and gold spoke volumes. I was not disturbed, and breakfast was delivered to me as well.

When I left the next morning I decided, whether I could help mages directly or not, I was going to make sure that *all* of their supplies for the soldiers, for battle, and for whatever else he planned would be destroyed. I'd burn it all to ash. *That* would be my contribution to preventing a war. They couldn't fight anyone if they couldn't feed their men.

Chapter 33

Slade

I stared at the ceiling. The lush fabric billowing down from it in greens and purples made it feel like I was laying in some kind of fantastical oasis, where I could forget the disaster that seemed to be brewing around me.

Mytharae was in shambles. Or at least, it felt that way. Homes were being raided. Mages were dragged out in chains. Neighbors turned on each other. Not a day went by where someone with magic wasn't being taken per the new king's orders.

The harlot I paid for the night reached over to trace her fingers along my chest. She'd more than earned her pay, but unlike most of her clientele I always made sure she enjoyed herself as well, and it seemed she wasn't done with me yet.

"It's been a while since anyone has seen you around," she mused. "We were starting to worry one of your...

assignments," she propped herself up on an elbow and looked down at me while her fingers trailed up the side of my neck, "might have gotten the better of you."

I sighed and let my eyes flutter closed. "I can assure you, that will never be an issue."

She chuckled at that. "Ah yes, the invincible Sàmhach Marbhadh is never concerned for himself."

My lips pulled down in a frown. "I'm sure I've told you how much I despise that name."

She hummed. "And yet you won't tell me what else to call you." She slid her leg up onto mine.

"You can call me whatever you want, except that."

"I'd like to know your name." She rested her head on my chest while her fingers traced down to where the blankets rested along the top of my hips.

Her persistence only reminded me of Liza. I came here to *forget* her, and yet I spent the entire night wishing that the woman next to me *was* her.

"Why would I tell you my name when I don't even know yours?" Even if I hadn't forgotten whatever moniker she'd chosen to go by in this brothel, I had no desire to learn or know the name she was given.

She seemed to consider the thought. "I suppose you're right."

I had expected her to fight me on it. I expected another question in return. A little more *fire*.

The realization had me sitting up and pushing her off of me. "I should get going." I grumbled, and walked toward the settee, where all my clothing had been discarded.

She pouted when I collected it all and began to dress. "Will you be in town for a while?"

"You know I can't answer that question."

231

She rose from the bed and began to collect her clothing, or what little she *had* been wearing. "Yes, yes." She chided. "Always so cryptic."

I rolled my eyes as I tossed my cloak over my shoulders and headed for the door. I couldn't tell her, but I wasn't ever coming back. All this did was remind me how much I craved a woman I would never have. Even if whatever initial spark I felt in that palace was a charm, the rest of it wasn't, and I realized it far too late.

*

I sat in one of the fancy armed chairs of the den in my estate in Larkspire. Zephyr would wake up soon, and I needed *someone* to talk to in confidence. I couldn't get her off my mind.

"Well, this is an interesting surprise." Zephyr mused, right on cue.

I lifted the glass of whiskey to my lips and let an amused smile rise to my face. "You say that as though you had other plans." I took a slow sip and let my eyes flick his way.

He leaned his forearms on the back of the other chair that faced the fireplace. "I always have plans. You should expect that by now."

I rolled my eyes. I knew very well his plans were simply to bring home whichever woman, or group of women, were interested in his company this evening. His plans were never really all that elaborate.

"Spit it out. You don't visit outside of our normal winter arrangement for no reason."

I grimaced.

"Oh, wait, let me guess." He stepped around and plopped in the chair. "It's that fire mage isn't it? I thought you were rid of her already?"

"I thought so too."

"Thought so, hmm?"

"She's like a plague. One I can't seem to escape." I glanced down into my glass.

"You've never been one to be distracted by a woman, or anything for that matter. Why is *she* any different?"

"If I knew that, do you think I'd be sitting here with *you*?" I shot at him, perhaps a little more forceful than I intended, but he was toying with me.

He scoffed. "You act like I'm not your only friend." I raised a brow at him. "Don't even try to pretend you've got anyone other than the whores you pay to warm your bed."

"I've never invited any woman to my bed." I snapped.

"My apologies." He chuckled. "I forgot you prefer to join them at the fucking brothel."

"I like my privacy. If they know where I live, they know how to find me."

He shrugged. "And yet, somehow I have a feeling you'd let *her* warm your bed.What is it about her that you're so stuck on?"

I glowered at him, because as much as I hated to admit it, she *was* the only one I thought I trusted enough to allow into my bed. "She's a storm of a woman, despite her aversion to violence. A light in the darkness, I guess. She's like the first ray of sunlight after a particularly miserable night. And she's caught up in a political disaster for no other reason than that she was at the right place at the wrong time. I'm not even convinced that her placement in the palace was an accident. It seems like a calculated move, though I have yet to figure out *why*."

"It is rather strange." Zephyr observed. "Moira has never been known for making mistakes, and her first order of business when she ascended her throne was to wipe out every last fire mage, so it is suspicious that she would have had one locked away in the palace all this time just to give it away."

I mulled that over while I took another sip of the whiskey. "A calculated risk maybe? She was there as a part of a trade agreement. If it went south, they may have just killed her."

I looked his way and he made a face that said it was plausible. "Perhaps. I would still question why she kept one alive in the first place. And how she was kept a secret until she appeared in Maeus."

A few moments of silence passed between us where I stared into the fire.

"How did you know *she* was why I was here?" I looked his way again with narrowed eyes.

"It was an educated guess. I have heard plenty of rumors about what's been going on in Mytharae and Emberwyn. It pays to be well informed."

I rolled my eyes. Whatever work he did for Queen Nyvara was a mystery to me, but he consistently surprised me in how much he knew about all of the courts.

"I couldn't leave her to rot in their dungeons. I turned her in and then I got her out. Discreetly of course."

I could feel his icy gaze on me. "You know better than to use your magic so openly. That was foolish."

"They had me by the balls, Zephyr. Was I just supposed to disobey their direct order to capture and turn her in?" I sat a little bit taller in my seat. "They would've put a price on *my* head next."

"You are out of reach here." He said it as though it was a guarantee.

"You don't know that."

"Have any assassins come here to fulfill a job?"

"I don't think we've ever had one that brought us here."

"And why do you think that is?" It was the infuriating condescending way he was looking at me as he asked the question that made me want to hit him.

"Perhaps because no one has put a hit out on anyone in Runelheim."

He shook his head. "It's because no one is stupid enough to run here, and even if they are, no one is stupid enough to follow them just for a bit of coin. Vampires are far more efficient at killing than humans. Besides, the guild is not welcome here."

"I have never heard of such a rule."

"It's unspoken, but it's there all the same."

"And what would have become of her if I had refused the job? Someone would've taken it."

He tried to fight a smile, and failed. "She would've been turned in as she should've been."

"She didn't deserve such a fate." I snarled.

He chuckled, and it made my blood boil. "You know, if I didn't know any better, I'd think you'd found a mate."

"I am not fae."

"No but–" He caught himself and shook his head. "Nevermind."

"What?" I demanded.

"Nothing. Perhaps if you are so stuck on her, you shouldn't have just let her go. Where is she now anyway?" He tried to adopt a bored look on his face, but I knew him well enough to know when he was purposely keeping something from me. I decided not to push him.

"She's probably in Emberwyn by now. The gods only know where. I put her on a ship and never looked back."

"Well, then you either need to forget about her and move on, or go find her. Since you're here, I'm guessing you're failing with the first one. Best of luck with that. Now, I had plans. You'll see yourself out, I'm sure."

He was gone in the blink of an eye, leaving me alone with my empty glass, staring in the fire, praying to the gods that I could forget the damned woman ever existed.

Chapter 34

Liza

I stopped caring which town I was in, but left a pile of ash in my wake for each one I passed through. If they had supplies from Emberwyn, I burned them. I destroyed anything that looked like it would help the guards or his army. The city I was in today was huge, but that meant there was an armory, and carefully lurking around taverns made it very easy to figure out where it was.

Now I stood in the shadow of the building next to the armory. It was not well guarded, which surprised me. Moira would never have left a building like this so unprotected. Stealth was not my strong suit, but I managed to confirm the building itself was filled to the brim with weapons of all shapes and sizes, as well as a stock pile of supplies shipped in from Emberwyn.

Fire wouldn't do anything to swords or daggers, but if I burned it hot enough, it *might* melt them. It would be a test for my limited control of my magic for sure. One I was prepared to take on, regardless of what it meant for me. This was the largest opportunity I had to slow them down yet.

A flick of my wrist had fire catching on the bottom corner of the building. It was wood, built like a barn, and it went up like a bit of kindling. I pushed as much power into the flame as I could, until it burned blue. There would be no mistaking this wasn't a natural fire.

Shouting began, and before I turned to run, a guard rounded the building directly ahead of me.

"Witch!" He shouted. Several others rounded the corner at the same moment.

"Shit." I spun around and ran. I let fire fly behind me, hoping to slow them enough to give me a fighting chance to get away. The sound of their shouts and metal armor clanging together spurred me on faster. I fumbled through crowds of people, rounding corners, and throwing myself down unfamiliar streets.

It was a stupid idea, to stand so close and try to cause more damage. Even just burning their supplies would have sufficed, but I had to do more. I never seemed to know my limits.

I saw a shadowed side street up ahead and made a beeline for it. I rounded the corner and slammed directly into someone. The man grabbed my arms and snarled at me.

"Watch where you're going you–" His voice stilled me immediately, and he stopped speaking when he'd pushed me back far enough to really get a look at me. I lifted my gaze up to lock eyes with Slade. A rush of emotions hit me all at once, none of which I could process in my current state.

His eyes had widened with shock. "Liza?" He gave me a quick once over. "What the fuck are you doing here?" His grip on me loosened, thank the gods.

I heard the guards closing in behind me. I needed to *move*, but he wasn't going to let me. An idea struck me and I didn't give myself time to think through the consequences before I threw myself at him. People *hated* public displays of affection, and no one would look twice at a man and woman kissing on a shadowed street like this. I looped my arms up around his neck and kissed him.

He went rigid, and for a split second I thought I made a huge mistake. In the next breath he scooped me up like I was lighter than a feather and hooked my legs around his waist. My back slammed into the brick wall of the building that had been beside us.

I gasped, giving him the freedom to deepen the kiss. He kissed me like he'd been dying to do just that from the moment that we locked eyes in the palace courtyard. My fingers intertwined in his hair. He rested one hand on my hip while the other slid up to cup my breast. I let out a breathy moan.

I barely noticed the clatter of the guards running past us. He was all I could feel, smell, and focus on. Cedar, leather, and whiskey. I was drowning in it.

When the sound of the guards faded, the hand that held my breast slid up and circled my throat. He squeezed just enough to startle me, but didn't stop my ability to breathe. It sent a spark of pleasure through me that I would never have expected. I was practically melting into his touch.

He ripped his lips from mine, but he didn't move far. I looked up at him through hooded eyes to find a blazing storm of fury in his amber eyes. Our mutually ragged breathing filled the space between us.

"You *used* me." He breathed and it was *definitely* whiskey I smelled on his breath. Had he been leaving a tavern when I slammed into him? I didn't dare to ask.

"You seemed to enjoy it." I panted.

His grip on my neck tightened. I should've been terrified, but all that did was fan the flames that were building inside me. He could kill me right here, right now. Snap my neck or strangle me. Yet somehow, I knew he wouldn't. Something about the empty threat turned me on far more than it should have. This was *not* what I intended but now I wanted to see where it led.

"I believe I gave Murdock explicit instructions to take you to Emberwyn and told those men to make sure you *stayed there.*" His lips remained a hair's breadth from mine. "Care to explain to me why you're *here* in *Mytharae* in *my* godsforsaken city?"

I struggled to steady my breathing with the way he held me. When it took me a moment to answer his grip only tightened. "It would–" I gasped. "Help– If I could– Breathe."

He surveyed me for another few moments, his eyes darting back and forth between my own before he relaxed his grip enough for me to breathe normally and speak.

"I couldn't just *return* to Emberwyn. It's far more complicated than that."

"So you chose to come *here*." He pressed.

"I chose to come back to Mytharae, yes. Forgive me if I don't exactly even know where *here* is. Nor did I know this was *your* city."

"Do you have a death wish?"

I smirked like an idiot and let out a breathless, "Maybe."

He pressed me harder into the wall once again putting pressure on my windpipe and gods damn it all, why did that have to be so fucking hot? I swore I saw him actually consider killing me for a half a second before he released me entirely and shoved my legs off of his hips. I nearly fell to my knees, but he grabbed my wrist and yanked me along behind him, further into the shadows of the otherwise quiet side street.

"Ow!" I nearly shouted. "What are you doing? You're hurting me!" I protested and tried to pull against him but it was futile. The man could snap me like a twig if he wanted. There was no way I was getting away from him with a grip like that.

"I'm taking you somewhere you *won't* get killed by a guard, since you seem so adept at pissing them off or getting yourself caught."

Ouch.

He pulled me into an exceptionally shadowed alcove and my stomach bottomed out as he shadow walked us to a different location. I thought I might be sick.

"If you're going to puke, at least do it in the bathing room." He motioned behind me, but I shook my head.

"I'm fine." That was a lie, but I was sure I wouldn't lose my lunch now at least.

"Gods," he started. He rubbed his face and began to pace in front of me. I had no idea where we'd ended up. Some kind of home, obviously, and we seemed to be alone. "I'm not sure I've ever met someone as idiotic and insane as you."

I frowned, but he didn't notice. He was too wrapped up in whatever he needed to spout off about. I crossed my arms and braced myself for the next insult.

"I thought Xavier was bad, poking the bear and threatening Leodric, but you–" this time he stopped and waved his arm at me. "You are another level." He shook his head and resumed his pacing. "Returning to the country where there's likely a new bounty on your head already. Granted,

241

they'd find you anywhere, but fuck. At least in the palace at Riodian you'd be safer."

He stopped and glared at me now.

"Are you quite finished?" I asked, one brow raised in annoyance.

"Am I finished?" He stormed closer to me. "You've yet to give me a single *good* reason you literally ran into me today."

"You haven't given me a moment to speak since we arrived wherever the fuck we are now." I gestured wildly at the room around us.

Shadows appeared menacingly flowing around the fist he clenched at his side. He followed my gaze to it and they quickly disappeared. He mumbled something under his breath followed by, "Why is it that anytime I'm around you I lose all my fucking sense and self control?"

The question was more to himself than me, but I answered anyway. "Not sure, but if it's all the same to you I'd be glad to leave you to… whatever it is you'd been planning to do and be on my way."

"Over my goddess damned dead body."

"You can't keep me here."

"You weren't all that hard to keep contained before, I doubt much has changed."

The bastard was baiting me, but I took it and flung a fireball at his head. It hit a wall of shadow and he hadn't even flinched. Shadows slipped up around me and yanked me down to my knees on the floor while he walked all the way over to me until I was glaring up at him.

"You're sorely outmatched, Firestorm. Don't test my patience again."

I thrashed against my binds and he just smirked. "You've made your gods damned point. Let me go."

He snorted, but the shadows dissipated and he wandered into what looked like a small kitchen. It had to be his house or his apartment.

He returned moments later with two glasses filled halfway with amber liquid. "Admittedly I do enjoy the sight of you on your knees, but do us both a favor and stand before I do something against my better judgement and continue what you started in that alley."

I flushed bright red, having not even considered the position I was in, and quickly rose to my feet. He offered me a glass. I stared at him blankly.

"I'm not letting you leave. You can either accept the drink and make yourself comfortable or you can continue to test my patience by *trying* to escape. And don't try to tell me that you don't drink whiskey, because we both know that's a lie."

I snatched the glass, nearly spilling it all over myself, and he just continued to smile smugly while he sipped on his own glass.

"I don't think you need another drink."

He raised a brow in question.

"I could taste the whiskey on you."

"You seemed to enjoy it." The bastard grinned in the most infuriatingly cocky way. I caught a glimpse of a single slightly elongated canine. I *knew* I saw that in the woods. I wanted to hit him upside the head with the glass for throwing my words back at me.

His gaze fell to my glass. "You're going to burn off all the alcohol."

I looked down to find that my glass was actually steaming and I hadn't even realized I'd done anything.

"Still haven't gotten control of your magic have you?"

"Oh fuck you!"

He huffed a laugh and then walked over to sit down on the plain gray but irritatingly comfy looking couch. I hadn't been able to sit on something so luxurious in ages. Like he could tell what I was thinking he patted the space next to him.

"So long as you promise not to set my couch on fire you're more than welcome to have a seat."

"I'd rather stand."

He shrugged and took another sip of his whiskey. "Now, I do actually have to go back out. If you're capable of keeping your hood up and your mouth shut I'll allow you to accompany me. If you can't, you'll be locked in here."

"I am not some *pet* you can lock up whenever you want." I glowered at him.

"No, you're more like a flea that I can't quite seem to shake off. I'll think I've done it, then you come back up and irritate me again."

"You bastard!" I chucked the glass at his head, but much like the fireball it bounced off the shadow he blocked it with and shattered all over the wood floor. The whiskey splattered everywhere but the couch which he also protected with the shadows he extended out of himself.

"Fire really is a fitting element for someone with such a short temper." He tisked. "You really should learn a little bit of self control, or, and I know this is a foreign concept for you, *self preservation.*"

I scoffed, my frustration getting the better of me. "Why do you even *care*?"

"It's a question I've asked myself about a hundred times since I helped get you out of those dungeons. Something you have yet to thank me for, might I add." He stood and finished his glass. "I suppose this means I'm going out by myself then."

"I will *not* stay locked in here while you go and do whatever it is your cold iron heart desires." I growled through gritted teeth.

"Then you will follow me, *in silence*, and keep your hood up. Can you handle that?"

"Yes." I seethed.

He disappeared.

"Good girl." He whispered in my ear, his breath tickling my neck and eliciting a response from my body that even my anger couldn't stop.

I spun on my heel and made to punch him in his irritatingly handsome face to knock that smug expression off of it, but he moved faster. He had me by the wrist, twisted my arm behind my back, and held me against him with his other arm across my chest.

How he managed to spin me around and end up behind me like that again, I'd never understand. He leaned in close to my ear.

"I'm starting to think you *like* when I overpower you."

"Let. Me. Go."

He released me immediately and took a step back. "Hood up, keep your mouth shut no matter *what* happens, and don't get in my way."

I turned to face him to find his hand outstretched. "I don't walk out of here. I've worked very hard to make sure no one knows where I live. I'll need to touch you to shadow walk us where I need to be."

I pulled the hood of my cloak back up and placed my hand in his. I was thankful it covered most of my face because I was absolutely mortified about the fact that I was beginning to realize he was right. In some sick and twisted way I *did* enjoy every single time he'd done that.

Chapter 35

Slade

Stupid, insolent, irritating, and *so* fucking distracting. That would be the best way to describe her. What was I thinking? I hadn't a goddess damned clue. I couldn't have just let them catch her, but I didn't have to push it that far. Should've skipped the whiskey, Slade.

But by the gods she tasted exactly like I thought she would. And the sound she made... I shook my head. I needed to screw it back on straight. Even the way she smelled was intoxicating. Juniper and smoke. It would haunt my dreams. I had to force myself off of her, and worse yet, she wouldn't have stopped me.

She was far too good for me, despite her wicked temper. I would ruin her. She needed to stay *very* far away from me. Perhaps I could find her somewhere safe in Runelheim. Zephyr would know somewhere I could take her.

If there was a price on her head, that would be another problem, but if what he said was true, no one would follow her there.

Who was I kidding? I couldn't send her away once I got her there. Leaving her on that ship had been harder than I expected. Now that I got a taste of her I wasn't letting her out of my sight, let alone sending her off again.

I shadowed us a block from Leodric's manor. Bringing her here with me was foolish. It was insane. And yet here she was, right on my heels as I walked through the iron gates and up the drive toward the front doors. Silent as I requested. I knew she wouldn't stay there. Just like I knew if I didn't show up like he requested I'd be in for a world of pain.

I walked through the foyer, ignoring Naomi entirely. I did the same as always and kicked open his door. I could see Liza flinch out of the corner of my eye, but she didn't utter a single noise. At least she *could* listen to me. When she wanted to, anyway.

"You're late." Leodric was facing the windows behind his desk. He spun around in his chair and sat down the glass of liquor he'd been holding.

"I was busy."

His eyes narrowed and he looked between me and the cloaked figure behind me. "Clearly."

"What was so important that I needed to come *tonight*?"

He heaved a heavy sigh. "I'll take an educated guess that's a woman. Regardless of who she is to you, she's not welcome for this discussion."

"Say what it is you needed or I'll be leaving now and returning tomorrow. I *do* have a life you know."

He raised a single brow. I prayed to whatever gods were listening that I hadn't just pushed him too far. I knew better than to deal with him when I had been drinking. He tested my patience when I was sober, but when I was buzzed, he could set me off with a single word.

"I have a new assignment for you. One that, I regret to say, is not optional."

Not optional? What had gone up his ass lately that I had now received *three* assignments I had no say in? "I believe you already know my feelings about this, but go on." I said as evenly as I could manage.

"A request directly from the king." He picked a piece of paper up off of his desk. "You've exceeded expectations in your last two assignments, apparently, and he'd like you to do one more. There's a fire mage that has really been a thorn in his side. According to his missive, you won't have to go far. She just set an entire warehouse of supplies on fire in this very city."

Well, that explained why she was here.

"No."

He smiled and seemed genuinely amused. "No isn't an option."

"I *said* no."

He moved quickly, but I was ready for it. I stopped the dagger he palmed and threw a split second before it hit its mark between my eyes. I sent it right back at him, but two more were already headed for me. I had little choice but to use magic to stop them. Had I ducked, they'd have hit Liza.

Leodric froze, his eyes wide at the two daggers held mid-air by shadow.

"You–"

I was behind him before he uttered another word and held one of his own daggers to his throat. "You are alive because I allow you to be. I will not be accepting this assignment, and if you come for me I *will* come back and follow through with killing you. Do you understand?"

He nodded his head slowly, careful not to move too much and draw blood on the dagger.

"Good. Now I'm going to walk out that door, and if you utter a word of what you saw here today, I'll also come back to kill you. Do you understand?"

Another nod.

"Excellent. I'd say it's been a pleasure, but honestly, it hasn't. You'd do well to forget I exist."

I tossed the dagger down into his desk, shadowed to Liza, opened the doors, and she followed me out. We walked to the same alley I brought us to when we arrived and I shadow walked us back to my apartment.

"Are you out of your fucking mind?" She flipped her hood back off of her head and stared at me in disbelief.

"Would you have preferred I just turned around and killed you then and there?"

The way her eyes practically bulged out of her head told me she didn't actually know what she'd wanted me to do instead. "He'll come for you. He'll most certainly just send someone else to kill me."

"He knows better than to come for me. You, on the other hand, are fair game now for him to assign anyone in the guild to kill you." I shook my head. "We'll leave tomorrow. I know somewhere we can go to lay low until I find *you* somewhere to hide."

"Oh no." She shook her head vehemently. "I am not going *anywhere* with you."

"You'll be killed within a week at most, or even a few hours if I let you walk out that door." I gestured toward the door that would lead her down into the storefront that's sat empty for nearly ten years now.

"I will ask again *why* do you care?"

I thought for a moment, doing my best to come up with something. "I owed you a life debt. You stopped your friend from shooting me with an arrow."

"You would've repaid that debt when you pulled me out of the dungeons."

"I did not save your ass for you to pull another stupid stunt and get yourself killed."

She seemed to be trying her best not to smile. "You *do* care."

"That is not what I said–"

She shrugged. "Fine. I'll stay with you. But I get the bed." She took off into the bedroom, where I'd indicated the bathing room was earlier.

"I am absolutely *not* giving you my bed. It was your–" I stopped dead in my tracks when I discovered she'd already removed both her cloak *and* her blouse. "Gods above." I covered my face with my hand. "You could have warned me."

"You act as though you didn't see me entirely naked at that lake. Now, if you'll excuse me, I'd like to take a *much* needed bath."

I grumbled a few curses under my breath. She disappeared into the attached bathing room and shut the door behind her. I removed my cloak and boots, and flopped down onto the bed. I was in way over my head, and was far too drunk by this point to think straight. Perhaps I should've just taken her to Larkspire tonight, but showing up *there* drunk, with her, would be a terrible idea.

I barely heard her return to the room. I was laying with a hand over my face while I tried to think through what the fuck I would do with her. What I would do with *myself* now that I'd lost it on Leodric.

The sound of one of my drawers opening pulled my attention back to her. I lifted my head and my hand just enough to get a glimpse of her. She stood in nothing but a towel and retrieved a tunic from the drawer.

"What are you–" I stopped speaking when she pulled it over her head and the towel fell to the floor. Now that I'd gotten a taste of her, seeing her like that, in one of my shirts no less, was nearly enough to shatter the sliver of self restraint I still had.

She turned and gave me an innocent look. "What?" I could tell by her tone that she knew precisely what she was doing. This was all a game to her, and despite my head telling me this was stupid, it was a game I was perfectly content losing.

"I am not giving up my bed." I tried to keep my voice stern, annoyed, even.

She shrugged, picked the towel up off the floor and tossed it over the top of the door. "I never said you had to." She walked around the bed and I tracked her every step. She pulled the duvet and sheets back, then crawled up onto the other side.

I drug myself back up to my feet, grabbed a pair of loose fitting pants from a different drawer, and forced myself to slip into the bathing room before I did something I would absolutely regret.

Chapter 36

Liza

I was asleep before he came out of the bathing room. The exhaustion from traveling alone combined with the cloud of a bed that he had was enough. I woke to the sound of footsteps, which seemed to be intentionally loud. There was a warmth at my back, and a weight across my stomach that I quickly realized was Slade's arm.

It tightened around me protectively as my eyes slowly opened. A woman dressed in black leathers leaned against the wall across from me.

"Well this is certainly unexpected." She mused. Her dark hair was tied up behind her head and weapons were strapped to her thighs, waist, and even upper arms. It reminded me of what Slade looked like beneath his cloak when he captured me. She had to be an assassin too.

"What the *fuck* are you doing here Selene?" Slade's voice was still groggy with sleep, but the bite to it hit its mark.

Her smile was mostly a show of teeth, like she couldn't wait for the chance to rip out his throat. "You should know that Leodric never misses a thing. This place has not been as much of a secret as you might think."

"I'm not going to ask my question again." He interrupted, sitting up behind me.

She sighed and rolled her eyes. "He's going to come for you. They all are, actually. Just thought I should warn you."

"And what would have possessed you to come and personally warn me?"

She lifted a single shoulder in a half hearted shrug. "I would hate to see the most famous assassin of this generation killed in his sleep tangled up with some washed up whore. It would be very anticlimactic to say the least."

"I'll take the warning into consideration." He said through gritted teeth. "Now get *the fuck* out of my apartment."

She made a pouting face, but pushed off the wall and headed for the door. "Best of luck, *Sàmhach Marbhadh.*" She mocked as she left.

"I'm going to fucking kill her." He muttered under his breath, then pushed himself off of me and rose from the bed. "We're leaving. *Now.*"

I quickly shoved myself up to a seated position and swung my legs over the edge of the bed. "Well I need to get dressed and–"

"No. We're leaving now."

"But I–"

He was in front of me in the blink of an eye. He pulled me up off of the bed, and then we were shadowing elsewhere. I barely had the chance to gain my balance before the floor fell out from beneath me. When my feet hit solid ground again I was standing on a slick wood floor in a darkened sitting room.

A fire blazed in the fireplace, and I nearly squealed when I turned around and found a man sitting on the couch in front of us, shirtless, with a woman straddling his lap. He lifted his head from between her breasts and looked around her to see who had interrupted his evening.

His blood red eyes narrowed when they landed on me. A vampire. I thought my heart may have simply stopped for a moment. "I wasn't expecting you." His gaze flicked to Slade. "Nor was I expecting you to bring anyone along with you."

"Plans changed." Slade growled. "Send the woman on her way. We need to talk."

The woman glanced around at us, an irritated look on her face. She was beautiful, and obviously human. Her blonde hair fell loosely down her back, and she, thank the gods, was at least still mostly clothed. She reached for her shirt when he tapped her thighs and indicated she needed to get up.

"Sorry, love." The vampire whispered. "Perhaps another night."

She shot us a glare, but put her shirt on and left the room. I glanced between the vampire and Slade. The vampire motioned to the two chairs.

"There's no time for that." Slade mumbled.

"You could at least introduce me to your new pet." He rose from the couch and started to walk toward me. "Did you bring her to share?" Something about the way he said it and the way he looked at me told me that he knew the answer was no. It seemed like somehow he knew who I was, but he was antagonizing Slade anyway.

Slade stepped between us. "She's the mage I've told you about, and I need you to keep an eye on her while I go take care of something."

"Absolutely not." The vampire and I said in unison, though my protest was far more vehement than his.

"Leodric knows about my magic, and he's planning to send the guild after me. I'd like to kill him before he gets the chance."

"You fucking fool." The vampire seethed, and if I didn't know any better, I'd think he was a mentor of some kind to Slade. He acted like he was thoroughly disappointed in him. "How did he find out?"

"He tried to kill me once already today. It caught me off guard and magic was my only defense."

A slew of curses, each worse than the last left the man's lips. "So there's a price on both of your heads now?" He shook his head. "I'll kill him myself."

"No." Slade growled. "He's mine. I need you to keep an eye on her while I go take care of it."

"It could be a trap." I didn't mean to say the words out loud, but they tumbled out of my mouth before I could stop them. Both Slade and the vampire turned to me. "Why else would that woman have come to warn you. It just doesn't feel right." I couldn't understand why I cared so much, but I didn't want him to go.

"Regardless, I'll kill them all if I have to." There was no telling this man no, and I just might kill him myself for that. I couldn't just let him shadow walk to his death because of me.

"She could be right." The vampire offered.

"Just keep an eye on her and don't let her leave." Slade glanced back at him, and whatever he saw in his face must've convinced him, because eventually the vampire nodded.

In a blink, Slade was gone.

"Idiot." I breathed.

"Couldn't have said it better myself." The vampire smiled at me. There was something knowing about it, and amusement shown in his crimson irises. "My name is Zephyr." He offered his hand to me.

I stared at it hesitantly. I had never met a vampire, much less been alone in a room with one, and the idea of that made my skin crawl.

"Relax, love, I don't bite." His smile grew wider, enough that one of his fangs stuck out.

"For some reason I don't believe that."

He chuckled. "Fine, I only bite those who *ask* for it. Is that what you're waiting to hear?"

I eyed his hand like it was the head of a snake. He finally relented and dropped it to his side.

"It would be helpful to at least know your name."

"Liza."

He nodded. "It's a pleasure to meet you, Liza. I've heard so much about you."

It was my turn to chuckle. "Somehow I doubt that." Seriously, how was this my life at that moment? Standing in an unfamiliar house, with a vampire, in a city I had never heard of. Waiting on an assassin who I was sure would rather kill me than deal with the chaos I caused him.

"Would you feel more comfortable in his bedroom?" He angled his head while he assessed my reaction. "I can escort you there if you'd like?"

I looked him over cautiously.

"If he doesn't come back in an hour, I'll go look for him. You have my word." He said rather resolutely. "But there's no reason you have to wait up for him."

I narrowed my eyes at him. "You're saying that so that you can lock me in there and claim to *keep an eye on me* without actually having to do so."

He fought to hide a smile. "Clever little mage." He took a step closer to me and I took a step backward. "I imagine it will also be more comfortable for you to wait in a room where I am not with you. His bedroom has no windows, much like mine, so I can *keep an eye on you* from the hallway while you sleep."

"Fine." I relented, though I was certain I wouldn't be getting any sleep.

"It's just that way." He pointed to the hallway leading off the sitting room behind me. He wasn't going to let me out of his sight, and I wasn't going to allow him to get any closer to me. Not that it would matter. He could clear the space between us and kill me before I even registered the movement. I knew that about them, at least.

They were frustratingly deadly creatures. I still did not understand why a human, like the woman he had earlier, would willingly hand themselves over to a vampire. I walked down the hallway he indicated and followed his remaining instructions until I pushed open one side of a double door. It led into a room far more lavish than even my accommodations at the palace had been.

I let the door close behind me, and he did not follow me into the space. There was a large four poster bed in the center of the back wall. Black silk was draped from the top of the bed, hanging down at each corner. The bed itself was laden with a duvet and sheets that looked just as silky and luxurious as the fabric hanging above it.

The rest of the space was decorated with candelabras and beautiful paintings of mountainous landscapes. It was hardly what I would expect of Slade, given what little I knew about him. The apartment he took me to was as bland and blank as I would expect of a man like him, while this spoke of an ancient sort of charm that I knew must've come from the vampire on the other side of the door.

I walked to the bed and let my hand run along the duvet. It was decadent, and I was sure I would feel like I was sleeping on a cloud. I climbed beneath the sheets, but sleep wouldn't find me now. Not while he was out doing the gods only knew what.

Chapter 37

Slade

It was definitely a trap. I was more irritated that she thought of it before I did. Selene would never have come to warn me out of some kind of professional courtesy. She *would* however agree to bait me into a situation that Leodric was sure would kill me.

It wasn't even midnight, which meant he would still be in his office. I shadow walked back to my apartment and pulled on my leathers, strapped on my knives, and sheathed my sword across my back. I should have known he wouldn't pay any mind to my threat. He thinks he's too untouchable.

I shadow walked into his office. It was dark and far too quiet. The thunk of a cross bolt firing caught my attention, but I moved too slow. In such a small space, there was no way I would've avoided it, but the bolt slammed into my thigh and I muttered a curse as I dropped to a knee.

Leodric tisked behind me and I twisted to face him with a snarl rising to my lips. "You of all people should know better than to threaten me." I could see the cruel smile on his face.

"Funny, I was going to say the same thing." I snarled. "Anyone with half a brain would've heeded that threat."

He laughed. There were at least five others in the room, from what I could tell, though I didn't take my eyes off of him to see who shot me.

"I thought you'd be smarter than this. That you wouldn't take the bait and I would be forced to send some of the newest recruits to Runelheim to kill you and that godscursed mage you drug in here with you. Yet, here you are, just like Selene said you'd be. I shouldn't be surprised I guess. I already knew you held no loyalty the moment you lied about killing Xavier."

I couldn't hide my surprise at that admission, which only spurred him to continue.

"I thought about killing you then, but when the assignment to kill Andras came up, I thought I would let the trash take itself out. It was a mystery to me just *how* you accomplished such a feat, but you made that quite clear earlier this evening. It really is a pity that you have to die. You were one of the best."

I smiled and ripped the bolt out of my leg. "And if I had let Zephyr come, you would all be dead already."

His eyes flashed, like he had forgotten that I was only here, I was only in *his* guild, because he owed Zephyr a life debt. He glanced around at the others hiding within the shadows. "Kill him. Whoever brings me his head gets to become the new Sàmhach Marbhadh."

I threw a knife at him, but he slipped out the door before it struck him and it pierced the wood of the door instead. The bloody coward couldn't even be bothered to kill me himself.

Selene was the only one that moved. She had a cocky smirk on her face as she stalked toward me, sword drawn. "I've waited for this moment for far too long."

"If you're quite finished gloating," I drew my sword. "I'd like to get on with my evening, and you'll be the first to die."

She scoffed and lunged at me. Her cockiness was always her weakness. She thought because I was already kneeling that she would have the advantage. She swung down with her right hand like she intended to cleave off my head. I twisted onto my uninjured knee and swung at her wrist, severing her sword hand. She screamed and bent over her arm, but I was quick to palm a knife and slashed across her throat.

Blood splattered my face when she tripped over my injured leg and fell to the floor. I shoved myself back to my feet.

"Who's next?"

The other five rushed at me from all sides. I yanked her body up to use as a shield and pushed through the two on my right. They fell to the floor. The thunk of crossbolts behind me had me spinning on my heel and sending up tendrils of shadow. I caught and spun them just in time. I didn't get the chance to aim, but one of them went down.

An explosion from a grenade behind me sent me flying forward into the book shelves. My ears rang and pain blasted through my body from the impact. I blinked to clear my blurry vision.

I coughed as I tried to rise and blood splattered the floor beneath me. *Fuck* I hadn't expected that. Who throws a grenade in such a small space? Fucking amateurs. I chuckled as I pushed myself to my feet, only further aggravating my shattered ribs.

"Is that all you've got?" I taunted.

The remaining four, seemingly unscathed from the explosion, came for me again. I used shadows to throw books at them while I threw daggers. I hit one of them in the eye. Levi, if I could see well enough in the dark. His scream was muffled by my still ringing ears.

I braced for the other three. Sam threw a punch. I ducked to avoid it, caught his arm, and twisted to swing him over me and slam him to the ground. I elbowed Connor in the jaw as he came up behind me. He staggered backward, momentarily disoriented.

I kicked him in the stomach and launched him backward. I shadow walked behind Levi and slammed his head into the wall, which shoved the knife I landed all the way through his skull. His body slumped lifelessly to the floor.

I used a tendril of shadow to return my sword to my hand, while Connor and Sam stood back up and unsheathed theirs. Connor swung at me, but I parried. I sidestepped to avoid Sam's blade and palmed a dagger.

Connor swung again, downward, like he might slice me in half. I caught his sword in the crossguard of mine. I spun and ripped his sword from his grip. Using the momentum of the movement, I swung for Sam and removed his head from his shoulders. I grabbed his sword as he fell and threw it into Connor.

Connor dropped his sword and stumbled backward. He tripped over the books littering the ground and fell back into what remained of the shelves.

"Please." He lifted his hands and gasped. Blood dripped from his mouth. "I didn't want to do this. He didn't give us the choice."

Firestorm

"You had a choice, Connor. Even if it wasn't given." I growled. "You chose the wrong fucking side." I drove my sword straight into his chest. On another day, I might've let him live, but with a sword through his gut, he likely wouldn't survive without a healer anyway. Killing him was more merciful.

The hinges of the office door creaked. "Looks like I'll have to do it myself." Leodric mused.

I turned to face him and sputtered another cough. It was getting harder to breathe. I let shadows collect around me.

"Oh come now, you really need your magic to fight me?" A cocky smirk rose to his lips.

I was a fool to play into his taunts, but I let the shadows disperse anyway. I didn't need them to beat him, but it sure as shit would make it a lot easier. He slid a set of brass knuckles onto his fingers.

I gave him a lopsided grin. "I'll take great joy in killing you." I lurched forward and swung my sword at him. Metal clanged as he batted it away. He swung at me with his free hand and landed a blow to my ribs that *definitely* broke something.

I stumbled backward and growled in pain. I pulled another knife from the strap on my chest and threw it at him. He tilted his head to the side and dodged it. My aim wasn't what it should be. I used a tendril of shadow to catch the blade and fling it back toward him. It stabbed into his left shoulder.

"Cheap shot." He seethed through gritted teeth.

"Says the one who sent six people in here to wear me down before you came in to finish the job."

Leodric ran at me now. I tossed my sword to the side and lowered into a defensive stance. The sword was only a hindrance. I could kill him with my bare hands. He went low, in an attempt to slip under and grab me, but I flipped over his

263

back and grabbed my knife instead. I ripped it from his shoulder and he snarled as he spun to face me.

He caught me off guard with a right hook to the side of my face. I landed a blow moments later, despite the throbbing in my head and blood trickling down my face from his fucking knuckles. We went blow for blow for what felt like an eternity before he landed an uppercut that sent me staggering. The room spun. He caught me by the arm and threw me through the large window behind his desk.

The glass shattered around me. A few shards stuck into me as I slammed onto the ground and rolled away. More blood filled my mouth and I was taken over by an excruciating fit of coughing while I pushed myself up to my hands and knees and tried to rise again.

Leodric placed a hand on the sill and threw himself up and out into the gardens with me. He stalked over to me and yanked me up by the collar of my leathers.

"You thought you could kill *me?*" He laughed. I found my footing when he released me, but he came right in with another punch. I staggered back a step.

"I'll admit, I admire your efforts." He mocked. I blinked and tried to clear my vision to swing at him, but he clocked me on the jaw again before I had the chance. "When I'm through with you, I'm going to enjoy torturing *her*. What was her name again?" Another blow had me losing more ground. "Oh right, *Liza*. I'm going to make sure she knows that you're the reason she has to suffer before I remove her head from her pretty little shoulders."

I tried to swing at him, but he caught my fist and shoved it away. He grabbed me by the collar again and leaned in close to me. "Any last words, Sàmhach Marbhadh?"

I still had the knife I pulled from his back in my left hand. I smiled. "Yeah." I muttered. "Tell Selene I said hi."

Firestorm

He had a moment to look confused before I swung the blade up and slammed it into the side of his throat. He stumbled backward and gasped, as well as one could anyway with a gigantic hole in the throat. His hands flew up to try to stop the bleeding, but it was too late for that. He crumpled to the ground. I used a shadow to drag my sword back to me while I watched him bleed out on the ground beneath me.

I shadow walked back to my bedroom in Larkspire and collapsed onto the floor.

Chapter 38

Liza

I was sitting on the bed hugging my knees into my chest when Slade shadow walked into the bedroom. His pained gasp startled me more than his sudden appearance, and I flung myself from the bed to run over to him. He stumbled and fell to the floor. He was covered in so much blood it was hard to tell what was his and what wasn't. His face was nearly unrecognizable.

"You were–" he grimaced in pain. "Right."

Zephyr burst through the door. I reacted instinctually and put a wall of fire between him and Slade. "Don't fucking touch him."

Irritation flickered in his eyes. "I came in here to help him."

I was about to snap back at him, when Slade muttered a barely audible plea for me to let him through.

I hesitated. "Vampires can't heal."

"Do you want him to *die*?" Zephyr gestured wildly toward where Slade lay between us. "Because he doesn't have all night. I can't heal him but my *blood* can."

I willed the fire to burn out, and thanked the gods that I had more control this time than I ever had before.

"You fucking idiot." Zephyr chastised as he knelt down next to Slade. He rolled up his sleeve, bit his own wrist, and held it up to Slade's lips. "Drink."

I cringed, and had to look away when Slade willingly obeyed. Either this had happened before, or he trusted this man far more than I ever could.

Zephyr pulled his arm away, and Slade let out a relieved sigh. His face had already healed completely. He looked like himself again, aside from the blood coating him anyway. "Thank you." He mumbled to the vampire.

I glared at him. Perhaps I should've been a little more relieved, but now that he wasn't actively at risk of dying I was just angry. Zephyr must've read as much from my face, because he left quickly and closed the door behind him.

Slade's gaze rose to meet mine and he visibly winced when he took in my expression.

"You could have *died*."

He pushed himself up to a sitting position and tucked one leg underneath him. That familiar cocky smirk rose to his lips. "I'm not sure why you care so much, Firestorm. It would've been an easy way to be rid of me."

I slapped the cocky look off of his face. I don't know what came over me. I was *not* a violent person. He seemed to bring that out in me. His face snapped to the side with the force of it, and he looked back at me in shock. He lifted his hand to touch his face, like I had actually *hurt* him.

"Oh gods." Realizing what I'd just done, I felt all the blood drain from my face. I pushed myself up to my feet and walked back toward the bed. I didn't know what to say, what to do, but–

He was in front of me, stopping my thoughts and me with a hand at my throat. He shadowed us, and then my back was pressed against the wall. He pushed my chin up with his thumb and his lips crashed into mine, forceful and desperate. Like he'd been holding himself back and waiting to do this again since I ambushed him with the kiss in the alley.

I returned the kiss just as fervently, my anger forgotten. My hands slid up to wind into his hair. I hummed against his lips, melting into his hold like I was made to be there. It was crazy, stupid, and maybe just a little bit toxic, but I loved every second of whatever the fuck this was. He was still covered in blood, but I hardly noticed it. All I felt was him against me, and I was sure I hadn't ever felt something so right in my life.

He removed his hand from my neck suddenly and braced it against the wall beside my head. He broke the kiss and rested his forehead against mine.

"You don't want this." He breathed. His face was clearly conflicted, like he couldn't understand what he'd just done to me. "You don't want *me*."

"What if I do?" I whispered.

His eyes locked with mine.

"What if it's *all* I want right now?"

The way his gaze shifted when I said that should've scared me. He looked like he wanted to devour me, and I wasn't sure that I was prepared for what that look meant. "You don't know what you're asking for."

"So show me." I dared him. Truthfully, I had no idea what I was getting into, or even what I was now asking him for, but I didn't care.

He searched my face like he still wasn't sure what to do. His eyes dipped to my lips. "Fuck it."

It was more than a kiss. It was a claiming. The spark that set my entire world on fire, and I was more than happy to burn up with it. A whimper of a moan escaped me when he slid his hands underneath the tunic I wore and he hoisted me up so my legs rested on his hips.

He pulled my lower lip between his teeth and I let out a shaky breath. He trailed kisses down my chin and neck as I pulled at his hair. He spun me away from the wall and I caught a glimpse of the bloody handprint he left there.

"Oh gods." I breathed. "You're covered in blood." I had forgotten already. I could feel it on my neck where he held me. The tunic I wore was covered in it where it transferred from him every place we touched.

His lips drug up the side of my neck, and I arched it to give him better access as my eyes fluttered closed again. "Does that bother you, my little Firestorm?" He breathed in my ear.

The sensation and the use of his infuriating nickname for me was nearly enough to make me forget what he was even asking about. My entire body felt like a living, breathing, fire and he was just fanning the flames. He didn't wait for me to answer the question. I heard the sound of running water as we entered the bathing room. How he turned it on, I wasn't sure.

He set me on the vanity and pulled away. His eyes traced over me with a longing I hadn't ever seen from anyone before.

"Take off that shirt." He ordered, while he began to unstrap the various leather belts that held his weapons.

It took me a moment to obey. I was too distracted watching *him* undress to remember that he'd asked me to do the same. I pulled his tunic over my head and tossed it to the floor to join the bloody remnants of his leather armor.

He kicked off his boots and removed his belt. My fingers itched to reach out and touch him, and yet I hesitated. He had so many scars. I remembered noticing them, even at a distance, but they were so much more gruesome up close. The largest, of course, from the cut and subsequent burn he got for the ambush that happened because of me.

I forced myself to lift my gaze to his face. His eyes were predatory as he dragged them over me, in a way that sent a thrill through me. I did my best not to flush under the scrutiny, but I hadn't ever had a man look at me like *that*.

"Gods you're too good for me." He breathed. "What the fuck am I doing?" He covered his eyes with one hand like he physically had to stop himself from looking at me. He took two measured steps back away from the vanity. "I'll leave you to get yourself cleaned up." He turned to walk from the bathing room. "I need to–"

I shoved myself off the vanity and caught him by the arm. "I don't know what makes you think I'm too good for you. Not that it should matter, but I'm nothing but a failure and a disgrace."

He jumped as though he hadn't expected me to grab him, let alone fight him on this. He glanced back at me. "You are nothing of the sort."

"You hardly even *know* me." I insisted.

He spun around now and backed me toward the counter I had just been sitting on. "You don't get it, do you? I kill people for a living, which means I also read people *constantly.* I can tell what someone is thinking, what their next move is, and what kind of person they are within a few minutes of observation."

He placed his hands on the vanity behind me, effectively blocking me in. "Even now, as I step closer to you, your heart rate increases. Your breathing is more erratic. You keep looking back and forth between my eyes like you're not sure if I'm going to fuck you or attack you. You don't know whether to run or be turned on by it. Are you going to tell me that I'm wrong?"

"Well... I..."

"You can't, because it's true. I spent more than a week traveling with you. You *wanted* to hate me. Maybe you *did* hate me, but at some point you changed your mind, and I still don't know what I did to make you think that I was redeemable. I don't know why you rushed over to me like you were actually concerned about me.

"You have no reason to care at all, but you *do.* Because you're a good person. A person who sees the good in everyone even if they're nothing but a killer with questionable morals. You deserve better than me, and I will not ruin you, as much as it pains me to walk away from you now. I'll have Zephyr arrange for you to have a room here. The longer I am this close to you, the less self restraint I have."

"By the gods, are you always such a self righteous and stubborn prick?"

He blinked and stared at me for a moment as if he didn't know me. That made it twice now that I'd done something he hadn't expected. At least I *could* surprise him.

"You don't just get to *decide* that you're not good enough for me, go on a ridiculous rant about why, and then walk away from me."

He opened his mouth to speak, but I put my finger over his lips.

"I'm not fucking finished, Nightshade."

His eyes narrowed into a glare at the nickname. It sent a thrill through me.

"*I* get to decide who is and isn't good enough for me. And you know what? Maybe you're right. Maybe I *shouldn't* want this. Maybe giving in to *whatever this is* is the worst mistake I'll ever make. But I wouldn't even be here right now if you didn't feel *something* too. So why would the gods throw me into you again if we weren't supposed to have the chance to figure that out?"

"If I recall correctly, *you* threw yourself at me. The gods had nothing to do with it."

"And I'm about to do it again, but I'd prefer if you'd wash off the blood first."

He stepped back, sighed, and turned to walk toward the large shower. There was a tiny step to prevent the water from getting all over the bathing room floor, and three of the four sides of it were tiled walls that came up to just above my hips. He pulled off his pants and tossed them onto the pile with the rest of our bloodied clothes, then he stepped into the shower.

I watched as he rinsed the blood off his body. Something nudged my shoulder and I nearly jumped out of my skin. I glanced back to find a tendril of shadow pushing me toward him.

"Get over here, my little Firestorm." His voice was a low growl.

I walked over to the opening of the shower. He turned around to face me and gave me another long look. I did the same to him. The shadow pushed at my lower back hard enough that I nearly tripped into the shower with him.

He pulled me under the water and his lips crashed into mine. One of his hands cupped the back of my head while the other grabbed my ass and pulled me against him. Both of my hands slid up into his hair. He kissed me slowly, like he intended to make this last forever. He guided me further into the spray of the water, then backed me up against the wall.

He slid his hand down from my head and brushed the backs of his fingers along my shoulder, my breast, and my stomach. I let out a shaky breath and he smiled against my lips.

"I wonder," he breathed between kisses as he trailed his lips down the column of my neck. "Will you taste as good as you did in my dreams?" He continued kissing down my body until he was kneeling in front of me.

"What are you…" my voice trailed off when he slid his hand from my ass down my thigh and hooked my leg over one of his shoulders. He kissed down the crease of my thigh and a soft whimper escaped me. By the gods that felt so good.

Shadows circled my wrists and pulled my hands from his hair. He pinned them above my head at the same moment he dipped his head between my thighs and ran his tongue along me. I pulled against the shadows and moaned.

He let out a satisfied hum against me. "Even better than I could've imagined." He circled my clit with his tongue and my hips bucked at the sensation that shot through me with his touch. He placed one hand on my sternum to hold me in place while the other gripped my thigh tightly.

He worked his tongue in and around me in ways I never could have imagined. A man hadn't ever kissed me like *that* and most certainly not *there*. My body hummed with ecstacy and threw me over the precipice of pleasure so violently that if he hadn't been holding my leg over his shoulder I was certain I would've fallen to the floor.

My legs were still shaking when he let my thigh go and stood back up in front of me. He claimed my mouth once more, with the taste of my orgasm still on his lips. He replaced his mouth with his hand and slid two fingers into me while his thumb circled my clit in an absolutely mind numbing rhythm.

"Slade," I breathed against his lips.

He kissed down my jaw. "You'll be screaming my name by the time I'm done with you." He whispered into my ear. He slid his free hand into my hair, grabbed a handful, and pulled my head to the side.

I gasped when he bit the crook of my neck. The jolt of pleasure heightened by the movement of his fingers inside me sent me over the edge again. I cried out in bliss.

"That's my girl." He released my hands from their bindings and I flung my hands around his neck. He caught me as I slumped against him. "We're only just getting started, darling."

He lifted me up and hooked my legs around his waist. He must have used his shadow magic to turn off the water, because it stopped on its own. He carried me out of the shower and back into the bedroom.

"Should I use my tongue again and see just how many orgasms I can get from you until you beg me for mercy? Or should I save that for tomorrow and fuck you senseless with my cock instead?"

"I'll take the second option." I croaked out. "Since I've only just learned what the first even feels like."

He let out a dark chuckle. "You've been severely neglected if that was your first time coming on someone's tongue, but fine. I'll let you have my cock. Tomorrow, I'll make you beg me to stop."

He carried me with him onto the bed. My back met the silk sheets and my head rested on one of his blissfully soft pillows. He hovered above me and pressed the head of his cock against me.

"Gods you're still so wet for me." He breathed, his lips brushing against mine. I rocked my hips up into him. He huffed a laugh. "Such an impatient little thing aren't you."

"You're enjoying making me wait." I whispered and nipped at his bottom lip.

"Hmm, perhaps I should make you beg…" He cupped one of my breasts and squeezed it gently.

"Please," the plea escaped my lips without hesitation and I moved my hips again.

He slid himself into me so torturously slowly. My hands flexed on his shoulders and I dug my nails into his skin. He was too much, and not enough all at once.

He groaned and breathed, "fuck you're perfect," into my ear.

I rocked my hips, desperate for him to move, to gain the friction I craved. He withdrew and thrust in again in the same slow and methodical way. He teased my nipple with his fingers and nipped his way down my neck. His other hand traced up my arm until he slid it into mine and pinned my hand over my head.

He picked up his pace slowly, sinking all the way into me with every thrust and hitting just the right spot. It was like he knew my body better than even I did. With each twist of his fingers on my breast, each nip, suck, and movement of his mouth on my neck, and his decadent movements within me I was buzzing with bliss.

Another slow thrust and I came with his name on my lips. He slid his hand up from my breast to my throat and squeezed. Breathing became a little harder. His lips trailed down to my other breast and he toyed with it with his tongue and his teeth.

He worked his hips faster as I rode the waves of my orgasm all the way into another one. I clawed at his back with one hand while I pulled against his hold with the other. He stilled above me when the shaking in my legs slowed and the aftershocks subsided.

"This time, my little inferno, I'm coming with you." He pulled out of me and flipped me onto my stomach. I slid my arms up so I was propped on my elbows. He lifted my hips in the air and slid himself into me again. A deep moan escaped me. I wasn't sure I *could* come again, but I didn't want him to stop either.

He pressed a hand to the small of my back, arching it further. He slid almost all the way out and slammed into me again.

"*Fuck*" I breathed. He slid his other hand down to circle his fingers around my clit. I called out his name.

"That's it." He encouraged me while he worked himself in and out of me. Slamming all the way to the hilt each time. I was so hyper sensitive already that the pleasure was almost pain.

"I can't," I gasped.

His pace picked up as he growled. "You *can*."

I clawed at the sheets. My senses worked in overdrive. My whole body was spun tight and ready to break. *"Please."* I begged. I didn't know if I was begging for release or for him to stop.

"Come for me, Liza."

I could do nothing but obey him. My entire body shook as the orgasm crashed over me. He followed me over the edge, the twitching of his cock only heightening my pleasure until he pulled away and we both collapsed on the bed. He pulled me into his arms with my back against his chest.

"Good girl." He whispered, just before sleep claimed me.

Chapter 39

Slade

The sensation of a finger trailing down my chest woke me. I caught her wrist, but managed to stop myself from flipping her over like I had done in that tavern. This was why I never let anyone share my bed. Why I never fell asleep next to anyone. I was taught not to trust anyone. If someone disturbed me while I was sleeping, they were likely doing so to *kill* me.

She froze, likely recalling the same moment I was. "I'm sorry, I shouldn't have… I should've known…"

I released her wrist and rolled to my side so I was facing her. "I'm sorry." I brushed a loose hair out of her face. "I haven't ever let anyone sleep with me like this."

Understanding flashed across her features. "I haven't either."

That intrigued me. I knew why I didn't, but I didn't understand why she wouldn't. She must've read as much from my face, because she laughed.

"Good to know I can still surprise you, Nightshade."

I glared at her. "I *really* am not a fan of that nickname."

"And that's precisely why I'm going to keep it." A victorious smile lit up her face, and I found myself wanting to find ways to see her smile like that more often.

I slid my arm underneath the sheets and traced a path down her side with my fingers until I could hook her leg up over my hip. She shivered under my touch and pressed herself against me. The marks I left on her neck last night darkened a bit. I worried for a moment that she might kill me for that.

She noticed where I was looking and tried to follow my gaze. "What? Do I have something *on* me?" Her voice went up in pitch.

I huffed in amusement. "No. I just, uh…" I cleared my throat. "I may have gotten a bit carried away and left a few marks."

Any lingering wariness from sleep left her and her sharp gaze widened on me in a way that actually scared me a little. "You *didn't*." It was disbelief mixed with ire, and it was incredibly amusing.

I half laughed and a grin rose to my lips. "I–"

"You bastard!" She shrieked and smacked my chest with the back of her hand. She struggled to hide a smile.

"I do like that there won't be any question that you're *mine*." I mumbled before I could think the better of uttering the words. She wasn't really *mine*. She had hinted at figuring out whatever it was we felt for one another, but we certainly hadn't done anything more than fuck.

She didn't flinch or shy away from the comment though. She came to some kind of realization though, the way her face changed. "Oh gods." She gasped. "I don't have any clothes."

There was a light knock at the door.

"Lord Grimsbane?" Abigail, one of the house keepers, called from the other side of the door. "Is it alright if I come in?"

Liza froze. Her breath caught in her throat. "Yes." I answered.

Abigail pushed the door open and wandered in quietly. She didn't even look toward the bed. Her gaze stayed trained on the floor in front of her, even as she brought the tray of food over and set it on the bedside table next to Liza. She pulled what looked like a neatly folded article of clothing from a pocket on her apron and placed it on the bed.

"Lord Nightingale mentioned that your female companion might need some clothing. I hope that this will work until you're able to find her something else. Based on his description, it should fit." She spun on her heel and walked back toward the door. "If there's nothing else you need, I will return to clean your chambers once you've dressed."

"Thank you Abigail, that will be all we need for now."

She nodded and slipped out, closing the door behind her.

Liza snickered. "*Lord* Grimsbane?"

I narrowed my eyes and glared at her. "I am *not* a lord, but they insist on calling me that."

"And Zephyr?"

"Works for the Queen. Doing what, I have no idea, but I think he does hold a title. I haven't ever asked."

She hummed. "Interesting."

"As much as I would enjoy nothing more than to spend the entire day in bed with you, we should get you some clothes." I slid her leg off of me and rolled so I could get out of bed.

"I don't have any way to pay for clothes." She protested. "Couldn't we just get my clothing from your apartment?"

"I don't ever plan to return to my apartment. I have everything I need *here* and I have plenty of money to buy you clothes." I walked toward the bathing chamber and stopped before I walked through the door.

She looked genuinely uncomfortable. "I can't let you buy me clothes. I have no way to repay you."

"If you're that concerned about it, you can certainly consider our late night activities as your payment." She looked genuinely insulted and chucked one of the pillows at me. It barely made it halfway. "Or, you can just accept them as a gift and leave it at that."

I didn't wait for her reply before I slipped into the bathing room to freshen up.

*

I had to reassure her at least ten times that I was not concerned about the cost of the clothing. I couldn't understand why she was so stuck on that. She gawked at what was displayed in Delilah's shop windows. The seamstress was one of the best in Larkspire, and her husband was a master at leatherwork, so between the two of them they could make almost anything I ever needed.

The fashion in Runelheim was drastically different from Mytharae, Elkridge, and Emberwyn. Almost all of the dresses, shirts, and pants were dark colors with black being

281

the most common. Every piece that Delilah put in the window was complimented with a leather belt, cowl, baldric, or bodice. In some cases, the pants were leather.

"Look, I know *you* seem to prefer leather, but I really don't need to walk around looking like an assassin." She whispered as I guided her through the front door and into the shop. The bell jingled to signal our entrance.

I chuckled. "You'll find that this is just the fashion here. It's practical. Do you think that Queen Nyvara is walking around in those pompous gowns you wore in Maeus?" We passed very few people when we walked down to the shopping district. Those we did pass were all dressed similar to the mannequins in these windows. She had been distracted by the architecture though, and hadn't noticed them.

"Well, I would've assumed she *did*. That's just customary for royalty is it not?" She looked around the shop until her gaze landed on the section I knew she would run to – the dresses. She started to walk that direction, until she noticed that even the dresses on those mannequins had some kind of leather accent, whether it was a bodice, leather over the shoulders, or leather accessories.

"Gods, even the *dresses* have leather on them?" She walked over and ran her hand down the shimmering skirt of the midnight blue gown with a leather bodice. "And everything is so *dark*."

"Slade." I could hear the smile in Delilah's voice. She walked out of her workroom to greet us. "It's been a while." Her black hair was peppered with gray now, but still tied up in a tight bun on the back of her head. She was paler than I remembered. Her brown eyes lit up as she took me in. When her gaze shifted to Liza, she raised a brow. "And who might this lovely little thing be?"

282

Liza looked back and forth between us like she wasn't sure how to react. Her hand fell from the dress and she tucked it behind her back like she was ashamed to have touched it.

"This is Liza. She's a…" I hesitated for a moment, unsure of how to explain whatever it was between us. "*Friend.*"

Liza's eyes narrowed on me, and Delilah laughed. "Oh of course. A *friend.*" She walked over and pushed the hood of the cloak I loaned Liza out of the way to get a better view of her neck. "Tell me, little bat, do you mark all of your *friends* this way?"

Liza backed out of her reach quickly and her face turned nearly as red as her hair. I hoped her embarrassment was enough to make her miss the nickname Delilah used for me. I never understood where it came from, but I didn't have the heart to tell her to stop using it.

A slightly embarrassed grin rose to my lips and I cleared my throat. "I was hoping you might be able to help her pick out a new wardrobe. She just arrived from Mytharae and did not have time to pack to bring clothes with her. I'll take care of everything."

Delilah gave me a suspicious glance, but didn't ask any questions, thank the gods. "Of course, little bat." She stepped closer to Liza and reached for the clasp of her cloak. "May I?"

Liza looked from Delilah to me. I gave her a reassuring nod. She turned her attention back to Delilah. "Sure."

Delilah unclasped the cloak and slid it off of her shoulders. "Well," she started. "You're a bit bustier than most, but I'm sure I've got a few things that will fit you. I see you were eyeing this gown. It would look stunning on you, and I believe I have one that should fit you. Would you like to try it on?"

"I, uh–" She looked at me again.

"I'm not asking him." Delilah chided and turned Liza's face back to her. "I'm asking you, dear. Would you like to try it, or is there something else you would feel more comfortable in?"

"I'm sorry," she breathed. She was nervously fiddling with her hands behind her back. "I'm really not used to clothing that's…" Her voice trailed off as she looked around the shop and tried to determine what to say. "Quite like this." She finally met Delilah's gaze once more.

Understanding flooded the older woman's face. "Well, unfortunately dear, I don't think I have anything that would be similar to the fashions of Mytharae. I could make something custom though if–"

"No, no." Liza cut her off quickly. "It's alright. I'll uh, I'll try whatever you recommend."

Delilah smiled. "Excellent. Let me take some quick measurements and I'll make a few selections." She pulled a measuring tape out of the leather pouch on her belt and mumbled to herself as she went.

"Slade, take her back to the dressing rooms. I'll be there in a few minutes with whatever I have that will work for her. I assume she will need undergarments too."

"Yes please." Liza answered before I could.

"Of course dear." She squeezed her shoulder and then hurried off to gather whatever it was she intended to have her try on. I picked up the cloak where Delilah had discarded it on a rack and led her back to the dressing rooms.

"Little bat?" Liza asked with a snicker once we were alone.

Embarrassment burned my face and I sighed. "I'm not sure where the name came from, but she's called me that from the moment that she met me."

"And when was that?" She smiled, and even though it was a result of my discomfort, it was a welcome relief after she had spent most of the day so unsure and timid.

"Honestly, I don't remember exactly. My mother worked for her and–" I looked away and cut myself off. It was a detail I hadn't meant to share. Why was it that with her I couldn't ever stop myself from sharing too much? When she'd asked me for my name I gave her my *real* name instead of an alias. I rarely disclosed my name to anyone outside of the guild, or those who knew me here. Even the women I paid at the brothel didn't know it.

"What?" Liza placed a hand on my cheek and turned my face back to her. "Why did you stop?"

"It's nothing." I deflected. "I've known her all my life."

She searched my face like she could see through my lie. It *wasn't* nothing. There was more history there than I was ready to share, and it was far too dark to disclose right now. She frowned, but dropped it and let her hand fall from my face.

"She seems nice. Delilah I mean." She traced her hand along the wooden frame of the couch that sat along the wall in front of the dressing rooms.

"She is. She's on the short list of people that I trust down here. And Zephyr is the only vampire that is on it too."

Her lips pursed. "Noted. Although I don't think you would've needed to worry. I wouldn't trust *any* vampire."

Delilah strode into the room now with her arms full of dresses, pants, and various other garments. "I can assure you dear, that most vampires really aren't as scary as I'm sure the

285

propaganda you were fed in Mytharae make them out to be. Queen Nyvara has very strict laws here. In all my time living here, there has only been *one* human death at the hands of vampires and all of the culprits were dealt with before they met Nyvara's blade."

She shoved through one of the curtains into the dressing room beyond and began to hang or lay everything out for Liza. "The blood sucking bastards were lucky that I wasn't here when it happened, because I would've made them suffer."

Something shifted in Liza's face, and I knew immediately that she'd been given enough information to put the pieces together. It made me wonder if Delilah had divulged the information on purpose. She might've been human, but she had hearing far better than any vampire I had ever met. She never missed a thing.

"Come on in, dear. I'll have to help you with the bodice on some of these. I tried to pick a few lighter colored pieces for you, but I think the lightest color I have is this dark teal. It will look lovely with your hair."

Liza walked over to her and Delilah slung the curtain closed behind her. I sunk down onto the couch and let my head fall back against the wall. I'd need to brace myself for the hundreds of questions that I was sure were going to come from Liza when we left.

Chapter 40

Liza

Delilah had me try on so many things that I genuinely lost track of them all. She refused to elaborate on what she had already told me, and scolded me for asking because Slade could hear us and was likely already irritated about the fact that she'd mentioned it.

He said his mother worked here, but then stopped himself from saying anything else. *She* said that only one human had ever died in her time living here, and Slade had never mentioned his mother before. Granted, I don't think we had a single conversation where it would have come up, but she confirmed enough by refusing to elaborate that my assumption it was his mother was correct.

Delilah insisted that I wear the dress I touched initially when we were finishing up. It had leather that covered my shoulders and neck, which covered most of the marks Slade left on me. Those that remained she attempted to cover with some kind of powdered makeup she had in her workroom. It didn't completely hide them, but they were far less noticeable. Slade shadow walked the trunk from her workroom to his closet, and then we walked back out into the main shop together.

By the time we left, the sun had set. I hadn't realized we woke so late in the day, but I also hadn't bothered to pay attention to the time in general. There was something weirdly freeing about being here. It was like stepping into a new life, and the idea of that thrilled me more than I expected.

Slade placed his hand on the small of my back and guided me down the street. "Before you ask," he whispered into my ear while we walked. "Yes, it was my mother that was killed. Yes, it was me that ended the vampires that killed her. It was how I discovered my magic. And yes, this is why I refused to discuss my first kill with you. I would rather not relive the details, so please, for the love of the gods, do not ask me to give you anything more than that."

I was shocked he had even given me that. I hadn't intended to ask, especially after Delilah had scolded me for asking her. I turned my head so I could whisper back to him.

"I wasn't going to ask about that. I was going to ask who knows that you have magic, though. You made such a huge deal about it being a secret, but it seems like a fair amount of people know."

He didn't spare me a glance. "Zephyr and Delilah were supposed to be the only two people that knew. That was Zephyr's decision. Another assassin found out. You obviously know that Leodric found out, but I killed him and anyone else who was involved in his plans to kill me, so that just leaves you, Zephyr, Delilah, and Xavier."

"How can you be so sure he didn't tell anyone else?"

His gaze flicked my way for a fraction of a second with a look that said he couldn't believe I thought of or voiced the question. "You know, you seemed pretty daft and naive when I observed you in the palace, but you're irritatingly insightful sometimes."

I smiled. "I'll take that as a compliment I suppose. I think of little things that most people don't when I am outside of the situation myself. That's what you get when you grow up around someone like Moira. You never know what she's going to do next, so you start to anticipate the worst."

He didn't reply. He turned me down a different street. I found myself eyeing everyone closely, especially as the crowd grew. I was desperate to be able to tell who was and was not a vampire. I was certain all of the people milling about around us were not human.

What was even more surprising though, was how clean and happy they all looked. I had expected Runelheim to be a miserable place, where humans were basically enslaved to a vampire that chose them as their personal buffet. Unlike every town I saw in Mytharae, there weren't any people sitting on the streets begging. All of the businesses and homes we passed were well kept. Children played in the streets, even after dark. It was just as shocking as the architecture and the fashion.

Slade took us to a tavern called Raven's Rest. It was a huge stone building, much like everything around it. The spires on the roof gave it a dark and mysterious look. The interior was far more refined than I had ever seen in such an establishment.

The bar itself was dark polished wood. There were several dark alcoves along the side and back wall that had lush purple curtains hanging beneath the archways that led into them. Some were drawn closed and others were tied back. The ones that were open revealed large cushioned seating areas with black fabric that looked just as decadent as the silk sheets on Slade's bed. In fact, they looked nearly the *size* of his bed.

"Go on, ask what *those* are for." His lips brushed my ear, and I jumped. I was too distracted taking everything in that I didn't realize how close he was to me.

Something told me I shouldn't take the bait, but I licked my lips and asked anyway. "What are those for?"

His hand slid down and around to my hip. His fingers brushed my hip just below where the leather bodice ended. "They're for the vampires mostly. If they find a willing human, they can feed and fuck with a little bit of privacy. But, this dress is making me want to claim one so I don't have to wait until I get you back home to rip it off of you."

My breath hitched. I hadn't realized what I wore affected him at all. Nor had I ever had someone so brazenly tell me how much they wanted me. And for some crazy reason, the idea of letting him do what he just suggested and having only a curtain between us and *everyone* in this tavern was as enticing as it was terrifying.

"So why don't you?" I asked before I could think the better of it.

His dark chuckle sent a shiver down my spine. "Because you're *mine*, and I don't even want anyone else to be able to hear the noises you make for me."

I leaned back into him. "So take me *home*." There was something about being wanted, *prized* so much that he didn't even want others to overhear me that was just intoxicating.

"Patience, little flame. The anticipation is part of the fun." He stepped to the side and put his hand on the small of my back again. He started to guide me to a table near the bar. There were two other men already sitting at it, neither of whom I recognized.

I had the sudden urge to stop, spin around, grab him by the collar, and demand he take me home and finish what he had just started with me. Teasing me to the point where I was ready to throw myself on top of him and then cutting it off like he could blow me out like a candle was irritating beyond belief.

One of the men at the table looked our way and did a double take. He had longer brown hair, almost shoulder length, which parted down the middle and framed his face. A smile rose to his face as we approached. His eyes were a bright gray. He stood from the table and stepped around it to reach for Slade's hand.

"Well I'll be damned. I didn't think we'd see you for at least two more weeks."

Slade removed his hand from my back and reached to clasp the other man's hand before they both leaned in for half of a hug. He had… friends? He seemed like he was always grouchy and miserable by himself.

"Good to see you too, Elijah." Slade looked toward the other man. "Kai." He nodded at him. He had auburn hair that was clipped close to his head with a well kept and short beard. His eyes were hazel and already a bit hazed from whatever he was drinking.

Kai's gaze fell to me and he whistled. "Not sure what's more surprising. You showing up before the solstice or the beautiful lass beside you."

Slade bristled at the words almost imperceptibly, but *I* saw it. "This is Liza. And she's *off limits,* Kai." The way he said it left no room for discussion. It seemed to sober the man enough that he nodded and diverted his attention to the mug in front of him.

"What brings you south so early?" Elijah asked and motioned for us to sit in the other two chairs.

"It's been a rough year. If I stayed north any longer I would've lost my head."

Elijah laughed, but I don't think he really understood the truth of the admission from Slade. Out of context, it meant nothing. It led me to believe they didn't know what he did in Mytharae.

Slade pulled out one of the chairs for me. Once I was seated, he took his place next to me and slid his arm around the back of my chair. It would leave no question that I was his, and it left me wondering why Delilah had bothered to cover up the marks on my neck.

Drinks were ordered for us, and I listened as they caught him up on everything that had happened in Larkspire while he was away. Slade told them about his travels, but didn't mention all of the people that he killed everywhere that he went. The way he spun the half truths for them was so effortless it was a little scary.

"Well, Zephyr's pet returned a bit ahead of schedule, it seems. And with a pet of his own." The voice was feminine, and had an air of a threat about it that made my skin crawl.

Slade's arm tightened around me.

"What the fuck are you doing here Jesabelle?" Elijah snapped.

I risked a glance over my shoulder. The woman was ethereal in her beauty. She wore a full leather body suit that reminded me of what Slade wore on our way to Maeus. Her eyes were blood red, just like Zephyr's, and a single fang poked out when she smiled down at me.

"She does look quite delicious."

"She's not on the menu, Jes." Slade growled.

She pouted. "Zephyr's pets never are."

I could practically *feel* Slade's rage, but he didn't correct her that I wasn't anyone's pet. I wasn't entirely sure where the term pet even came from, but I didn't like it at all.

"Find someone else to harass, Jes. None of us are interested, and never will be." Kai growled at her.

"Spoilsport." She grumbled, but she walked away.

"Why did she call you Zephyr's pet?" I whispered to him when I thought she was out of earshot.

"It's a term used for any human that lives with a vampire or is under the protection of a vampire." Elijah explained. "It can be a term of endearment, but for someone like Jes it is always intended to be derogatory. She doesn't keep 'pets'. She prefers to choose someone different anytime she feeds."

"Surely she'll run out of options eventually, won't she?" I turned my attention back to the table now that I lost her in the crowd.

"She already has." Slade grumbled.

*

We started to walk home shortly after midnight. Slade hadn't had another drink after Jesabelle had interrupted the evening. I hadn't either. I walked with my head resting on his shoulder and my arm around his waist. His arm was draped over my shoulders. It was quieter, but there were still more people in the streets than there had been during the day. It was so bizarre.

"Does everyone here operate on a vampire schedule?"

We turned down the road his manor sat on. It was beautiful out here, even at night. There were fewer homes the further we got from the center of the city. Each one sat on a large plot of land. Some had lush gardens while others were just grass.

"Everyone is different, but most of the businesses operate on a schedule that's about halfway between a normal human schedule in Mytharae and a vampire's schedule here. So they'll open at five and close around two in the morning. The taverns open around five too, but they stay open until sunrise."

We turned to walk up the path to the front door. Slade's manor had gardens with flowers that were beautiful in the sun, but even more stunning at night. Some of them glowed, and some of them had opened now that the sun was down.

"Did you design the gardens?" I tilted my head so I could look up at him.

"No. They were Zephyr's creation. I help to tend to them when I'm here at times, but the house keepers do most of it." He stopped on the front porch and pulled me around so I was between him and the door. "Do you have any more questions you want to ask before I *finally* get to take this dress off of you?"

The way he was looking at me heated me to my core. If I had any other questions, they were forgotten the moment he pinned me against the door.

"No."

"Thank the goddess." He breathed and brushed his lips against mine. "I'm not sure I would've had the patience to answer them." He pushed the door open and spun around to pull me inside. The moment that it closed behind us he shadowed us to the bedroom.

He took my face in his hands and kissed me like I was the air he needed to breathe. His tongue traced across my lips and I opened them for him with a moan as he slammed me back against the wall.

I furiously yanked at his leathers, pulling him against me harder. I needed him closer, with nothing in between us. Shadows snaked up around my legs. The feel of them was soft and decadent like he was tracing along my skin with a feather. One of them lightly caressed me over my panties and I groaned against his lips.

He unbuckled the choker that held the top of the dress in place without breaking the kiss. His hands slid down to my hips and he yanked them away from the wall so he could untie and loosen the stays of the bodice. The shadows didn't cease their teasing movements.

He trailed kisses down my jaw as more shadows snaked up around my neck and shoulders to push the dress down until he could shove it over my hips with his hands.

I cried out when his hand replaced the shadow and he rubbed my clit through the lace of my underwear. The friction it created left me begging him for more. Another shadow snaked around my thigh, just above my knee and yanked it up to rest on his hip. I was forced to brace my hands on his shoulders to keep myself in place.

"Gods, the things I want to do to you." He breathed in my ear and bit the sensitive spot between my neck and shoulder.

His name left my lips as a whisper. No, a plea.

"I want to pin you to my bed and fuck you with my shadows while I watch as you writhe with pleasure."

I whimpered, the idea of it sending a new wave of thrill through me that left me aching for him to do just that.

"I'll edge you until you're begging me to let you come, and then I'll keep you going until you beg me to stop."

"Please." I breathed.

"What do you want first, my little flame? My cock?" He rolled his fingers aggressively against my entrance, my underwear still in his way. I rocked my hips against his hand, desperate for more.

"My tongue?" He licked the side of my neck and nipped at my ear. I let out a shaky breath and licked my lips, the anticipation of any of it was absolutely driving me mad.

"My fingers?" He pulled the lace aside *finally* and rubbed his thumb against my clit. I dug my nails into his leathers hard enough that I was sure I left marks on them.

"Or my shadows?" The featherlight touch of a shadow brushing against my clit had me crying out.

"Everything." I breathed. "I need *all* of you."

His dark chuckle against the sensitive skin on my neck sent a shiver down my spine. "One at a time, my greedy little brat." He wrapped a hand around my throat. "Answer the question."

"I–" His grip on my throat tightened and he traced his fingers around my entrance. Every tangible thought I had fled my mind so swiftly that I forgot what he'd even asked me.

"What do you want, Firestorm?" He pulled back so he was looking into my eyes. "I won't ask you again."

I stared at him through hooded eyes, my vision hazy with pleasure already despite that he had barely touched me. "Shadows." I managed to whisper. His grip on my throat loosened a touch as he smiled. "And I want *this,*" I pulled at his shirt, "off."

The shadow holding my leg at his hip disappeared and he stepped back. I nearly toppled over at the sudden loss of his weight against me. I hadn't realized he was the only thing holding me upright until he was out of my reach. I braced my hands against the wall behind me to steady myself.

That only seemed to amuse him, because the smile on his face grew into a wicked grin. "Get on the bed."

I narrowed my eyes at him. "Make me."

His gaze turned predatory. I wondered for a moment if I had made a mistake, but the next thing I knew he had tossed me over his shoulder, walked us to the bed and thrown me down. He yanked my panties off. Shadows circled my wrists and ankles. They drug me up toward the pillows and spread my legs for him. I was pinned just as he said, with my hands stretched over my head toward either of the bed posts.

More shadows danced over my skin now. Some were more forceful than others. My hips bucked and I sucked in a breath as one circled my clit in the same way he'd done with his tongue last night.

He hummed. "If you can be a good girl, I'll take off my leathers, but if you're going to keep being a brat, I'll make you wait until you've earned it." He propped his knee on the bed and leaned down over me until his lips almost brushed mine. One hand circled my throat again while he held himself over me with the other. "What's it going to be, my little flame? Can you be a good girl for me?"

"Yes." I breathed.

"That's my girl." He released my neck and a shadow settled over my eyes like a blindfold. His weight disappeared from the bed. I could hear the sound of his belt unbuckling, and him pulling off his clothes, but I couldn't see past the gods damned shadow. I pulled against my binds.

He gripped my jaw and turned my head toward him. "Ah, ah. You told me you would behave."

"You didn't tell me I would be blindfolded!"

The dip of the mattress next to my head told me he was leaning on the bed again. His breath tickled the side of my neck as he chuckled. "You asked for my shadows. You didn't specify exactly how you wanted me to use them."

I was about to snarl at him in frustration, but he loosened his hold on my jaw and traced his thumb across my chin. "Do you trust me?"

The question was startling, but I nodded without hesitation. "Yes."

"I would never do anything to hurt you. If you want me to stop, all you have to do is say the word, and I will stop everything immediately. Understand?"

"Yes."

"Do you want me to stop?"

"No."

He released my jaw and without warning, the shadows that had been slowly teasing me scattered across my body. The multitude of sensations spiraling through me sent me soaring into a never ending feeling of bliss that I almost couldn't tell what was shadow and what was *him*.

I jerked against the binds as I desperately tried to rock my hips harder against the shadows that circled my clit and moved in and out of me. He worked me right to the precipice of an orgasm, but wouldn't do what he knew I needed to fall over the edge.

"Look at you." His breath tickled my neck. I arched toward him and his lips ghosted across my skin. "Wound so tight and desperate for release." He trailed a finger up my stomach, the sensation so different from everything else that I could identify that at least. "Beautiful." He breathed. "Just breathtaking."

The shadows circling my clit moved a little faster, but still not enough to bring me to a release. I whimpered and yanked against the binds holding my wrists.

"You know how to get what you want." The bed dipped between my legs and one of his hands fisted in my hair. He pulled my head to the side and trailed his teeth down the column of my neck.

I arched my back up off the bed and let out a low moan.

"Beg." He demanded.

The shadows pulsing in and out of me stretched me further and I cried out. It was almost as thick as his cock. They brushed against the most decadent spot inside me and I writhed beneath him, but it still wasn't enough. I was *so* painfully close, and yet so far.

"Please," I finally relented.

"Please, what, Firestorm?" He pulled my bottom lip between his teeth.

I growled in frustration.

"Tell me what you want." He whispered right into my ear.

"Please let me come." I relented. "Please, Slade."

He laughed in triumph, the sensation of his gods damned breath on my skin only furthering my frustration and need. "That's my girl."

He *finally* moved the shadows the way he knew would give me what I craved and I came so hard that stars peppered my vision. The aftershocks were nearly debilitating.

The bindings around my hands and ankles disappeared, and the blindfold faded to nothing. His mouth closed over mine and he worked me into two more orgasms with his fingers before he finally let me have his cock.

Chapter 41

Slade

Gods, I hadn't ever witnessed something so magnificent. And the chorus of moans and gasps as I worked her with the shadows had me almost coming just watching her. My cock *ached* for her, but I made her wait.

When I finally relented and gave it to her it took me no time at all to have her clenching around me as another orgasm ripped through her like a fire would blaze through a stack of kindling. I was a moth, and she was the flame. I would let her burn me down to nothing if it was what she wanted. I'd give her everything I had, including the heart beating in my chest if she asked for it.

I flipped her over, yanked her hips into the air and slammed my cock back into her. Her scream was muffled by the pillow her face pressed into and she gripped at the sheets like it was the only thing tethering her to this world. I fisted one hand in her hair and yanked her head up while my other hand slipped down and around her hips so I could work her clit while I pounded into her.

"Slade," my name left her lips in a whimper. "Please." She breathed. "I can't."

"You can." I pinched her clit between my fingers and she cried out again. "You're doing so good for me, my little flame." I leaned down to whisper in her ear as I thrust deeper. "Come for me one last time."

One final thrust of my hips and pinch with my fingers had her shattering beneath me in an orgasm so violent that I growled my own release as I followed her over that edge.

She slumped down into the pillows, completely spent. I pulled out of her and helped her roll to her side as I collapsed behind her.

"Such a good little Firestorm," I breathed in her ear while I gently cupped and caressed one of her breasts.

She sighed and her head rolled back against my chest. She slid her hand up and pulled mine off of her. "No more, please." Exhaustion plagued her voice. "I can't take it."

I hooked my finger on her chin and turned her head so she was looking up at me. Her eyes were half shut and hazy. "I know." I assured her. "Let me get you cleaned up."

Her eyes fluttered closed and she gave me a weak nod. I used shadows to turn on the water in the large soaking tub next to my shower. I scooped her into my arms and carried her to the bathing room.

The water was warm as I sank into the tub with her, but it turned molten as she settled back into me. Steam rose up around us and it was *almost* too hot, but her contented sigh kept me from complaining. I washed her hair and then massaged out every bit of tension from her back until she was nearly nodding off. I let the water drain from the tub, gently dried her off, and carried her back to the bed. She was asleep before her head even hit the pillow.

*

Zephyr was working on a painting in the den. It was of the very same cliffs that I lied about throwing Xavier off of. Liza was laying on the couch watching him work, with her head in my lap. I was mindlessly running my fingers through her hair with my attention more on her than the painting taking shape in front of us.

"Is that somewhere in Runelheim?" She asked him, her voice barely more than a whisper.

He didn't turn from the canvas. "No, these are the cliffs on the western side of Mytharae."

Surprise lit up her face. "You've been to Mytharae?"

He chuckled. "I've been around for millenia, I've seen every part of this continent."

"So you're painting that from memory?"

Zephyr nodded and dipped his brush into a darker glob of paint to add more depth to the cliffs. I hadn't ever taken the time to admire them from this angle. He had to have been on a ship.

"I am sure that we could sail that way, if you wanted to see them in person."

She rolled back and turned her head so she was looking up at me. "If you're suggesting we sail with those pirates again, I think I'll pass. Sleeping in the cargo hold was *not* fun."

The corner of my lip twitched up into a grin. "You wouldn't be stowing away as a fugitive this time. I can promise he would give us better accommodations if I asked for it."

She narrowed her eyes at me. "So you *could've* had him put us somewhere nicer."

"No. He wouldn't have given any extra comforts to fugitives. Even if they were on his ship to fulfill the debt he owed me."

A knock on the front door halted her next question. Zephyr and I looked at one another. We almost never had visitors here, unless he or myself brought them home *with* us. Liza sat up and looked out into the foyer toward the door. I rose from the couch.

"Stay here." I ordered as I strode around her. "I'll get it."

Zephyr put down his painting supplies and walked over to rest his shoulder against the threshold of the Den while I opened the door.

Jesabelle stood on the stoop with two other women behind her. One had blonde hair and blue eyes. She had a pale blue gown on that resembled what the royalty in Emberwyn typically fashioned. The other had brown hair with golden eyes. She wore leathers that solidified my assumption they were from Emberwyn. The royal crest was stamped on her chest.

I leveled my glare on Jesabelle. "I don't appreciate unexpected visitors. What do you want, Jes?"

"Oh, don't look at me. I'm just the chaperone for this visit." She stepped to the side, allowing me a much clearer look at the two women. "Ezra and Princess Amelia would like a word with you. May we come in?"

"You already know the answer to that question is and always will be *no* for you."

The brown haired woman stepped forward, breaking my death glare with Jesabelle. "Slade, is it?" She asked. I nodded. "I'm looking for Elizabeth Cutwater. If we could speak to her, whether inside or out here, I would appreciate it."

I surveyed her a bit more closely. Her body language suggested she was irritated, but her tone made her seem far too cordial about it. The attire and the fact that she was traveling alone with the princess told me everything I needed to know about her. Emberwyn had an agreement with the fae. I wanted a fae in my home just about as much as I wanted Jes in here.

"There's no one here by that name. I'm sorry to say that you've wasted your time." I started to step back and close the door. "Have a good—"

The woman caught the door with her hand and stopped me from closing it. "Don't lie to me *halfblood.*" The insult was slung with a sneer. It didn't hit the nerve she intended though. "I can *smell* her all over you. Just the same as I can smell your sire lurking in the shadows behind you."

My entire body went rigid. To my surprise, Jes did too, and her gaze flicked between the fae and myself. My *sire?* Zephyr was the only other male in the manor at the moment. He said I was a *mage.*

The fae seemed to notice the change in my posture, because her eyes lit with amusement. "Oh, it seems neither of you were aware of that. Forgive me for pointing out the obvious. Regardless, the princess would like a word with her half sister, so if you'll please have her come to the door, we can get on with why we're here and we'll be on our way."

I couldn't stop myself from looking back toward Zephyr with a glare that could've killed him. His face was set into a deep frown, one that told me he never intended to reveal that particular detail. My gaze fell to Liza, who stood partially behind him in the threshold. Her expression was a combination of horror and pain. Like she had also intended to keep this secret from me.

How did I end up here, with the only two people I trusted in this world having kept secrets from me that uprooted every single thing about my life? Against my better judgement, I opened the door back up and stepped back.

"The fae and the *princess* may enter." I pried my eyes from Liza to look at Jes. "You are not, and will never be welcome in my home."

Jes didn't even appear offended. She nodded and stepped back. "I will wait outside."

The fae glanced at her with a raised brow and a hint of concern.

"He will not harm you. Zephyr is a part of Queen Nyvara's inner circle. He's several ranks above me. I can assure you you're safe with him."

The fae entered first, followed closely by the princess. They both looked around before their eyes settled on Liza. I shut the door behind them. The way the fae looked at Liza made me uncomfortable, and despite her betrayal, I didn't trust either of them. I walked over and stood next to Zephyr, putting myself between Liza and the newcomers.

She stepped partially behind me, and placed one hand on my arm while the other gripped my hand nervously. She must have read from my expression that we would be having a *very* long talk when these people left.

The fae clocked her movements, but her half sister hardly paid them any mind.

"Get on with it then." I demanded through gritted teeth.

Amelia looked at me with a hint of disdain, then her gaze fell to Liza once more. "Mother sent me to retrieve you." She started. "War is brewing. She regrets her decision to banish you to Maeus to secure a union with the prince. She wants you *home*, where she can protect you. She's been worried sick about you since we got word of Edward's efforts to enslave the remaining mages in Mytharae."

Chapter 42

Liza

My blood ran cold. First they show up here and blurt out who I *am*. A secret I had successfully kept from everyone for almost the entirety of my life. *Then* they demand that I return with them to Emberwyn. Moira had made it quite clear that I was unwelcome to return if I failed. She rarely regretted a single decision she ever made. I clung to Slade like my life depended on it. After their reveal of my heritage, I got the feeling I might not be welcome here either, but he didn't shove me off when I touched him.

"It's unlike her to regret anything." I muttered, when I finally shook off my disbelief. Even if it were true, I couldn't just leave with them. I couldn't leave *him*. I didn't really understand why, or when I began to see him and this place as *home*, but I didn't want to leave now. In fact, I had forgotten all the responsibility I felt for preventing the war. Runelheim seemed untouchable and I was safe here. I was safe with Slade.

"Well she does." Amelia demanded indignantly. "She'd like you to return with us *immediately*."

My eyes nearly bulged out of my head and I had to fight the urge to step entirely behind Slade.

"What aren't you telling me?" I willed my voice to remain steady. Even if it was true, there had to be a catch. Moira locked me away in the palace. I was forbidden from using magic. It would be no different than turning myself over to Edward, the more I thought about it. The only difference would be that I didn't have a cuff on my wrist.

"Is it *that* hard to believe that mother cares for you?" Her voice increased in pitch, like she hadn't expected this to be so difficult. I don't know what ever gave her the idea that I would've listened to a word she said. She always turned her nose up at me. She was in the small group of people who got to know the truth about me, but she *hated* it.

"You and I have had very different experiences with her and you know it."

She rolled her eyes. "I don't, actually, because I don't enjoy spending my time with someone as pathetically powerless as you."

Ezra shot her a glare and she quickly adjusted the look on her face as well as her tone. She cleared her throat. "I'm sorry, I'm just tired. I'm not usually up this late." She rubbed a hand down her face in frustration. "Mother can't bear the thought of you out here defenseless when the humans are being so volatile. She can protect you. You're far safer within the palace walls of Riodian than in this dreadful place."

Zephyr and Slade both visibly bristled at her words. Slade's hand closed around mine. This place was not dreadful.

In fact, it was the first time I had ever witnessed a place where all beings were equal, healthy, and happy.

Ezra cut in. "I can see you need some time to think this over. Why don't you consider this tonight and we will return tomorrow?" Amelia turned toward her to protest, but she raised a hand. "She's obviously been through a lot in the last few months." She gestured toward me.

I was suddenly all too aware of the lack of hair falling down my back. It had grown some since I cut it, but it was nothing like it had been the last time either of them would've seen it. I didn't even know if the way it grew made it look more evenly cut, or if it was still as haphazard as it had been when I cut it. I hadn't taken the time to look at myself in the mirror beyond that evening with Delilah, and even then, I had not focused on my appearance outside of the clothing she put on me.

"Moira was very clear that we–" Ezra silenced her with a hand again.

"I was there when she demanded we retrieve her. I know what she said. Aside from forcibly pulling her away we aren't going to get anywhere, and I get the feeling that neither of these men intend to allow that to happen."

"Lay a single fucking hand on her, and I'll remove your head from your shoulders before you've even realized I moved." Slade's tone was just as terrifying as it had been that night in the woods when he'd threatened the men who ambushed us. Amelia's face went white as a sheet.

"Of course, she can have the evening to think it over. We will come back tomorrow, at the same time." She gave him a weak smile. "If that's alright?"

He gave her an almost imperceptible nod. "You can see yourselves out."

Ezra ushered her toward the door. She sent me an apologetic look over her shoulder as they walked out and closed it behind them.

Slade dropped my hand and shoved me off of him. He walked over and clicked all of the locks of the door into place. "Well," he started. "This has been an enlightening evening."

"Before you get started, let me explain." Zephyr pushed off the wall and took a step toward Slade.

"Oh no." He raised his voice at the vampire. "You don't get to talk until I'm finished. You've lied to me my *entire* life. And *you*," his attention turned to me, "*you* had every opportunity to tell me why you couldn't return to Emberwyn. Every single opportunity to tell me who you *really* are. The infuriating part is, I wouldn't have cared. Fuck, everything you've said about being a disgrace would've made a whole lot more sense, but you chose to keep that from me."

"Slade, I–"

"You're a fucking *princess*, Liza."

"No!" I advanced a step, my frustration getting the better of me. "My birthright was stripped from me the moment my magic manifested. It's a curse I've had to live with for nearly seventy fucking years because I'll never be good enough to live up to the title I *should* have."

Slade blinked, the only sign of his surprise. I'd rendered him speechless, despite the growing frustration building in his eyes.

"Fire magic is not a curse." Zephyr turned to face me. "It was one of the most sought after magics of the dark times. Second only to blood magic, of course."

I scoffed. "That's impossible. Moira said it made me weak. That I was a mistake. A disgrace to the royal bloodline. She was so frustrated about it that I found out she tried to send

Desmond to find the mage she was certain was my father and kill him."

Zephyr shook his head and frowned. "Would you consider me to be weak? Am I also a mistake?" Shadows swirled around his hand as he raised it and watched them. The way they moved reminded me of the way fire would. "I *was* a fire mage, you know. Nyvara turned me. I was one of the first few that she freed when she took this land back. She recognized the power I held and offered to turn me. To include me in her court." The shadows dissipated.

"She appointed the water mage she freed when she liberated the land now called Emberwyn. She named it after her late sister. Had there been a fire mage she felt she could trust in those dungeons the royal line may very well have been made of fire mages."

"That's not how it's written in our historical records." I weakly protested.

He huffed an unamused laugh at that. "Of course it isn't. I'm sure that Moira rewrote some of that history when she made the decision to wipe out the fire mages. I don't know what got in her head, but at some point she decided they were a threat. It's one of the reasons Nyvara has refused any audiences with her since then. She sends one of us instead."

I stared at him in disbelief. I knew it was true that she wiped them out, because he wasn't the first person to have said as much. I couldn't believe, though, that fire mages were more powerful than water mages. It went against everything I had ever known.

Slade laughed now, but it was tinged with irritation. "Well, are we going to keep adding to the secrets you've never decided to share with me, or is that all?"

"Your mother didn't even tell me *you* existed. Forgive me if I carried on the illusion that you weren't mine. It was startling enough to have found you surrounded by the corpses of her killers and sobbing over her body."

"But you've known this *entire* time." He stepped closer to the vampire. Zephyr stood only an inch taller than Slade, and now that I took in the two of them more closely, the resemblance was hard to miss. "I could understand not telling me as a child, but *now?* You made me find this out from a *fae?*"

"You were never meant to find out at all. No one other than Delilah was meant to know, and the only reason that *she* knows was because she was who Carissa confided in when she was pregnant with you. I still don't know how she managed to keep that secret from me." Zephyr turned away from Slade and walked back into the den. "Nyvara is going to lose her mind. I am sure Jesabelle will run and report this to her immediately."

Slade brushed past me as he stomped after his father. "And what fucking difference would it make if Nyvara knew?"

"I have been Nyvara's consort many times. I am permitted to fuck whoever I please but I am *not* allowed to procreate with *anyone* without her explicit approval. She knew I had a mate, but I never sought approval to have a child because it was never something I wanted. It wasn't ever something that Carissa mentioned wanting either."

Slade froze a few paces past me. "And what does she do to offspring she hasn't approved of?" The edge to his voice had me quickly putting the pieces together.

This was far worse than what Ezra had just revealed about me. For all intents and purposes I was still just as much of a disgrace as before. Even if Moira wanted me to return, I still wasn't a princess unless she decided to return my title to me. Zephyr's bombshell was far more dangerous.

"She's not going to come and cull you, if that's what you're asking." Zephyr picked up his paintbrush and began working again, as if this conversation bored him. "She's more likely to call upon *me* and demand answers before she deals out a punishment. I'll have to present you to her, but she won't harm you. Halfbloods can't reproduce, so you won't ever have to worry about that at least."

He tossed out the last sentence like that might cool the rage building in Slade. That made the fertility suppressant I was taking effectively pointless. It seemed Zephyr only had the maids prepare it to keep up the facade that Slade was a mage.

"You know that I have no issue keeping secrets. Why would you keep this from me anyway?" Slade clenched his fists.

Zephyr sighed and his brush halted midstroke. "By the time I felt I could share it with you, I knew you would be just as irritated with me as you are now. It didn't seem worth the frustration. It was easier to keep up the image that you were a mage."

Slade spun around to storm out, but when his gaze fell on me he grumbled a curse under his breath. He brushed past me anyway. "I'm not finished with *you* either, but I need some air."

I wanted to rush after him, but I knew when to quit before I made things worse. I watched helplessly as he unlocked the door once more and turned the knob to go out. When he opened it, he stepped back in surprise. Standing outside the door, reaching for the knocker, was Ezra. *Alone.*

She looked startled, but then glanced over at me. "Could I speak to you for a few minutes?" She glanced at Slade, then back to me. "Alone."

"Anything you have to say to her, you'll say in front of me." Slade answered before I could. "I will not let her go anywhere alone with someone like you."

"Slade, she's a friend." I walked over to him to reassure him that she could be trusted.

He held up a hand to signal for me to stop. "She's a fae, Liza. The fae are known for being untrustworthy."

Her face scrunched up in frustration. "If you know so much about the fae then you should know that we can't lie."

"You cannot outwardly lie, but you are excellent at twisting the truth and I will *not* allow you to be anywhere near her."

"Fine." She growled and tried to push past him into the foyer. He had her pinned to the wall by her throat so fast that she hadn't seen it coming. Her feet dangled beneath her. She glared down at him.

"I did not say you could come inside."

I rushed up to him and pulled at his shoulders. "Slade. I told you she's a friend. Let her *go*." I appreciated his possessiveness most of the time, but right now it was concerning.

I expected him to shove me off, but he released her like I asked. He radiated rage like a dark aura around him.

Ezra brushed herself off and shifted her focus to me. "Look, if you don't want to return, I can't say I blame you, but she really didn't intend for us to give you that option."

Slade huffed in annoyance and Ezra shot him a glare.

"Well she doesn't own me. She stripped me of any title I had." I almost hesitated to say the next few words, but I forced them out. "And I'm happy here, Ezra. I don't want to go back. I thought I wanted to earn her approval, but I couldn't seem to do anything that would do that. There's no sense in continuing to try."

She studied me for a few seconds. "I know you, Liza. You can't be happy to just give up. She may have irritated you at times, but what if there *is* a way you can win her favor again?"

I half laughed and shook my head. "I've tried everything, Ezra. There's nothing else that will change her mind."

"But there *is*." She was insistent enough that it intrigued me.

"Fine. Tell me whatever it is you came here to tell me, but I can promise you it isn't likely to change my mind."

"The dragons are disappearing. They're leaving, to be more specific. They're being called to another realm. Azazel told us about it. If Edward decides to push his army through the mountains, hundreds of thousands of people will die before they reach the capitol. Moira can't send out her forces to the mountains and risk them coming from the sea instead. She doesn't have the manpower to split them."

"I'm failing to see what this has to do with Liza." Slade cut in.

Ezra gave him a dismissive scowl. "Azazel knows where they're going, and who controls them. He told me how to find her. If you can go to this other realm and convince them to fight for Moira, she may very well give you your title back."

"What makes you think they would even care?" I hadn't expected anything like that. I *had* done a pretty good job at winning Andras' favor. This seemed plausible *if* they would be sympathetic to my cause. A flicker of hope lit in my chest.

"Azzy was there, Liza. He watched them fight off a king much like Edward."

"If Azazel was there, why didn't *he* ask them to come to fight for your queen?" Slade questioned.

"He didn't know what was happening here until he came back. He wouldn't have known to ask them. For all he knew, it would open it up for us to push north with our armies and take Mytharae back. But he saw Edward's forces on the other side of the mountains. They'll move as soon as they feel it's safe enough to do so."

It was plausible, understandable even.

"And why wouldn't you or Azazel go to do the very thing you're trying to convince her to do?" Slade motioned toward me.

"Because Moira can't spare the resources. But you could go. I could tell her you disappeared and we couldn't find you. It would buy you time to go and try to convince them."

I stared at the floor while my mind whirled. I had given up on the idea of reclaiming my throne. I actually started to see a life here. I actually started to really enjoy Slade's company, and appreciate *him* in a way that I hadn't ever felt about anyone else.

"You could save so many people." Ezra urged. She stepped toward me but Slade blocked her. "*Your* people, Liza. Don't you want to protect them?"

As if Slade knew that would pull at my restraint, his posture softened and he turned toward me. I looked up at him and his expression was conflicted and unreadable. Taking this chance might mean losing him, but not taking it meant that Edward might make good on the promise he made to his people, and I didn't think I could live with myself if I let that happen.

"How do I find them?"

Nearly an hour later, with heavy bags packed and slung over our shoulders, Slade and I stood next to Ezra in a cold and dark cave. The cavern was large enough for two dragons to walk side by side, wings stretched up and out behind them. At least, if the golden dragon I ran into was a good estimate on the average size of them. I had to wonder how no one but Azazel had stumbled across this. It was even more suspicious that it wasn't guarded. By dragons or by mages.

"How did he find this?" I glanced at Ezra.

"He didn't say."

I took a deep breath. "Alright, who or what are we looking for? Are you coming with us?"

"Azazel was able to give me a mental image of the mage you'll want to find. I will follow you through until we find her. After that, you'll be on your own. I can't be gone long. They don't know I'm helping you."

"How can you go with us till we find her then?" Slade's suspicion was hard to miss.

"Time moves differently there. Ten days for them is only one for us. I could be gone for more than a day and it would only be a handful of hours." Her explanation made sense, and yet, the idea that we'd find this mage in just a day felt a little too optimistic.

"How long will we realistically have to find her and convince her to come and help us?"

"That's a hard question to answer. I wouldn't imagine you'll have long though. A month at the most. That would be about three days here."

That was reassuring. A month seemed far more realistic. Though I hoped it didn't take that long.

"Lead the way." Slade gestured toward the portal.

Ezra seemed startled that he wanted her to go first, but she nodded and took a few steps toward it. She glanced back to make sure we were following. I stepped forward and kept pace less than a step behind her. Slade was a bit reluctant, but stayed right behind me. Truthfully, I hadn't expected him to want to come with me.

When we emerged on the other side it was damp and cold. The cave was dark, and it took a few seconds for my eyes to adjust. Ezra strode forward confidently, like she knew exactly where to go. Slade was suddenly right behind me, so close that I could feel his breath brush against my hair.

As we walked it got brighter, and we rounded a corner into a space that opened to the outside world. Before I could take in the landscape a green dragon spun around and growled at us. Its eyes darted between the three of us quickly. It was half the size of the golden dragon.

Slade shoved me behind him and made a move to draw his sword.

"No!" Ezra whispered quickly. "Don't threaten it."

It was clearly threatening us. Returning the favor hardly seemed like it should be an issue, but still, his hand paused on the hilt. Tense seconds passed. They felt like minutes. Anytime we attempted to move the dragon snarled again.

Finally, it tilted its scaly head and looked behind it. Other dragons came into view, flying in our direction. One was so dark it almost looked black, but the scales gave off a violet shimmer in the sun. The other dragon was blue, like the most brilliant sapphire. It was smaller, but not by much.

The green dragon huffed. It turned quickly, ran a couple of steps and dropped off the cliff at the edge of the cave. I would've run forward, were it not for Slade blocking my path. It took me a moment to realize that it was making room for the other two dragons. They slammed into the cliffside. The violet dragon had blood red eyes that seemed to stare directly through me. The blue dragon's eyes were a brilliant emerald.

Both approached with their teeth barred. They looked like they intended to devour us, but then three people materialized in front of them in what looked like a quick puff of smoke. One of them moved just as quickly as Zephyr could. Before I registered what they were doing, two of them were beside Slade and I. Slade had drawn his sword, and the female was snarling.

They all wore black leathers, similar in design to Slade's, but they each had a metal chest plate with a crest engraved on it. It bore a crescent moon, lotus flower, and a sigil I didn't recognize. One of the males was holding back the female. Ezra was nowhere to be found.

"Goddess curse that fucking fae." Slade muttered under his breath.

The female looked at us, and I stumbled back a step in horror. Her eyes were as black as night, with dark veins streaking out away from them. She had fangs, just like Zephyr. Her black hair was braided and hung down her back. Her sword had blood dripping from it as though she'd already slashed at Ezra before she disappeared. The male holding her had short black hair and icy blue eyes. He surveyed us as he released the female.

Slade, of course, was not deterred, but her snarled words chilled me to my core.

"WHERE IS AZAZEL?"

Acknowledgements

Wow, where do I even start with this one? My husband has been the biggest supporter of this particular adventure. While he has not read the books, he has sat and listened patiently as I went on and on about all the ideas, the plot twists, the character arcs, and the world building. He critiqued my politics, the lore, and even choreographed the epic fight scene between Slade and some of the assassins from the guild. He drew the initial sketches for the map you see at the front of this book, *and* tolerated the excessive number of times that I played Taylor's music in the car because I always daydreamed new scenes when he was the one driving. (This man seriously deserves a medal… He does not like her music at all and my playlist for Firestorm was full of it!)

Then there are the couple of friends that have become my trusted "alpha" readers. I sent this out to them when it was still very much in a *rough* draft version. I hadn't finished some of the spicy scenes, and I hadn't done a very thorough edit of a lot of what I'd written. That didn't deter them though. They read through it and were hooked within the first few chapters. So, to Rachel, Mandie, Abbey, Chloe, and Jeffery – I owe you big time! Especially for all the words you pointed out that I overused and the suggestions you made to enhance the yearning/tension. You guys are the best!

I have to give a massive shoutout to Fantasy Fox Maps, who created the stunning map for this series. My husband may have laid the framework initially, but Fantasy Fox brought that to life and I am forever grateful that I won the contest to have a black and white map drawn.

I also, of course, have to thank my incredible illustrator for all of her hard work. She has created every book cover for my books, and she's brought every single idea of mine to life so perfectly that I am not sure where I would be without her help.

The pressure is on now to make the second book just as incredible as this book was!